Natalie Normann grew up  coast of Norway and always
she wanted to smoke ci
Hemingway but settled fo
glass of Baileys.

Her writing journey started with short stories in women's
magazines until her first book was published in 1995.

Summer Island was her first romance written in English.

 twitter.com/NatalieNormann1
 facebook.com/NatalieNormannAuthor
 instagram.com/natalienormann

Also by Natalie Normann

Summer Island

CHRISTMAS ISLAND

NATALIE NORMANN

One More Chapter
a division of HarperCollins*Publishers* Ltd
1 London Bridge Street
London SE1 9GF
www.harpercollins.co.uk

This paperback edition 2021
First published in Great Britain in ebook format
by HarperCollins*Publishers* 2020

A catalogue record of this book is available from the British Library

ISBN: 978-0-00-836274-4

Printed and bound in Great Britain by
CPI Group (UK) Ltd, Croydon CR0 4YY

To my beautiful grandmother Elise, who always made Christmas so special for us. To my always funny grandfather Waldemar, who was the best – and scariest – julenisse ever.

To Maria and Anan for the Christmases now.

Chapter One

A huge spruce or fir or whatever it was called stood on the pier, swaying in the wind. It looked as miserable as she felt despite the blinking white fairy lights.

Holly Greene dragged the suitcase behind her through the slush on the concrete pier. What looked like patches of snow was ice and half-melted sleet. She looked down on her brand new winter boots and realised she would have been better off with wellingtons or even sneakers.

The lights from the ferry cast a strange, white light onto everything, but didn't reach very far from where she stood.

As far as she could see, there were only a few houses near the harbour. She could see lights in their windows. Also all sorts of Christmas lights: hanging stars, wreaths, and even menorahs.

She looked back at the ferry. It was still there. Perhaps she could return to town, get a nice warm hotel room, preferably with a humongous bathtub, and come back in the morning? It had seemed like a good idea to catch the last ferry. Now she wasn't so sure.

She already regretted the whole trip, but Jack had been so eager for her to see his new life, she couldn't refuse. *Come meet Ninni and baby Rosie, stay for Christmas,* he had said. *Please.* She had a strong feeling her dad and Jack had conspired to get her away from London, but truth be told, she hadn't protested much.

'Damn it,' she muttered.

Why was it so dark? And bloody wet? This was Norway in December, for God's sake. Shouldn't there be snow-covered mountains, wild ski slopes, snowmen with carrots in their round faces and angels in the snow? Instead it rained or snowed or both; it felt like ice barbs against her face. Apart from those few cosy windows, everything else was pitch black.

And damn Jack for not being here.

'To hell with this,' she muttered and turned around to see the ferry cast off and sail away. Leaving her to fend for herself. She felt like bloody Robinson Crusoe.

Time to call for help. Holly stopped to look at her phone. Battery was almost dead and here she was, facing the great dark north all by herself. She couldn't even call Jack because he was in Spain showing off Rosie to Ninni's mum.

Holly took a deep breath. Jack had said all she had to do was take the path past the shop, and walk straight ahead until she came to a rack of mailboxes, go past the rack and Ninni's house would be on the top of the hill.

She was going to send him a harsh text. Her hands were shaking from the cold and before she managed to stop it, the mobile slipped out of her fingers and landed in a puddle of slush.

'Oh, blast it,' she said, almost bursting into tears.

When she picked up the phone, it gave away one last, green light, before turning completely dark. Holly tried to shake off the water, only to lose the phone again.

She finally shoved it in the pocket of her new winter parka, before giving the suitcase another pull. The pathway between the houses wasn't difficult to find. A huge sign on a building revealed the shop. "Joker", it said. *Strange name for a shop,* she thought.

Holly regained hope. She looked at the houses as she passed by.

They look kind of nice, she thought. Perhaps the lights in the windows were all part of the *hygge* thing the Danes raved about. Did Norwegians also do that? She had no idea.

Soon the houses and the pier disappeared behind her. The wind picked up and she discovered that a parka bought at a charity shop was woefully inadequate for proper, shitty weather.

If I'm going to survive for whatever time I'm here, I need one of those anoraks that Inuits use, the ones made of polar bear fur, she thought. Preferably one with fur inside and outside. Which probably was against the law and constituted animal cruelty, so no. Might be better to get a space suit. *They were built for outer space, which was probably as cold as this,* she thought.

The suitcase suddenly stopped and she almost fell forward. She pulled hard at it, and it slipped loose from the wet ground with a loud "glup".

Holly looked around, realising she stood in complete darkness. She caught her breath. Once, when she was little, Danny had pushed her into a cupboard and slammed the door. The darkness had seemed so vast, so huge, that she had been sure she would never see lights again.

The only thing that worked was singing, so she started singing 'Jingle Bells'. It seemed appropriate.

Jingle bells. Jingle bells. Jingle all the way.

Above her head, she spotted a few stars through the clouds. Somehow that helped.

The problem was, she couldn't see more than a few inches ahead of her. What if this was the end of the island, if there even was such a thing, and what if she took another step, only to plunge into the ocean? Her next thought was how on earth it could be so dark at seven in the evening? It was insane.

Holly dug into her pocket to find the phone. Even it's pathetic torch would be better than this darkness. She pressed the buttons and hoped for a miracle. Not even a shimmer of light from the screen.

'I'm dreaming of a white Christmas,' she belted out, trying to keep the shaking under control.

When she drew her breath for another verse, she became aware of a weird sound behind her. A growling sound. And she dropped the phone for the third time. It made a squelching noise as it hit the ground. Holly forgot all about the sound she had heard.

'Oh, damn this. Why the hell did I come here to the middle of nowhere?'

She bent down, trying to find the slim, black phone case

4

in the dark. *It's probably ruined anyway*, she thought. The slush was freezing cold and she kept picking up stones, but no phone.

'Where are you, wretched thing,' she muttered to herself.

The growling got closer and she froze. The search was forgotten. What the hell was that?

Holly turned around, trying to determine where the sound came from or even what it was.

The sound continued and then she saw them. A pair of glowing eyes in the dark. What kind of animal did that? Holly couldn't remember if they had wolves in Norway. Did they? Or perhaps it was some kind of giant lynx? She had no idea if a lynx would attack people.

She stood, feeling a bit safer standing.

The growling grew louder and the eyes came closer. Werewolves? Oh, crap. Vampires!

Holly stood completely still, unable to move, unable to breathe. *Perhaps I can stand like this until morning*, she thought.

After a while the cold seeped through the soles of her fancy winter boots. *Bloody useless they are*, she thought.

I have the choice of either freezing to death or being eaten by a wild predator or some kind of mythical beast. And to think I could have been in my warm flat in London, enjoying a glass of wine and some mind-numbing Christmas movie on the telly, talking to Jocelyn and having a grand time. Thanks, Jack, she thought.

Instead she was about to die because her brother convinced her that a trip to a bloody island in the middle of the North Sea would do her all sorts of good.

Or actually, it was all Brian's fault for behaving like an utter bastard in the middle of the hospital.

'Hopefully I will die quickly and painlessly,' she mumbled, swallowing the fear. *That way I don't have live through the humiliation and frustration I'm experiencing right now.* The thought cheered her up a little.

Another sound broke through the panic. It sounded like rustling. *Wolves,* she thought, *were-bloody-wolves. Or trolls.* Trolls were a thing in Norway, she knew that much. *I'm going to die in complete darkness.*

She would so haunt them all after she was eaten.

Chapter Two

Holly couldn't get her eyes away from the glowing orbs. They seemed to grow bigger by the second. And the damn creature was still growling.

The other sound came again and then the hellbeast jumped behind her and Holly lost it. She screamed.

A voice cut through the panic.

'*Stå i ro*,' he yelled.

Holly hiccupped and forced herself to breathe. She had no idea what the words meant. All she understood was that there was a giant beast of some sort leaning against her legs and a screaming man in front of her.

His voice was so brash, so angry, she forgot to panic. Holly drew her breath.

'Who... who are you? Are you real?'

The man came so close she could see his face. A full beard hid most of his features. His head was covered in a woolly bobble hat and his eyes were stern. But she could see he had short hair and surprisingly brown eyes. Also, he

7

towered over her. A proper Viking. The thought almost made her smile.

He changed languages and spoke English. 'Are you mad? What are you doing out here?'

'Out where?' Holly knew that if she hadn't been so scared, she would have run. But she could still not see what kind of creature was behind her. 'I came from the harbour. I'm trying to find my brother's house.'

'You're on the wrong side of the island, woman. How did you get here?'

'How do you think I got here? By bus? I walked. Why is it so bloody dark everywhere?'

He looked as annoyed as she felt.

'It's late evening. You're on an island. There are no street lights out here. Give me your hand,' he said.

Holly hesitated. 'Why?'

'Because you are standing on the edge of a cliff and if you step backwards, even a bit, you're going to fall into the sea,' he said.

Holly couldn't feel her feet, much less take a step. 'I can't move,' she whispered.

He looked like he was about to roll his eyes, but he didn't. Instead he held out his own hand and grabbed her, none too gently, and pulled her towards him.

Holly gasped when she fell against his chest. She realised she was safe, and then all the fear and stupid panic welled up and she erupted.

'What are you doing, you idiot? You scared me half to death. You bastard!' she yelled. 'There isn't even an edge, is there?'

He held her, despite her wriggling to get away from him, and turned her around with one easy movement. 'Look,' he said and turned on a powerful torch.

Holly swallowed. There really was an edge there, and the drop seemed to go on forever.

'Oh, dear god,' she said.

Then she looked down and almost screamed again. A giant black cat stared up at her, its eyes glowing in the torch light.

'This is Frøy. He won't bite. He won't bite you, I mean,' the man said.

Holly wasn't convinced. 'Is… is he some kind of lynx?'

'Have you ever seen a lynx?'

'No, not really. Never a Norwegian lynx, anyway,' Holly said, trying to find her bearings.

'Frøy is mostly a Norwegian Forest Cat. He's also the one who saved your life,' the man said. 'He heard you sing and followed the sound.'

Holly looked at the cat who now sat on the ground, the tale around his legs, looking like a huge, fluffy, black cloud. *How on earth did I think he was a werewolf?* she thought.

'Where do you live?' the man asked outright.

'London,' she said.

He gave her an exasperated look and pointed at the ground.

'No, where do you live here, on the island?'

By now Holly realised she was shivering from the cold and most likely also shock. 'I was on my way to Ninni Torps's house. She's my brother's partner,' she said. 'I thought it was close to the pier, but it was all dark and there was no signs to follow and I got lost.'

'The harbour is all the way on the other side of the island. How long did you walk for?'

'The boat or ferry or whatever it's called, docked at six-thirty, I think, and I've walked since then.'

'And it's now almost eight o'clock. Didn't you notice that you were lost?'

Holly couldn't take it anymore. Eight o'clock? That didn't make sense. And being berated by some bearded stranger was too much. 'If you could please show me where Ninni's house is, I'll find my own way, thank you very much,' she said in her most sarcastic voice.

He seemed totally unaffected. 'Sorry, can't do it. I don't know anyone here.'

'You don't know anyone? How is that possible? It's a damn island!'

Holly remembered Jack saying that everyone on the island had been there for ages, generations even, and they all knew each other.

'It's possible because there is this thing called renting a house for a limited period of time,' he said, his voice dripping sarcasm.

Holly glared at him. 'So, what am I supposed to do? Stand here until the sun comes up?'

'Which, if we had been further north, would have meant you would be waiting until spring,' he said, looking at his watch. 'If you prefer to remain here, daylight will commence in about fourteen hours. Best of luck and good night.'

He turned to leave and Holly couldn't believe her eyes. 'Are you really leaving me here, in the bloody dark?'

'Isn't that what you wanted?' He did stop, she noticed.

Holly swallowed a few choice words. 'No, not really. I really don't want to fall off that cliff, thank you.'

'Then you have no other choice than to follow me.'

'I... I need to find my phone. I dropped it when your cat growled. Could you please use that torch to help me find it?'

He seemed to hesitate, then turned the torch to the ground.

Holly heaved a sigh of relief when she spotted the phone. It was most likely beyond repair, but still. Maybe it was salvable if she could put it in a bowl of rice or something.

'Take it with you. I'm leaving now.' The man didn't look well pleased when he turned around and started walking away from her.

What was his problem? Holly thought.

'You know, my brother said that the islanders are really nice people,' she said, trying to keep up the pace and still dragging the suitcase behind her.

'I wouldn't know. I'm not an islander.'

The giant cat ran along beside them, sometimes disappearing into the dark, but always returning to his owner's side.

Holly told herself that serial killers wouldn't have giant, friendly cats. But then again, cats were rumoured to be psychopaths. It was a hard call.

'I'm Holly Greene. What's your name?' Holly tried to smile at him.

He was having none of it, but at least he answered.

'Tor,' he finally said.

Holly gave him a disbelieving look. 'Your name is Thor? For real?'

He stopped and glared at her. 'No, it's not Thor, it's Tor, like in... in torpedo. No bloody, lisping h, for God's sake. Don't know where they got that spelling from. There are no "Thors" in Norway, and if there are, the bloody h is silent in all of them.'

Holly couldn't hide her giggles. She pressed a hand against her mouth.

'What, you think it's amusing to make fun of my name?' He didn't smile at all.

'I think it's funny that you take it so seriously, yes. I'm sorry if I offended you,' she added, in case he was so annoyed he changed his mind and left her there. 'What's your last name?'

'Rude. And before you laugh again, it's spelled r-u-u-d.' He turned his back and kept walking. *Boy, did he have the right last name*, Holly thought.

After a while she spotted a single light in the darkness.

'Where are we going?'

Tor slowed down his pace and took her suitcase from her without asking.

'My house. It's too late to get you to the other side of the island, and frankly, I don't want to wander around, knocking on people's doors. Tomorrow morning you can return to the harbour and ask for better directions.'

'If you have a mobile phone that works, I can call my brother and ask for directions right now,' she said, not too keen on spending a night with a total stranger in this horrible place.

'Don't have it with me. How can he give you directions if he's not here? Does he know the island that well?'

They were climbing a sloping trail of sorts and Holly was gasping for air. 'Maybe not Jack, but Ninni does. She practically grew up here,' Holly said.

'Don't know her and I don't have a phone with me. Now, if you don't mind, I'm cold and I'm going home. The harbour is back the same way you came.'

'Are you some sort of psychopath? Are you seriously going to send me away into the darkness after you and your cat saved me from almost falling off the edge?'

Tor frowned. 'No, I'm not. But neither am I trekking along the pathway in the dark. I'm trying to tell you it's safer to come with me.'

'You're not right in the head,' Holly muttered.

She almost stumbled over the cat who had placed himself in her path, looking at her with those luminous eyes.

'Fine. I would prefer to come with you, please,' she said, without looking at Tor.

'Good choice. You can use my phone when you get to the house and if you have a computer, you can try that. Both phone signals and Wi-Fi are erratic on this side of the island, I'm afraid.'

Erratic signals and eccentric Vikings, Holly thought. This was mad.

She hoped she would wake up from this nightmare soon.

Tor pulled the heavy suitcase behind him. He had no idea what had made him go outside. He never did after dark. It was too... isolated and rough, and he missed the street lights back home in Oslo.

With street lights you knew where you were, you could see everything. Nobody could sneak up on you and you were in no danger of falling off cliffs if you made a wrong turn.

But Frøy had made such a ruckus he had had to go outside. At the time he had thought perhaps there were foxes or something, scaring the cat, or more likely, pissing him off.

Except the minute they stood outside, Frøy ran ahead of him, occasionally stopping to look back, making sure he was coming. Then he heard the singing. The voice was crystal clear, with perfect pitch, and he wondered if the island had sirens he didn't know about.

And when he stopped, he did so in front of a woman who seemed as out of place as he was. The thought that she could have tipped over the edge, falling into the sea and probably to her death without anyone on the island knowing about it, was sobering.

He was glad they had found her when they did. Although, he wouldn't tell her that. She was annoying. An intrusion in his quiet life. And he liked his life quiet, thank you very much.

All he had to do was make up the sofa, leave her to herself and maybe feed her. Then, in the morning, he would point her in the right direction and happily return to his peaceful existence.

He could hear her struggling behind him. The path up to the house wasn't exactly a paved road. It was barely a path, littered with gravel and holes.

Again Frøy ran in front of him and sat in the middle of the path. Tor sighed. 'Troll,' he muttered.

'Sorry? I couldn't hear you,' Holly said.

Tor almost growled at the cat before turning to her. 'Give me your hand.'

She stopped. 'No,' she said.

He held out his hand. 'We're coming to an icy stretch. Your chances of not falling on your bum are better if you let me help you. Your boots are not suited for the weather conditions on the island,' he explained.

She looked down on her boots. 'They were supposed to be perfect for snow,' she said.

'I'm sure they are, but what we have here is ice and rain and sleet, and under that, partially frozen mud. If you don't have metal studs on the soles, you will fall. And if you hurt yourself, there's no doctor on the island.'

'There is now,' she said, grabbing his hand.

'What?' Tor was only half-listening when he pulled her over a hole in the ground.

'I'm a doctor,' she said, leaving out a few crucial details.

'Good for you. But I don't think it will help if you get hurt. You're not Doctor Rogozov,' he said.

Holly narrowed her eyes. 'And this is not the South Pole and I doubt a fall will require me to cut out my own appendix.'

He almost smiled then. 'You know about that?'

'Of course I do. All doctors know the famous Russian doctor who had to operate on himself because they were in the middle of a South Pole winter,' Holly said.

He was puzzled by that, but didn't say anything more. 'Come on, we're almost there.'

And it was true. A few minutes later, they reached a gate, hooked on both side to an odd, diagonal kind of picket fence.

The light in the window came from the kitchen, the only window facing the pathway. 'It's warm and you'll be safe,' he said before opening the door.

'Thank you,' she said, following him inside the house.

Frøy shot past them into the lounge and flopped down on the sofa. He obviously considered his job done.

Tor turned around and looked at her. She stood still in the hallway and looked bedraggled. 'Take of your boots and coat, and go into the lounge. Are you hungry?'

She nodded. 'Yes. Thank you.'

Tor found the constant thanking unnerving. 'You don't have to thank me all the time. We don't really do that here. Also, it's Frøy you should thank. If it wasn't for him, I'd be asleep on the sofa and you would be in the water.'

Holly smiled slightly. 'Okay. I can do that.'

Tor watched her as she sat on the sofa, as close to the fireplace as she could, and reached out a hand to pet Frøy.

He held his breath. Frøy was a friendly cat, but sometimes he'd bite if he wasn't in the mood to be petted.

'My phone is charging by the television. Feel free to use it,' he said, all the time watching Frøy.

When the big cat rolled around and put a paw on her hand, he smiled. *Silly cat,* he thought before going to the kitchen.

'Thank you,' she called after him.

Mad woman, he thought.

Chapter Three

Holly picked up Tor's phone from the charger, but didn't call anyone right away. Instead she stroked the cat. He was fluffy as a cloud and soft as a pillow.

'You look like a pillow too, don't you?' she said and smiled when he swatted her hand.

It took her a second to realise that the grumbling sound she heard now was the cat purring. He sounded like he had an engine in his throat.

'You are so beautiful. I'm not actually a cat person. We never had any pets. And most cats are so... so weird,' Holly said.

The cat's giant paw stopped her when she tried to pull away her hand. So she leaned against the sofa back and closed her eyes.

I really should have stayed at a hotel, she thought.

Everything would have been easier if she had arrived on the island in daylight. No scary edge, no weird cat and no angry, bearded man.

She was almost asleep when Tor returned with a tray and put it on the table in front of her.

'It's just soup. I'll get you some bread. Did you make your call?'

'Uhm, no, not yet.'

Holly's stomach growled and made the cat lift his head.

'I'll call my dad after I've eaten,' she told him.

She took the spoon and pulled the bowl closer. It smelled divine.

'What kind of soup is this?' Holly lifted her spoon.

'It's fish soup, with a few different types of fish, some fish balls, and then some crab and shrimps, some veggies and cream,' he said, reminding her of Jack's way of listing ingredients.

'Fish balls?' Holly gave the soup a suspicious look.

She thought he smiled, although it was difficult to see through the beard.

'No, it's fish dumplings. Made of flour and fish, and cooked in a broth,' he said.

'Did you make it?'

He looked surprised by the question. 'I'm the only one here. Uhm, I forgot something. Be right back.'

She found one of the dumplings and tasted it. It was good, she decided, and was halfway through the bowl when Tor returned with thick slices of brown bread, buttered and covered in almost equally thick slices of cheese.

Holly smiled at him. 'I have to thank you for this. I haven't really eaten anything since I left London. This is really good, by the way.'

'It will warm you up,' he said.

'Aren't you having anything?' Holly got worried he had given her all of his supper. 'I don't want to leave you with nothing.'

'No need to worry. There's plenty of soup. I always make enough to last me for days. I'll get you some blankets and pillows. Be right back,' he said again.

Holly took one of the bread slices and sniffed it. It smelled so good, it was impossible to think about anything else. Not toast, but it would do.

She emptied the bowl before she checked her phone. Dead as a dormouse. She sighed. Perhaps it would help to let it dry out and then trying to charge it again. And if that didn't work, maybe Jack or Ninni had an extra phone she could use. Or she could buy one in town. Or maybe just learn to live without it. She did have the computer, but still. It wouldn't be the same.

Tor's phone worked. She almost sniffled when her dad answered.

'Hi, Dad. I've arrived on the island. No, everything is fine. I'm at the house,' she lied.

'How do you like the island?' Paul loved to hear about the place.

'I wouldn't know. I... It was dark when I came here. No street lights. It's like staying in a house that floats through space.'

That made him laugh, as she had hoped it would. 'I'm so tired, Dad. Can we talk tomorrow? I need to eat something and sleep. And my phone got wet.'

Holly squeezed her eyes closed. *Shouldn't have said that*, she thought.

'That's why the number screen said unknown number? I thought it was because you're in Norway. Who's phone are you using?'

'Jack or Ninni must have left it here. I found it a few minutes ago.'

'Good. You should always have an extra phone in your handbag, you know. I've told you that so many times.'

It was her teenage years all over again. He would catch her lying and then make a big fuss.

'I really should. Good night, Dad,' she said.

'Good night, poppet. Don't let the bedbugs bite,' he said.

Holly put Tor's phone back on the charger and returned to the sofa. It was good to talk to her dad but if he knew what really happened, he would worry. No need for that.

She took a bite of the bread and closed her eyes. It was too good to eat fast. 'Oh, my god,' she muttered.

The cat lifted his head and looked at her, blinking slowly.

'Too bad for you, cats don't eat bread. Not sure if I can offer you a piece of cheese either,' Holly said.

Frøy rolled around, turning his back on her and waving his tail in her face.

'Lovely,' Holly said, pushing the tray away. She was wondering if she should call Jocelyn, then remembered that she was on the night shift.

She looked up when Tor came back, his arms filled with bed sheets and pillows and even a duvet.

'I'm not sure I'll have to eat anything else in my life,' she said, remembering not to say thank you.

'You'll be hungry again soon enough.' Tor dropped everything on top of a chair. 'I don't have an extra toothbrush.'

He's awfully practical, Holly thought. It was sweet.

She nodded at the suitcase he had placed by the door. 'I have everything I need in there.'

'You look concerned. Is there something wrong?' Tor glanced at her.

Holly smiled. 'I hope I'm not too much of an inconvenience for you. You were probably not expecting guests tonight.'

Tor looked at her. 'I'm not used to company, to be honest. I hope you'll be comfortable enough on the sofa. There's only one bedroom, I'm afraid.'

'Next time I'll text you in advance,' Holly said, trying to lighten the mood.

'That would be good,' he said, and Holly caught him smiling, which was quite a feat, considering all that scraggly beard.

'I couldn't anyway since my phone is dead,' she said, suddenly embarrassed. 'I'll have to get a new one, I think.'

'Ah, sorry, I can't help you there. Did you make your call?'

'Yes, thank you. My dad worries if he doesn't hear from me when I travel. I guess that's what fathers do.'

'I wouldn't know. Do you need the phone again?'

Holly shook her head, wondering what he had meant.

Perhaps he had lost his father at some point. But she couldn't ask him that.

He picked up the phone and put it in his pocket, then went over to the fireplace and put another log on it. 'I brought an extra blanket in case it gets cold in here. This is an old house and I have found there to be drafts in the window frames.'

Holly was comfortably warm. 'I'm fine, thank you.'

'Good. I have work to do, I'm afraid, so I will leave you to it. My room is upstairs. The bathroom is on the other side of the hallway. And feel free to use the kitchen if you get hungry or thirsty. Good night.'

Holly didn't know what to say. 'Uhm, thank you?' she said.

He smiled again. 'No need. I'll take away the tray.'

'No, please let me. I can do the dishes, you know,' she said, trying to make him smile again.

'I'm sure you can, but you are my guest, and as such, you will not do the dishes. I'll take the tray.'

She cocked her head, watching him. *He sounds like an old butler,* she thought. 'Okay. I'll see you in the morning then, I guess.'

'I'm up pretty early, so don't get spooked if you hear me in the hallway.' He held one hand on the door handle – *ready to bolt,* Holly thought.

'Of course. Uhm, Tor. What about Frøy?' Holly looked at the gigantic cat splayed out in front of the fireplace.

'Frøy goes where he wants too. Just leave the door ajar and he'll wander off when he feels like it.'

'Thank you.' Holly smiled her best smile.

He didn't say anything, just nodded and left. The cat stayed behind.

Holly listened to his steps up the stairs. There was no reason for her to worry about him attacking her while she slept. The stairs was so squeaky she would hear him a mile away. *All good then*, she thought. Not that she thought he would ever do something like that. She didn't get that kind of vibe from him. Holly sighed. Not that her 'vibedar' got it right every time. Brian was a perfect example of that.

No, not thinking about Brian now. Better to focus on Tor the Viking.

She wondered what Tor was working on in an old house on a desolate island. An artist, maybe? She looked around. He had said the house was rented, so presumably what was in here wasn't his.

'Which is really good,' she told Frøy. 'Because this is a strange place.'

Now that she was alone, she could take a proper look around. One wall was covered in floor to ceiling bookshelves. That wasn't the strange thing. The small pieces of what appeared to be carpets hanging on the wall was.

Holly got up from the sofa and walked over to them. No, not carpets, weaving of some sort. All sorts of patterns and stripes, and very colourful. They looked nice on closer inspection, but why on the wall? Why not on the table, or used as throw pillow covers?

On one of the shelves she discovered playing cards and an assortment of board games. All worn out from use. *Nice*, she thought. Probably a family lived here, instead of the grumpy troll upstairs. Or maybe it was some kind of permanent holiday let? Could be.

She opened a few drawers and discovered silver cutlery next to an even bigger assortment of match boxes and lighters. 'Either he's a pyromaniac troll or someone who lived here used to smoke a whole lot.'

Frøy had climbed on top of the sofa again. His tail flicked behind him. Holly smiled. 'You're like a guard cat, aren't you?'

A troll cat, perhaps. Her eyes fell on a few framed drawings on the wall by the door. She smiled when she saw them. They were drawings of creatures with long noses. *Trolls,* Holly thought. *Actual fairy tale trolls.*

'You know, Frøy, I like these a lot better than cyber trolls,' she said, walking over to the cat.

She scratched his head while she tried to decide whether she should attempt to sleep or watch TV. She decided to go for the entertainment.

It wasn't exactly the latest in smart-TV technology with its small screen and chunky backside. But she found a remote control.

Holly plunked herself down on the sofa and turned it on. She made the cat and herself jump when the sound maxed. She turned it frantically down and laughed at the cat who turned his back and swatted her with his tail.

She flipped channels only to discover there was about five to choose from. News in Norwegian, so she couldn't understand a word. Then there was another channel, more news, one channel that looked like a cooking channel, but wasn't, and then she found one with old episodes of some American comedy show.

She left it there, and pulled the duvet over her lap. The cat decided that the blanket was what he wanted. He slid down the sofa and landed in her lap with a thud.

'Oh my god, you weigh a ton,' Holly said, laughing out loud.

Tor heard her laughing through the floor. He couldn't remember the last time he had heard someone laugh, especially a woman.

It was almost painful to listen to.

Mostly it was annoying. After Linn and everything that had happened, he wanted to be alone. He had come to the island to be away from everything, especially women.

He sighed, pushing away the drawing he was working on. Hearing her laugh reminded him too much of what he had lost.

She was talking to Frøy now and laughing again, as if the cat had responded. The cat was impressive, but he couldn't talk.

Tor looked at the drawing again.

It looked wrong. He couldn't get the floorplan to fit the vision in his head.

Holly laughing and talking to Frøy did nothing for his concentration.

'If I don't finish this, the bills will not be paid; no

electricity, no food. Not even cat food,' he reminded himself.

Tor found his earphones and put them in. The music blared in his ears.

He had no time for other people – not after all that had happened – and he had no intention of being distracted by a woman his cat had saved. That was out of the question.

Tor picked up the pencil and the ruler again, and started drawing.

He could still hear her.

It was freezing cold and someone had left a motor running. It sounded so close. Holly opened her eyes and realised the cat was sleeping across her chest.

She tried to move, but Frøy flicked his tail and she fell back onto the pillow.

It was a nice sight, watching the cat sleep. Only she had to pee something awful.

The cat looked at her. Holly smiled. 'You're mental, that's what you are.'

She stroked his head and scratched him behind the ears. 'I'm sorry, Frøy. You have to move otherwise I'm going to have an accident in the sofa. Tor's not going to like that.'

She sat up, properly this time, and the cat slid behind her. *Perhaps cats really are liquid*, she thought.

It was pitch dark in the lounge. She turned on the lamp on the table and looked around. The fireplace was cold and apparently there was no other source of heating.

Holly tiptoed out in the hallway. She heard nothing from Tor's room. In the bathroom she peed and hurried out again. Everything was freezing cold.

She huddled down on the sofa again, pulling the duvet and the blanket Tor had given up to her chin. It was barely six in the morning and still dark outside.

'Think we'll ever see daylight again, Frøy?'

The cat blinked at her, then kept purring. Holly put a hand on his fluffy belly and smiled when the purring reverberated through her arm.

'I had the most horrid dream, Frøy,' she said. 'I was back at the hospital and going mental all over again. God, I wish I had hit the bastard. That might have made everything well worth it.'

She closed her eyes, not sure if she would be able to fall asleep. And then she did.

Chapter Four

The sun shone right into her face. Holly pried open her eyes and squinted towards the windows. Actual daylight and loads of it. *That's a relief*, she thought.

The cat was nowhere to be seen. All he had left behind was black hairs everywhere.

Holly pushed herself up from the sofa. She felt awful. *I must look a fright*, she thought.

The door opened and she turned her head. Tor was in the doorway. 'I have coffee for you, unless you prefer tea. I have that too, but I'm not sure how old it is.'

'Coffee will be fine,' Holly said.

Tea reminded her too much of the hospital anyway.

'Okay. I'll be in the kitchen while you... um, freshen up,' he said and disappeared.

Now I know for certain I look a fright, Holly thought.

She stood and it was still freezing in the room. She wrapped the blanket around her shoulders and peeked out the window. The sun was shining on what looked like a barren moon landscape with patches of snow and grey stone. Not even a tree or a brush in sight.

It took her eyes a second to realise the window faced the sea. Everything was grey, even the water, and the patches of snow were actually chopping waves. She could see a boat moored to a wooden pier, just below the house. Half the boat was covered in blue tarp. She wondered why only half. It seemed odd.

I so have to get back to London, she thought. *I'm in the bloody wilderness.*

She had slept in her clothes, not at all comfortable undressing in a surly strangers house. It wasn't as if she wasn't used to falling asleep wherever she fell down between shifts at the hospital, but that was different. That was civilisation.

A quick trip to the bathroom to pee, brush her teeth, and drag a brush through her hair, made her feel a lot more human.

Holly almost fell over the cat when she walked into the kitchen. She sat and scratched his head. 'You don't have to rescue me from the evil door.'

Tor sat by the window. 'Coffee is ready,' he said.

Holly looked at him. He seemed so uncomfortable and she realised the last thing he wanted was to sit with her for a coffee. *Right back at you, mate*, Holly thought. She gave him her most reassuring smile.

'You know what, I think I'll take a rain check on the coffee. I'm more of a proper tea person, you know? Could you perhaps point me in the right direction? You don't have to follow me back to the harbour or anything. I won't get lost in daylight.'

He couldn't hide that he was relieved. 'I can do that. Are you ready now?'

Holly nodded, perfectly happy to end their little adventure.

'Yes, I am.'

A few minutes later they were outside Tor's house and walking up the path. Frøy went up front, Tor carried her suitcase this time, and Holly tried to keep up. Her boots were still wet and becoming more uncomfortable by the minute.

She looked around and decided it absolutely looked like the moon, especially since there was no snow anywhere.

They walked through the gate and soon arrived at a wider pathway. Tor looked at her. 'This is where we found you.'

Holly could see the tracks from the suitcase wheels. She had to see the edge where she could have – potentially – fallen to her death. Tor didn't say a word while she passed him. He knew where she was heading.

'Oh my god,' she muttered when she looked down.

It was worse than she had imagined. The drop seemed to never stop. At the bottom, she spotted a narrow strip of beach.

'The fall is about fifty metres down,' Tor said behind her.

She jumped, almost completing what could have

happened the night before. He grabbed her arm. 'Please don't do that.'

'You scared me,' she said. To collect herself she smiled at him. 'Do you ever climb down to that beach?'

'No, you have to use a boat to get to it. Also, it's not permitted to swim there. There's a bird mountain on the other side,' he said.

'What's a bird mountain?' Holly couldn't see any birds from where she was standing.

'It's where birds meet to... to procreate,' he said, frowning.

'Like a *Love Island*, only for birds?' The idea made her laugh.

Tor frowned even more. 'They are mostly protected species.'

Perhaps he was an eco-warrior. One of those weirdos who sits on his computer all day and writes about the environment. Or perhaps he's the Norwegian equivalent of the Unabomber. With that beard, she wouldn't be surprised.

'I have taken up more than enough of your time, I'm afraid. I think I can find my way from here, for sure,' Holly said when it became awkward.

'Yes, I think you will. As soon as you come further down the path, you will see the other houses. Walk towards them. Goodbye.'

He had already turned his back at her before she managed to even thank him.

'Thank you!' she called after him.

He didn't turn around.

Wanker, Holly thought.

She took a better grip on the suitcase handle and started walking away from him and the edge of the world. Hopefully it wouldn't take three hours to go back. Her feet were freezing.

Tor climbed up on one of the larger boulders. He came here every day to look at the sea. It was fascinating to him that the next stop from this point was somewhere on the North American continent. Maybe Canada, he wasn't too sure. Also, Shetland was between them, anyway, or maybe Greenland.

The sea changed all the time. He never tired of it.

Frøy jumped up and sat beside him, his paws primly set in front of him. The wind smoothed his fur and he closed his eyes, turning his face towards the sun.

'Troll cat,' Tor said.

He looked towards the harbour, but couldn't see her. The path twisted and dipped between slopes and outcrops.

She would be fine. It was daylight, for God's sake, and the path only went one way. She couldn't miss it even if she tried.

He looked down at Frøy who had also turned his head in the same direction. Tor sighed. 'You're such a nagger.'

Slowly he made his way down the boulder and strolled after Holly. *I'm only going to make sure she's on the right track,* he thought. Just until she was safely back to where the other people lived.

Twenty minutes later, he spotted her. He was on higher

ground and could see Holly walking towards the small cluster of houses. Far out to sea, he caught a glimpse of the ferry coming towards the island.

Frøy sat and started cleaning his paws. His thick fur almost never got muddy. Tor stood still until Holly disappeared among the houses.

He looked at Frøy. 'Let's go. We can make it to see the rain come in and still be on time to pick up the supplies.'

Frøy jumped ahead and ran up the path, the way they came.

Holly couldn't recognise any of the houses from the night before. But she did recognise the scraggly Christmas tree with the fairy lights. It did not improve with daylight; if anything it looked even more miserable.

She stopped and looked around. The pier was smaller than she had imagined. There was a large building on one side. Probably the community building Jack raved about. He was building a restaurant in there.

Good luck with that, she thought. The building looked ready to keel into the sea.

She turned around, looking for the store. It should be in one of the houses. She smiled when she discovered the Joker sign. *I remember that,* she thought.

There would be someone in there who knew where Ninni's house was and also how to get to Jack's farm. She was really curious about his farm and wanted to check it out as soon as possible.

She had to do something to get her mind off other things.

Inside the store, she stopped to look around. Groceries on one side, and more DIY stuff, arts and crafts, and Christmas stuff than in all of China.

Holly couldn't help smiling. Also it smelled sensational in there. She followed the intense temptation of fresh baked goods and stopped in front of a display of cakes and bread. 'Oh, my word,' she said, almost laughing.

'*Kan jeg hjelpe deg?*'

Holly twirled around, feeling guilty for some reason, and gawped at the woman eyeing her. She, in turn, raised her eyebrows and repeated what Holly sensed was a question.

'Oh, I'm sorry. I don't understand.' she said.

The woman's face lit up in a warm smile. 'You must be Jack's sister. Am I right?'

Holly nodded. 'Yes, I'm Holly.'

'I asked if I could help you.' The woman smiled and held out her hand. 'I'm Alma. I run this store. Are you hungry?'

She didn't wait for an answer, only grabbed a paper bag and tongs. 'Which one would you like? Do you like coconut or chocolate? Danish or wheat bun?'

Holly couldn't make up her mind. 'Ehm, they all look delicious. I'm not really used to eating cakes for breakfast.'

'Coffee then,' Alma said. 'You can take a few buns with you for later.'

Holly followed her to a small corner of the shop. A couple of wobbly tables and a few mismatched chairs stood next to an old-fashioned coffee maker. 'It's fresh. Sit down and get warm. I'll bring you a cup,' Alma said.

Holly didn't mind. She had no place to go and nothing to do. It was such a strange feeling. She discovered there was a panel oven on the wall and she stretched her legs towards it.

'Did you come with the ferry now? I didn't see you. Jack phoned earlier and I'm afraid he was a bit worried. He said he had tried the house and didn't get any response, also your phone, I think, and your computer. No one seemed to know where you were,' Alma said, bringing two cups to the table.

'I came in on the last ferry yesterday and then I got lost. My phone died and then I lost it in the snow three times. It's dead by now,' Holly said, flinching at how stupid it sounded.

Alma nodded as if this was exactly what she had expected. 'But where have you been all night? You must be freezing.'

Her voice was so filled with concern, that Holly almost burst into tears. *Oh, this won't do,* she thought, pulling herself together. 'No, I was found by a man and his cat,' she said.

Alma frowned. 'What man? Oh, you mean our hermit?'

'Is that what he is? He seemed a bit odd.' Holly could picture Tor as a hermit. The beard and the cat, and living on his own on what looked like the most remote place on the island.

'He is a strange one, yes. He showed up a few weeks ago and for a short time we thought he was like Jack, but no, he rents the house out there, never talks to anyone, and pays us to deliver him groceries to the house. Sometimes he brings us fish and crabs to sell. Most odd,' Alma said.

Holly smiled. 'Well, Tor was nice to me. His cat saved me from falling over the edge and down onto the beach.'

'Where did this happen?' Alma looked concerned.

'Right by the bird mountain. Tor called it that,' Holly said.

'You walked all the way out there in the dark? You are a lucky girl.' Alma smiled at her.

'Yes, he told me so. It was that amazing cat who found me. I've never seen anything like him.'

'Yes, he is lovely, isn't he? He comes to visit the shop, you know. Of course we give him treats. You would think it was the cat who would hide from us, not the man, but it's clearly the other way around.' She interrupted herself and looked out the window. 'Excuse me, I have to make waffles. The ferry is leaving soon and people love warm waffles. You know, to take on the trip. Stay here, I'll take you to Ninni's house later.'

'Really, you don't have to. All you have to do, is point me in the right direction,' Holly said.

'And have you fall off another edge? Ninni would never forgive me for losing Jack's sister. Enjoy your coffee and tell me how Jack and Ninni are doing,' Alma said.

She had a waffle iron next to the coffee maker and fetched a mixing bowl from the fridge. Then she poured batter in the iron and closed it. The smell was unbelievable and Holly tried not to look at it.

'Uhm, I think they're doing fine. They're going to spend

another week in Spain with Ninni's mother, and then come here before Christmas,' Holly said.

'I'm not sure it was such a brilliant idea to take the baby all the way to Spain in the winter. But young people always think they know better,' Alma said, opening the waffle iron and pulling out a golden waffle.

Holly swallowed. 'Rosie is thirteen months old. I think they'll be fine.'

Alma was interrupted by a customer, who threw Holly a curious look then was handed the warm waffle, wrapped in paper, and a cup of coffee. Other people followed. They all exchanged a few words in Norwegian, and then the customers nodded goodbyes before they ran out to catch the ferry.

Alma kept saying Jack's name whenever she spoke to them. Holly knew she was being introduced to the islanders already. She wasn't so sure what she thought about that.

Holly considered sneaking out, but it wasn't really an option and she didn't mind the wait.

She was warm, the coffee was good, and Alma talked about how it was beyond her why anyone would pick Spain over the island.

'Especially this time of year,' she said and handed a new waffle to another customer.

It didn't take long before Holly tuned her out. She studied the shop. Hopefully they had frozen pizza. It was the only thing she was able to cook on her own.

'Here. Eat this. You look starved.' Alma sat a paper plate on the table in front of her, followed by a jar of red jam, and then sugar and butter.

The waffle clearly wasn't a Belgian waffle. It consisted of five hearts and they smelled of cardamom and vanilla, and made her stomach rumble.

Alma handed her a knife. 'For the butter. Pull them apart or just fold the whole thing over.'

Holly buttered the waffle and dropped a dollop of jam on it.

'Do you make these every morning?' She pulled one of the hearts away and put it in her mouth. 'Oh, my god,' she said, chewing slowly to savour the taste. 'These are fantastic.'

'Yes, they are. I make them every morning during winter. People like something warm with their coffee.' Alma filled the waffle iron again and pressed down. The stack of waffles grew rapidly.

Holly licked her fingers. 'Most mornings I eat a stale sandwich from one of the coffee shops on my way to work,' she said.

'That's not good for you,' Alma said.

Not sure if waffles are good for me either, Holly thought, but didn't protest when Alma placed a second hot waffle on her plate.

A few more customers came in while she sat there. They didn't have time to chat, but left with waffles and coffee, and a curious glance at Holly.

'Want to try some brown cheese on it?' Alma said with a glint in her eyes.

'I'm not sure,' Holly said. Jack raved about that cheese, but he had a strange palate.

41

Alma put down a square of caramel-coloured cheese, with a cheese cutter on the side. 'Enjoy.'

Holly didn't want to admit that she hadn't used one of those things before. The only place she had seen that kind of cheese cutter was in Ikea.

She kept her hand steady and cut too deep, making a thicker slice than she had intended. Aware that Alma was watching her and being far too self-conscious, Holly put the cheese on the last waffle heart and bit into it.

It was weird. 'Like soft, sticky toffee,' she said.

'Better than that,' Alma said.

Not going to argue with an old woman about her cheese. Holly nodded. 'Good.'

She discovered something when she took another bite of the waffle. She did not like brown cheese. It stuck to the roof of her mouth. Like peanut butter, but without the salty flavour.

Alma laughed. 'It's an acquired taste. Please, you don't have to eat it.'

They both looked up when the ship's horn sounded. 'There she goes. I guess that means we can get you to Ninni's house. That's where you're staying, right?'

Holly nodded. 'Yes, Jack said that's the nicest house and also that the farm wasn't really fit for living in yet.'

'Oh, absolutely not. The farm is still very much an old bachelor pad, and hasn't been refurbished in forty years or so. Agnar didn't believe in spending money on "unnecessary things", as he called them.' She shrugged. 'But then again, he didn't have any family to take care of.'

Holly knew the whole story. Jack had struggled with

coming to terms with this unknown father leaving him his farm. 'Jack has been so busy with the restaurant,' she said, feeling a need to defend her brother.

Alma smiled at her, a smile that lit up her face. 'Of course he has and a grand job he's doing of it too. You'll come and see it when you have settled. Don't get me wrong, my dear. We are all so happy to have Jack and Ninni on the island. We need more young people here.'

She took off her apron and slung it over a chair, then fished a set of keys from her pocket. 'Let's get you to the house.'

'Do you sell mobile phones here?' Holly said before they left.

Alma shook her head. 'You'll have to go to the mainland for that, I'm afraid.'

Holly nodded, feeling a bit resigned and a lot silly. *Just as well*, she thought. If anyone wanted to get in touch, there was the laptop and social media.

Detoxing from the phone, she thought as she followed Alma outside. *That's a new one.*

Chapter Five

Alma insisted on walking her to Ninni's house. She had also made sure they brought with them a bag of groceries, despite Holly trying to explain to her that she only ever ate food that could be microwaved.

Those were not the magic words. Alma, she learned, did not believe in microwaves.

The walk to Ninni's house was short. Holly couldn't understand how she had managed to get it so wrong the night before. Alma seemed to know what she was thinking.

'You got it wrong right over there,' she said, pointing at a fork in the gravel road.

Holly smiled. 'It was awfully dark last night. I'm not used to not having street lights.'

'I don't know how you can live having them, to be honest. You can't see the stars or the sky in London, can you?' Alma said.

'Sometimes we can, but not like this. Light pollution

they call it. Oh, that's lovely.' Holly stopped to admire the huge wreath decorating the front door.

'Yes, I think Ninni has gone completely Christmas mad this year,' Alma said.

The house was small and white, and the black sleet roof was partially covered with patches of snow. A redbrick chimney pipe made Holly think of gingerbread houses with icing.

The illusion grew stronger when they entered the house. The first thing that caught Holly's attention was a grinning doll sitting on the last stair of a staircase. He had on a white shirt, a red vest, black trousers, and Holly was sure he also wore clogs. On top of his curly, white hair, perched a red woollen bobble hat. 'What is that?' she said.

'Oh, it's a *nisse*.' Alma looked at the doll with a frown. 'Not sure how I can explain that in English. You probably don't have those in England.'

Holly wondered why the *nisse* grinned like a maniac and only had four teeth. 'Are they some kind of goblin?'

'Not sure what that is. They are a part of Norwegian folklore. According to the stories, they belong to the underground creatures, and they live at farms where they take care of the farm animals, and make sure that the farm is thriving. Do you have anything like that?'

Holly had to think about it and remembered her nana's stories. 'Yes, we do. They're called brownies.'

'Isn't that a cake?' Alma smiled.

'Brownie the cake is American. Brownies are supposed to be mean spirits who live on farms and work at night. You have to give them sacrifices: food and drinks, I think, or they will make trouble,' Holly said.

'The *nisse* is not an evil spirit. He, or she, works with the farmer. They have the same goal, after all. They want the farm to be prosperous and the animals to be happy and well taken care of,' Alma said, frowning slightly. 'But, if the farmer disrespects them or mistreats the animals, they can be mischievous. And if they get really mad, then they have been known to give the farmer some serious trouble.'

Holly wasn't sure Alma was completely sane. She sounded like she thought they were real.

She gave the *nisse*-brownie one last look, just in case he was up to something, then followed Alma into the kitchen.

It looked like a Christmas shop had exploded in there. The curtains were red and white and there was an embroidered tablecloth on the table. Holly discovered the pattern was red poinsettias with green leaves. 'This is nice,' she said, touching one of the flowers.

Alma nodded. 'Petter's mother made that, along with the curtains. She was good at crafts. You will want to be careful not to spill anything on it. It's probably from the sixties. Ninni has made an effort this year, I see. It must be because of you.'

Holly was delighted. 'She's very thoughtful.'

'That she is.' Alma lifted the bag of groceries onto the counter. 'I think you'll be fine here. Now that you know where we are, please drop by if you need anything else or even if you're simply bored. Anything.'

'Uhm, I'll do that,' Holly said. 'Thank you,' she added quickly.

'You will find that we are nice to people out here, and you are Jack's sister, so that makes you one of us right away,' Alma said, smiling.

'Thank you,' Holly said again, amused by the idea of being an islander by proxy. They had really taken Jack in as one of the family.

Alma disappeared quickly and Holly closed the door with a sigh of relief. She locked the door too, despite Jack and Ninni insisting nobody ever did that.

There are maniacs everywhere, she told herself. She was still not convinced about Tor.

She put away the groceries and marvelled at all the stuff she had no idea how to cook. Vegetables that needed peeling and cutting and boiling, meat that looked far too advanced for her capabilities, and all sorts of cheeses with names she couldn't pronounce anyway.

'Not in a million years,' she said and put most of the items away in the fridge. They would probably survive until Jack returned.

At least there's pasta, she thought after a quick rummage in the cupboards. And luckily a jar of some sort of pasta sauce. Not Jack's, obviously, as he hated those. Oh, no, for the great chef only homemade sauce would do, and all the time while he cooked it, he would be karaokeing the hell out of some poor Italian ballad.

Not having the energy to even think about food, she left the suitcase in the hallway and went exploring.

In the lounge there were even more Christmas decorations. Every table seemed to have candles in candlesticks, decorated with what looked like scrunchies at the base. *Way too much of a fire hazard,* she thought. But they looked cheerful. No elf on the shelf anywhere, but a few more of the *nisse*-brownie; this time females with long skirts and white aprons and the silly grins that seemed to be a trademark. It was a bit unsettling.

On the mantlepiece there were family pictures. Frikk the dog and Ninni's daughter Rosie featured in all of them. She hadn't met Frikk yet and she had only seen Rosie the two times they had been to London to meet the family. And even then she barely had any time to spend with them.

There had had to be a disaster, like her whole life collapsing, to get her to the island. And then Jack and Ninni had decided to go to Spain with Rosie before she arrived. Although she didn't mind it so much. Being alone felt good. At least for right now.

Holly turned on the TV as the silence was getting to her. Leaving the hospital and the small apartment she shared with Jocelyn to end up in an empty house in the middle of the North Sea was almost too much.

There was baby stuff everywhere and it made her smile. Cuddly toys and boxes of more toys, and a crib in the corner. Next to the crib she spotted a comfortable dog bed, also filled with toys. Either the dog's or Rosie's. Hard to tell the difference.

She loved seeing Jack with baby Rosie. He seemed so happy, and Ninni was all she could imagine in a partner for him.

For herself, on the other hand, she saw nothing. Not the way things were now. Staring down that edge earlier was almost as bad as staring into the abyss that was her life right now.

'No, nothing like that anymore. I'm done crying and being miserable. I'm going to take a nap on that comfortable couch and then eat... something and find a bottle of wine if there is any here.'

The little speech helped. Holly fell down on the couch and pulled with her a large, woollen blanket.

She fell asleep in seconds.

It was snowing. Tor looked up at the grey sky and pulled up the zipper in the heavy down jacket he wore. *No matter, it will soon stop*, he thought.

Frøy waited by the door, giving him a slightly impatient look.

'Yes, we are going,' Tor said, before pulling the woollen hat over his ears, winding a scarf a few times around his neck, and finally pulling on his boots.

He could have sworn the cat smirked at him.

'We don't all have a thick fur coat, you know,' Tor said, opening the front door.

Frøy was out the moment the door cracked open. Tor followed him, locking the door behind him.

It was almost impossible to see the cat in the darkness. He blended in too easily. Tor caught his movements, but that was about it.

Frøy kept coming back to make sure he was coming,

running and skipping next to him while he walked down to the pathway.

'Don't worry. Your treats will be there. Otherwise we will go to the shop and get them tomorrow.' He hoped not. It had been his firm policy to stay away from people as much as possible. The whole point of coming to the island was to get away from everyone, including well-meaning strangers.

The people in the store were nice, but the small talk was hell. To avoid it, he had made arrangements to have groceries delivered. One of the kids on the island brought it twice a week. So far she had never failed him.

Frøy disappeared again.

When Tor caught up with him, he sat as pleased as Punch on their box. The girl had put the box on top of the fencepost and hung two carrier bags on the side.

'You look like a demented hellcat,' Tor said.

Frøy jumped down from the box and looked at him as if to ask for his prize.

'No treat until we're back at the house,' Tor said.

The cat gave him a scornful look and ran towards the house.

'You could carry a bag,' Tor called after him. 'The goddess Frøya had two cats pulling her wagon. How about I get two cats that can do that and give them all your treats?'

I'm losing it, he thought, shaking his head. *Talking to the cat. That's the first sign. Perhaps I do need to go to the store once in a while, to talk to other humans. Perhaps I can talk to Holly again. Ask her how she's doing, if she managed to find a new phone.*

Or perhaps I should stay inside and not bother people, he thought.

When Holly woke up from her nap, it was dark again. She could see the windows from the sofa. There was something disturbing about not seeing daylight. How on earth did it get so dark so soon?

Without thinking, she reached for the phone, then dropped her arm. Damn. There had to be a clock somewhere.

She cringed when her neck felt stiff and painful. She had dreamt again, and – as always – it was about the hospital. She knew it was too early to hear from them, but the waiting was so stressful. She was officially suspended for four weeks, but that didn't mean they would use all four weeks before they got back to her with their decision. Right now, she just wanted it to be over.

The house was so quiet and she suddenly felt totally alone in the world. *I need a shower,* she thought.

Get clean. It always helped to get clean. She dragged the suitcase upstairs and looked around. The master bedroom had room for a double bed and a baby cot next to it. It made Holly smile.

The bathroom was between the two bedrooms, but before she went in there, she pulled the suitcase into the guest room.

'Weird,' she said when she discovered toy planes hanging from the ceiling and all the books on the shelves. She pulled one out. Hardy Boys, but in Norwegian. The books seemed used and really old.

Twin beds in here, she noticed. Ninni had said that there were no king size or queen size in Norway, and that a double bed was twin beds. *At least it's roomy*, Holly thought and sat to test the mattress.

Nice. She quickly unpacked and headed for the shower. No fiddling with the boiler for once as there was no boiler as far as she could see.

It was the same in the kitchen when she came back down. No boiler in sight.

She looked at the clock on the wall and frowned. Five o'clock?

'But it's dark outside,' she said.

Her eyes fell on a *nisse*-brownie perched on the windowsill. It looked identical to the one on the stairs. Holly stared at it, not sure if it had been there before. It didn't move, of course, and Holly shook her head.

'Time to do something constructive,' she said to the doll.

Her stomach insisted it was time for food. Holly opened the cupboards and rifled through the amazing amount of boxes and tins more thoroughly this time. And then, in the back, triumph.

Holly pulled out an unopened package of Jaffa cakes.

'Thank you, Jack,' she muttered.

Stuffing a Jaffa cake in her mouth, she checked the rest. A package of Norwegian crisps looked promising.

'*Potetgull*,' she read. No idea what it meant, but there was a picture of crisps on the front.

If I had a phone, I could translate that word, she thought.

She also discovered a bottle of white wine in the fridge and took one of the cheese packages to taste. There was a lot of food in there, even several foil packages. *Probably left by Jack*, she thought. *I'll check those later.*

Holly brought the haul into the lounge, dropped it on the table and turned on the TV. They were bound to have some kind of mind-numbing movies she could binge watch and not have to think too much about anything until she got tired enough to sleep again.

She changed channels and landed on a news channel, a Norwegian one, and found it unnerving not to understand anything they said. A cheery Christmas movie popped up and she let out a sigh of relief. She could live with that even if it had subtitles.

Holly pulled out her computer from the bag and connected to the broadband. Ninni had said it was a mobile broadband since there was no cable on the island and that it could be temperamental.

Working perfectly fine now, Holly thought. She checked her emails, nothing from the hospital. What if they didn't come back to her until after Christmas? How would she cope until then?

Better not to think too much about that. Instead she sent an email to Jocelyn, explaining her lack of mobile phone, and that she was fine. She also sent one to Jack and Ninni, asking them if they by some miracle had an extra phone in the house.

Danny had sent her a message on Messenger. Her baby brother could always make her smile. It hadn't always been like that. She remembered being fiercely jealous of him when he was a baby.

'Good thing I outgrew that,' she mumbled as she opened the message.

A gif popped up, a dancing Viking making rude pelvis movements. Holly snorted. 'You are silly,' she wrote back, happy Danny didn't know about Tor. He would go mental over that.

The wine was delightful and she felt no qualms about drinking in the afternoon. It was her first holiday in... in years. She couldn't remember the last time she didn't have work or have to worry about exams.

She eyed the table of snacks and popped another Jaffa cake in her mouth while opening the bag of crisps. They were salty and good. Holly sighed. Fine, then. She would just sit on this couch and eat until she couldn't move anymore, then nothing would matter anymore.

Problem was, she had been so disciplined for so many years, studying and working towards a goal that now, just as her life as a doctor was starting, the whole thing could be ripped away from her because of Brian. And she couldn't stand it. Especially because she had nobody to blame but her own stupid self.

Holly frowned. What on earth would she make of herself if she couldn't be a doctor? She had no idea. There had never really been an alternative for her.

There was nothing else she wanted to do.

'I could retrain to be a veterinarian,' she said, but she

couldn't quite picture herself with pets or farm animals. *Maybe if there were cats like Frøy it wouldn't be so bad,* she thought.

Her mind shifted to Tor. Alma had called him a hermit, even to the point of arranging groceries to be delivered. Why would he do that? He looked scruffy, like someone who didn't care anymore. Depression, perhaps? He had that haunted look on his face, hidden behind that beard, anyway. And also, isolating himself with only a cat for company wasn't healthy. He had been there for weeks, Alma had said.

No wonder he seemed so unwilling to help when he found her.

Tor glared at the computer screen where his friend and partner talked without ever catching his breath.

'So, you see, Tor, you have to come home for a bit,' Henrik finally said, smiling at him.

'No, I'm not leaving this place. You can do this on your own, Henrik. All you have to do is take the meeting, show them the plans and sign the dotted line. You could talk the fur off a polar bear, for God's sake.'

Henrik scowled at him. 'You really should show up at the office once in a while, you know. It's not good form for one of the partners to be hiding in a cave.'

'It's not a cave and I'm not hiding. Besides, I saw you three weeks ago. Do the meet and greet, and let me know how it goes. And if they're still miserable, let's have a digital meeting.'

Henrik sighed. 'Fine. You're bloody lucky you're such a talented bastard.'

'Yes, and I'm lucky you're such a social bastard. How are the kids and Kari?'

'They're doing just fine, as you would know if you ever checked your social media accounts. Kids are trying so hard to behave for Christmas, it's giving them stress levels higher than mine. Kari sends her love and told me to tell you that the beard has to go. You're too old to be a hipster.'

Tor frowned. 'No, I'm not and tell her I happen to like the beard.'

A blonde woman popped up behind Henrik's shoulder. 'You look like a barbarian. Please, shave it off. Even the cat must be fed up with it by now,' she said, smiling at him.

'Frøy likes my beard. He thinks it makes me part of his pride,' Tor said, smiling back.

'That's probably because mice are nesting in there. When are you coming home? You've been out there for ages. I never figured you for a nature boy.'

'I'm not in nature, I stay inside. Except when I'm out fishing.' Tor grinned at her when she rolled her eyes. 'I'm happy here, Kari.'

'Fine. But you look miserable, not happy, and I don't like it when you're so alone. It's not healthy, you know. Soon you'll be muttering to the cat, forgetting to take a shower and not eating anything but the food Frøy throws on the floor.'

She had a point with the cat and the showers.

'Thank you for the fortune cookie advice, which is not at all helpful. I'm not that isolated actually. Frøy and I saved a woman yesterday.' Tor could have bit his tongue as soon as the words left his lips.

He shouldn't have told them that. Kari's face lit up. 'Oh? Tell us all about it. How did you save her?'

Tor tried to backtrack. 'It wasn't a big deal. Frøy found her. She had taken the wrong turn from the ferry and couldn't find her house in the dark.'

'How old is she? Is she staying on the island? Will you see her again? What's her name? Is she attractive?'

The barrage of questions had him laughing. 'Would you please stop? I'm not going to see her again. She's a guest of someone on the island. Someone I don't know and have never spoken to, and never will.'

He thought that would make her shut up, but he should have realised nothing could.

'What's her name?' Kari had a deep frown on her forehead.

'I... don't remember,' Tor said.

'Ha, you do so know her name. Come on, tell us.'

Tor gave in. 'Her name is Holly. She's from London and her brother lives here on the island.'

'She's visiting him for Christmas? How lovely,' Kari said.

'I'm sure it is, but it has nothing to do with me.'

Tor could see Henrik rolling his eyes and Kari getting ready for more questions. He raised his hand before either of them could get another word in.

'You've had your fun. I'm not likely to meet her again, so you don't have to bother with it. Goodbye.'

Kari tried to protest, but he waved at them and shut down the computer.

Not bloody likely, he thought.

He looked at Frøy who lounged on the edge of the desk, taking up more than half the space. His fluffy tale wafted at the computer.

'You agree with me, don't you?'

Frøy ignored him.

Tor stood to go downstairs. He hadn't cleared away the bedsheets from the lounge yet. Frøy looked up, then decided that perhaps something interesting was going on.

He followed Tor into the lounge and immediately flopped down in front of the heater.

Tor gathered the bedsheets together and brought them into the laundry room.

She wore perfume, he could smell that. Then he felt funny about smelling her bedsheets, and chucked them into the washing machine. He turned it on and looked at it for a long time.

He was going bonkers, no doubt about it.

Chapter Six

Holly woke up and almost fell out of bed. She couldn't remember where she was for a second, then spotted the toy aeroplanes dangling from the ceiling.

Her head was pounding. 'Urgh,' she muttered.

She climbed out of bed and opened her eyes wide. One bottle of wine had quickly turned into the second one she had found in the lounge, only it was red, and then she had devoured most of the snacks. A really bad idea. She felt bloated, hung-over and miserable.

The shower was hot and the water plentiful, and she stood there until her head cleared.

When she came downstairs, the sun was shining. Holly put on the kettle for tea, and looked out the window.

Tufts of brownish grass covered most of the ground as far as she could see. From the window, she could see the ocean. It was as blue as the sky, and glittering from the sunshine falling on it.

'Lovely,' she said and couldn't help smiling.

It was time to explore the island, to see what all the fuss was. To discover why on earth Jack had fallen in love with this place.

She dressed quickly, adding a woollen sweater and a thick down jacket from the hallway. Holly looked at the row of boots and tried a few, eventually settling for a pair that were a bit too large, but an extra pair of socks solved the problem. She was not about to fall on her arse, hiking alone. A woollen bobble hat completed the look.

'I'm the abominable snowman,' she said to no one, and ventured outside.

Good thing Jack and Ninni will be back before Christmas, she thought. *I'll go barmy if I have to keep talking to myself.*

Outside, she stopped and looked around. The sun was shining, but it wasn't warming anything. Instead the wind chill made her pull up the zipper on the down jacket.

A walk would do wonders. And maybe a trip to the store wouldn't be amiss. Some more fizzy drinks would be great, and maybe they would have more of those buns or Christmas cakes. Perhaps they even had some wine.

She stuffed her hands in her pockets and walked towards the pier. On the way, she stopped to look at the few houses close to the beach.

Jack's farm, she thought. It looked small from up the road. It was weird to think that her big brother owned the place. Not only did he own it, he loved it. She knew that tiny farm was the best things that had happened to him. She could only wish something as exciting as that would happen to her. *Fat chance*, she thought.

He had left the key, she knew that, and so she would

take a look later, if only to satisfy her curiosity. And those sheep. She had to see the sheep for herself.

The thought made her smile. Their dad kept pretending he was convinced they were goats. It annoyed Jack, and it always made him happy to annoy his children. *Dads*, she thought, shaking her head.

The wind was harsh. She decided to do the shop later, and walked the other way instead. When she got closer to another cluster of small, white houses she spotted a set of swings in a yard.

A playground. It was filled with kids playing in the few patches of snow. They yelled at each other and tried to make snowballs. It was almost impossible with the slushy snow. Didn't stop them, though. They had a full-on war happening over there.

It looked like they were having fun and Holly couldn't help stopping to look at them.

A woman came out of the building and clapped her hands.

The teacher, Holly guessed. She was a friend of Ninni's. Jack had talked about the people living on the island, but she had their names all jumbled up.

The teacher noticed her and waved. The snow fight stopped and every kid turned and stared at her. Some of the little ones also waved.

Holly didn't have any choice but to wave back, feeling like a proper idiot. After, she burrowed her hands in her pockets as she realised the teacher was coming towards the fence.

'Hi! You must be Jack's sister,' she said in English.

Holly nodded. 'I guess I must be.'

Behind them the snow fight started again. So did all the yelling. The teacher ignored it. She smiled at Holly.

'Alma said you arrived. I'm the local school teacher, beer brewer, and general annoyance.'

Holly couldn't help smile back at her. 'Nice to meet you. And yes, they have mentioned you and everyone else.'

'Yes, and I'm guessing you have no idea who any one of us is.'

Holly nodded, slightly embarrassed. 'Guilty,' she said.

'I'm Britt and these munchkins are my kids. They are not half as bad as they look, and sometimes they're even half human. And now they're showing off for you.'

She called something in Norwegian and the kids slowed down. Not much, but enough for Britt to turn to her again.

One of the kids came up to Britt, leaning against her hip and gawking at Holly. His woollen hat was askew and he looked pretty snotty. He said something to Britt.

'This is Ole. He wants to know your name,' Britt said.

'Hi Ole. I'm Holly.'

Ole giggled and ran away. Britt shook her head. 'Kids are so weird,' she said.

It made Holly laugh. 'You're a teacher.'

'That only makes me extremely qualified to say just that,' Britt said.

Holly smiled. 'I'll be getting on. I'm out for some fresh air, and you're working.'

'That I am.'

One of the kids threw a snowball and hit one of the

others right in the face. He went down with an impressive scream.

Britt turned around immediately. 'Oh, shit,' she said.

Holly didn't hesitate. She jumped the fence and ran towards the screaming boy. He was clutching his face.

Britt reached him at the same time as Holly. She was talking a mile a minute. The other kids formed a half circle around them.

Holly sat on the other side of the kid. He was clutching his hand to the side of his head and drawing breath for another scream.

'Let me look at it, sweetie. I'm a doctor,' Holly said.

The boy looked at Britt who said something to him. He turned his head towards her.

'What's your name, sweetie?' Holly waited as Britt translated for him.

He swallowed. 'Emil.'

He looked about ten years old, and he slowly took his hand away. Holly smiled at him and held up her hand. 'Can I touch your face, Emil?'

He pulled away and Britt talked to him again.

'Go ahead,' Britt said.

She took his other hand.

A quick exam showed nothing was broken. Holly smiled. 'You'll probably have quite the shiner, Emil, but that's about it.'

Britt looked at her. 'Are you sure we don't have to get him to the hospital in town for an X-ray, or something?'

'Of course. That's up to the parents, and you should tell them that I'm not licensed to be a doctor in Norway. From what I could feel, nothing is broken. The snowball looks like it hit the outer edge of his eye. Put some ice on it and give him an over-the-counter painkiller. If the swelling or the pain gets worse, then they should take him to the hospital. They will know that by tomorrow, anyway.'

Britt talked to Emil, who nodded slowly. He grabbed a handful of the snow with his mittens, and pressed it against his head.

'Or he can use snow,' Holly said, trying not to smile.

She stood and watched while Britt sent the other kids inside. An older boy took Emil with him to sit on the steps.

Britt turned to Holly. 'Thank you. That helped a lot.'

'I'm sure you would have managed just fine,' Holly said.

'Yeah, but I would have been a lot more worried for him. I'll call his dad and have him come get him.' She shook her head. 'They get hurt all the time, thankfully only bruises and minor cuts, but it freaks me out when it happens.'

Holly nodded. 'Happy to help. Uhm, I'll be on my way now.'

Britt followed her to the fence. 'Listen, if you need something or you're bored, I live here, next to the school. Feel free to come by any time. Also, I feel I should warn you. People will come and say hi to you.'

'Why will they do that?'

'For one thing, you helped Emil. So his parents will want to say thank you. And also because you're Jack's sister. That makes you practically family. Don't worry, you can tell people to bugger off if you prefer to be alone.'

'Right,' Holly said, not believing she could to that for a moment.

Britt looked back at the two boys, then leaned over the fence. 'Alma said you know our local hermit,' she said.

It wasn't really a question, more of a statement. Holly couldn't believe she was part of the local gossip already. She frowned. 'I don't know him. He helped me when I arrived, that's all.'

'The kids think he's a warlock,' Britt said.

'Why would they think that?' Holly couldn't hide her surprise.

'Because he has a beard and that giant cat of his. It's because Frøy's black and they have seen too much TV about witches, I'm afraid.'

'Frøy's a gentle giant.'

'We know. Frøy comes by on his own to say hello to us once in a while. Don't you think it's weird when a cat is more social than his human?'

Holly couldn't help nodding. 'Yes, a bit. He was all over me when I met them.'

'I'm guessing you're not talking about the hermit when you say that? We respect privacy here, but he's on an extreme level, that boy.' Britt realised that all the kids had come outside again. 'Time for class, I'm afraid. I'll catch up with you later, Holly. Lovely to meet you and thanks again for your help.'

She turned around, heading for the school house.

Holly waved at the kids who waved back with enthusiasm. They were adorable, all of them.

Chapter Seven

Holly followed the road past the school, and didn't really worry where she ended up. It was daylight and she was on an island, so how lost could she get?

The cold wind cleared her head. She felt better looking at the views and understood more about why Jack loved it so much. Although to settle here for good was taking it too far, in her opinion.

She came to a dry stack that seemed to go on forever, consisting of layers of uneven stones. On the other side, there were fields, with spots of rock sticking up from the earth. It reminded her of Scotland. Even the dry stacks looked the same.

At the top of the road, she stopped to admire the ocean. The sky was clear and so blue it almost hurt. She filled her lungs with the fresh, cool air and instantly got a coughing fit, coughing so hard her eyes filled with tears. She bent over and tried to catch her breath.

When something hit her leg, she screamed and almost

fell over. Frøy rubbed against her legs, then sat in front of her, watching her with those yellow eyes as if he wondered what on earth she was up to.

'You are like a ghost, you silly cat,' she said, crouching down to pet him. 'If you weren't so gorgeous, I'm not sure I would be able to forgive you.'

Frøy rubbed his head against her hand, purring loudly. 'Charmer,' Holly muttered.

She looked around to see if Tor was with him, but she couldn't see him. 'Are you roaming the island alone today? What are you doing? Catching birds or mice?'

Frøy flicked his ears.

Tor felt like a massive idiot, hiding behind the drystack. He knew someone was coming when Frøy bolted out into the road. It was stupid, he knew, but he couldn't pop up out of nowhere now, could he? She would think him a prat if he suddenly stood from his hiding place.

And she'd think he was an even bigger prat if she found him hiding. He couldn't make up his mind. Instead he watched her through a crack in the drystack.

She was sitting on her knees, petting Frøy, who obviously was enjoying himself.

'Traitor,' Tor muttered.

She was the first stranger he had talked to for more than five minutes since the news. And he couldn't help liking her. She was very good-looking, but it was more than that. She seemed... real, somehow.

He pulled away, annoyed with himself. *I'm not a peeping Tom*, he thought. Sneaking around, lurking at strange women wasn't what he did. This was stupid and immature.

He decided quickly and stood from the hiding place.

The only one he saw was Frøy who ignored him and kept washing his paws. There was no sign of Holly.

Frøy suddenly started walking away from him with his tale looking like a fluffy flagpole.

Tor hesitated for a second, then followed him.

Holly climbed carefully down the slope to the beach. It was muddy and slippery, and she didn't fancy ending up in a gooey heap at the bottom.

She was pretty sure she could follow the shoreline back towards Jack's farm and the house. At least she hoped so.

The wind was even stronger down here. She pulled the hat further down over her ears and pulled up the collar. Next time a scarf would be a good idea and a pair of those mittens she had ignored earlier.

Walking along the shore quickly turned out to be a monumentally bad idea. There was no place to climb up again. It was all sharp-edged stones and a lot more difficult to climb than she had anticipated.

'Why the hell don't they make a pathway for normal people to use?' she said aloud, while trying to climb over a boulder larger than herself. She tried to walk around it, but it jutted out into the water and she was not in the mood for a swim.

The stone was wet and covered in a thin layer of some kind of moss, making it slippery.

She was halfway over when her boot slipped and she fell. She tried to grab hold, but there was nothing to grab onto, and she tumbled down back on the beach.

'Fuck.' Holly tried to stand, but slipped again. 'Fuckety fuck,' she said.

She realised her knee hurt and found blood and a tear in the jeans. Holly sighed. *If this continues, I'll be so out of fucks*, she thought. *Before I do anything, I have to clean this. God knows what kind of bacteria will be in the mossy thing*, was her next thought.

She took off the backpack and dug through it for the wipes and the bottle of water she always carried. *No Band-Aids*, she thought. *My standards must be slipping.*

She looked at the tear. Damn, these were expensive jeans. She couldn't bear to tear them even more.

Holly looked around, and then up, and couldn't see anyone. To hell with modesty. This was an emergency.

She turned around and pulled down her jeans. It was bloody freezing, but at least the jeans would be saved. She started to wipe off the blood to inspect how bad it was.

Tor stopped so abruptly, Frøy bumped into his feet and gave him a disgruntled look.

What the hell was she doing?

She was bending down, looking at something, with her jeans around her ankles.

72

He held his breath for a long second, then realised he was acting like a real peeping Tom this time and took a step to the side, only to step on Frøy who let out a blood-curling scream and scratched his ankles.

It felt like slow-motion. Tor watched Holly turn, stumble in her own jeans and fall forward on her face. Tor couldn't move. This was a situation where he had no idea what to do.

She lifted her head. 'Are you fucking insane? What's wrong with you?'

Tor hesitated. She clearly wasn't asking Frøy and he wondered if the best thing he could do was to retreat and run up the hill.

But watching her struggle to get up, hindered by the jeans that were still around her ankles, he had no choice.

'Uhm, do you need any help?' He walked towards her, shielding his eyes so she wouldn't think he was staring at her bum.

'You think?' She gave him a scorching look, much like the one Frøy often used. 'If I've broken anything, I'll sue you for damages.'

Tor sat in front of her. 'I have no money, so good luck with that. Here, take my hand.'

She huffed, but allowed him to pull her up.

'You're bleeding,' he said when she stood. 'I'm sorry. I saw you, and when I tried to leave, I stepped on Frøy's tale.'

'You didn't cause this. I fell from the boulder and scraped my knee.' Holly sighed.

'So, you were checking the wound when I stepped on Frøy?' he said.

'Yes, I don't usually drop my pants in public and bend over. Especially when it's also freezing like this,' she said.

Tor frowned. 'Of course. Sorry.'

Holly raised her eyebrows. 'Would you mind turning around? I realise it's a bit late, but still. If you please.'

Tor turned around at once, feeling even more like a pervert than before. 'How... how did you end up down here?' he said after a while.

'I followed the slope. I thought that I could walk back along the beach and that there would be some kind of pathway,' Holly said.

'No, we don't have anything like that, I'm afraid. When you're a stranger, sticking to the more regular paths is the best choice.'

'You sound like a traffic warden. And why can't I explore? If it's dangerous for people to walk along here it should be fenced off.'

'The islanders know everything about the island and don't need fences. In fact, you are in a country where we have a world famous mountain cliff with no fences or protective barriers at all. We trust people to be sensible. And also, there's no shame in turning back,' he said.

Holly walked up to him, fully clothed again, he noticed.

'Why should there be any shame in turning back?' she said.

'There isn't. That's the whole point. If you come to a boulder like this or some kind of hindrance that could potentially be dangerous, you either walk around it, or you walk back the same way you came. You don't risk getting hurt.'

Holly looked at him. 'Are all Norwegians like you?'

'Like what?' Tor frowned.

'Like you have a long, logical explanation for everything. You did the same thing when you saved me from the cliff,' Holly said.

Tor wasn't sure how to respond to that. He wasn't sure if it was bad or good. 'Uhm. I don't think so,' he finally said.

'Never mind. Does it mean I have to go back up the same way? Is that even possible?' Holly said.

'Yes, and I'm afraid so.'

Holly sighed. 'Why are you down here? You must know that there's no path here.'

Tor had no idea what to say at first. 'Uhm,' he said. 'Oh, I followed Frøy. He's the one who found you.'

'Again? I now owe Frøy at least one can of tuna.'

Frøy suddenly showed up and plunked himself on Holly's boots. She bent down and stroked him. *Traitor,* Tor thought and scowled at the cat.

'You must really have hit a sore point on his tail.' Holly looked up at him.

'I did, and now he's mad at me, as you can see,' Tor said.

Frøy rolled around, letting Holly scratch his belly.

'He'll forgive you,' Holly said.

'Not so sure about that. Last time he got mad, he ignored me for a week. Look.'

Tor bent down to pet Frøy who immediately rolled away from him, jumped up and ran ahead of them.

Holly laughed. 'I see what you mean. Poor you.'

'Yeah, I'll have to get more treats for him now, I guess.'

They walked slowly back the way they came and when

Holly looked up the slope, she frowned. 'Are you sure that's the only way up?'

'Unless you want to swim. The water is probably three or four degrees. Celsius, that is. I have no idea what that is in Fahrenheit. You'll get hypothermia before you get past that headland you were attempting to climb,' he said and frowned when she burst out laughing.

Tor waited until she stopped. He could not see the humour in what he had said. It was necessary information, so why was she laughing?

Holly could see he had no idea why she laughed and that made it even funnier. She pulled herself together in case he would be insulted.

'Okay, so where's the easiest path up?' she asked, looking up at the slope that now looked more like the side of the Matterhorn than the easy hill she had come down.

'Put your feet where the rocks are,' Tor said and pointed. 'You go first, and then, if you fall, I'll catch you.'

She smiled at him. 'And who will catch you if you fall?'

'As long as I don't fall on Frøy, I'll be fine,' he said and smiled back.

Holly quickly looked down to hide her surprise. His whole disposition changed, even through the beard.

'Right. I'll go then,' she said, sounding a lot more confident than she was.

Walking upwards was hard. It strained her ankles and thighs, and the aching knee didn't exactly help either.

And she also knew that if she fell and he had to catch her, she would die from embarrassment before either of them could plunge to their death.

As if to demonstrate how easy it was, Frøy scooted past her and ran straight up, then stopped at the top to look at her.

'I think your cat is laughing at me,' she said to Tor, panting as she climbed.

'You're probably right. He does that a lot. He's very judgemental of humans, I'm afraid.' Tor didn't sound out of breath at all.

Holly looked down. He seemed to have no trouble climbing up the slope.

For a second she could see herself falling down, into his arms. He would save her, again, and they would gaze into each other's eyes and... and then they would tumble down, ending up at the bottom with their necks broken.

Get a grip, Holly.

Chapter Eight

Leaving the house after lunch the day after the knee incident, Holly was determined not to be saved by Tor and Frøy again. She would take a look at Jack's farm and then perhaps visit the shop. And she wouldn't go anywhere near Tor and Frøy's house.

She had found Band-Aids aplenty at the house, most of them colourful and clearly meant for Rosie, but they did the job. The knee was a bit stiff, but nothing to worry about.

The key to the main house was easy to find. Jack had put a little note on it that said "farm". She stuffed the key in one of her pockets.

Jack wouldn't mind if she had a look.

Not like I care if he does, she thought. *It's his fault that I'm here.* Jack had told her there was a pay as you go phone in a drawer, thanks to their dad, and armed with that, she headed outside. The phone was barely useful for texting and had absolutely no internet or even a camera, but it was working. It would do until she could get into town.

The farm had its own beach. How insane was that. Right now it looked grey and bleak, reminding her of all those Scandinavian crime series. But she had seen pictures from when the field was green and filled with wildflowers, and loads of people swimming in the clear, blue water.

'Bet it's freezing now like Tor said,' she muttered.

She also remembered Jack telling her about the boathouses. Ninni's was on one side of the path, his on the other. Apparently there were row boats in both of them.

'Trust me to come when the weather is awful and freezing,' she muttered.

Holly found her way down to the yard in front of the white house. The farm looked smaller than it had done in her head. There was the weird house on stilts; Jack loved raving about all the cured meat stored in there.

I'm not going in there to look at meat, Holly thought.

All she wanted was to try to understand Jack's fascination with this island. It was so strange that he had a whole new life, one that had nothing to do with any of them back home.

The key fitted in the outer door of the white house. Holly pushed it open and went inside. It seemed weird to go into an empty house like that. *Just a quick look, and I'm out of here,* she thought.

Everything was old and outdated. The furniture seemed worn down and ancient. She wrinkled her nose. Everything was dusty and in serious need of a good scrubbing down.

Holly decided not to go upstairs. It was too much of a ghost house.

She texted Jack.

Your farm is weird.

It took a few seconds before he replied.

I know. There are ghosts in there.

Shut up. There's no such thing.

Really creepy Norwegian ghosts of dead fishermen climbing back on land. They're called 'draug'.

Holly looked around. Something called *draug*, didn't sound nice at all. *Shut up*, she texted again.

He called then and Holly could hear him laughing.

'You are such a tit,' she said.

'Don't forget I spent the first night on the island sleeping in the garden,' he said.

He had sworn her to secrecy when he confessed to that little embarrassment.

'I'm not sleeping here. I just wanted to see your house. How are Ninni and Rosie?'

'Rosie has decided that sleep is for losers and keeps us up every bloody night. Ninni is so sleep-deprived she makes no sense most of the time.'

'You sound happy,' Holly said, smiling as she said it.

'Of course I'm happy. Being a dad is scary and exhausting, and I'm loving every minute. Of course, it helps to love the tired mum as well.'

'Good for you. When are you coming back?' Holly

looked out of the windows in the lounge. The view was stunning. 'I think I can see your goat island from here.'

'No, you can't. The islet is a lot further out than you think and also, they're sheep. We're coming back soon, long before Christmas, you know that. Ninni's mum is besotted with Rosie and keeps trying to get us to stay for the holidays though. It's getting on Ninni's nerves.'

'Well, maybe that's why the baby isn't sleeping. She's stressed.' Holly dropped the flimsy curtain and turned to leave the house.

A tall, burly man stood in the doorway, glaring at her.

Holly shrieked and dropped the phone.

Frøy was still ignoring him. He had found a spot in the window where he could enjoy the sunshine and ignore him at the same time.

Sneaky bastard, Tor thought.

He felt restless and slightly annoyed, despite spending two hours in the boat. And it was her fault. Why would a woman he had met and talked to twice have any kind of effect on him?

But here he was, thinking about Holly when he was supposed to be working.

There was something about her. She seemed happy enough, but she was also sad. Something was bothering her.

Tor went into the kitchen and put on the coffee machine. He glanced at the papers on the kitchen table. There wasn't much to hold his interest at the moment.

A nap might be the best option, or the book he hadn't finished.

Frøy appeared behind him. He flicked his tail back and forth while glaring at Tor.

'Yeah, I'm not giving you a treat. You're still mad at me for the tail. It was an accident,' Tor said.

The cat never begged for food. All he did was sit there.

Tor shook his head. 'I'm to blame, Frøy.'

Time to make peace with the cat, the only company he had at the moment. He took a piece of dried fish from the cupboard and dropped it on the floor.

Frøy tapped the fish with one paw, almost like he was checking the "best before" date. Then he snapped it and swallowed in two seconds before leaving.

'I guess you're too cool to chew,' Tor said.

He filled a thermos with the coffee, picked up the papers from the table, and walked up to the office again, determined to focus on buildings and not think about attractive sad women.

———

The big man stared at Holly with pure terror written on his face. He lifted his hands in front of him. *'Unnskyld,'* he said.

Holly took a deep breath. 'I have no idea what you just said.'

'Oh. I saw the door was open and I became worried. It's always locked.'

Holly picked up the mobile from the floor. Jack was still

there. 'I'm fine,' she said. 'Some man came in and scared the... scared me.'

She looked at the man who now looked mortified. 'I don't know who he is.'

'I'm Tobben. I work with Jack,' he said.

Holly smiled at him. 'It's Tobben, Jack.'

He made her laugh before saying goodbye, and she put the phone in her pocket. 'He says you're okay.'

Tobben visibly relaxed. 'Oh. Yes, I own the meat production business together with Jack and some other islanders. Did you know he's planning to open a restaurant here next summer?'

'Yes, he's mentioned it a few times.' *About a million times*, Holly thought.

'He's a bit mad, isn't he?' Tobben shuffled his feet a few times. 'Well. Uhm. I'll be going out again now. Sorry I frightened you.'

He turned around and disappeared, surprisingly quiet for a big man.

Holly shook her head. Jack had said the islanders were charming. So far, they had mostly been weird.

She waited for a couple of minutes before going outside herself. There was no sign of Tobben.

Holly stood still, not sure where she'd go next. It was all so quiet everywhere. How did they manage with all this silence? She was used to getting out of bed by six in the morning, and working ten to twelve hour shifts, surrounded by doctors, nurses, paramedics, patients, and all the rest of the people that made up a hospital. There was hardly a quiet moment anywhere.

Here the sky seemed endless. She could see trail from aeroplanes flying overhead, heading for the little airport where she had landed.

She sighed. At least Jack had been able to swim in the ocean when he first came to the island. Now it was too bloody cold.

Even so, she went down to the beach, walking between the two boathouses. Both houses had small, wooden piers sticking out into the water. Holly sat on the edge of one and looked down. The water was surprisingly clear and she could see all the way to the bottom.

'Fish,' she said when she discovered a small shoal swimming in between the seaweed. 'Itty, bitty, tiny fish.'

She sighed again and looked ahead. Nothing but water and sky.

I could so easily go stark mad by staying here, she thought. *There's absolutely nothing to keep me distracted. Just me talking to myself.*

She pulled out the phone and looked at it. No signal. Absolutely perfect. For a second she considered throwing it into the water, but stopped herself. Without it she'd definitely lose her mind.

Still, as she sat there, looking at the view and the water, her shoulders relaxed and she smiled to herself.

Tor entered the shop with a bit of trepidation. He hadn't been in there for days now. He knew they thought he was odd and they were right. He sighed with relief when he saw Jens inside. He preferred dealing with him.

The old man sat behind the desk, reading a newspaper and muttering to himself. Apparently he didn't like someone's politics. He looked up when Tor entered.

'Good morning,' he said, as his eyes fell on the bucket Tor was carrying. 'Is that for us?'

'Yes, I caught some cods today. Unfortunately the crab pots were empty,' Tor said.

Jens took of the lid and peered inside. He looked up at Tor. 'These are nice. We might keep them for ourselves.'

'You're welcome to them. Did you receive Frøy's treats?'

'Sure. They're on the shelf. You know where to find them.'

Tor passed him, nodding slightly, but didn't say anything else. He could feel Jens's eyes in the back of his neck. The old man was curious, but he didn't push, and he was grateful for that.

All I want is a treat for the damn cat, he thought.

'Got mail for you today,' Jens said, suddenly standing right behind him.

Tor looked at him, then at the envelopes and magazines Jens held out to him. 'Okay. Thanks.'

Jens beamed at him. 'Are you looking for anything else apart from the treats for Frøy? A varied diet is a healthy diet, you know.'

Tor had no idea how to respond to that. 'Do you have those cans of tuna? The ones in water. Frøy likes them,' Tor said.

'Of course we have. Frøy also likes fish pudding, if you want that?'

Jens chatted while he walked ahead with Tor trailing after him. 'Yes, give me one of those as well,' Tor said. 'I hope Frøy isn't a nuisance to any of you.'

Jens laughed. 'No, of course not. He's a delight. He comes to say hello when he's in the mood and we give him his little treat. I hope that's okay.'

'I'm sure it is,' Tor said.

He looked around, not wanting to chat with any more people.

Jens finally dug out a multi-pack of canned tuna and handed it to him.

'Anything else I can get you? Something for yourself? We have freshly baked Christmas bread today. And also Alma's speciality, the wort beer bread. It's one of my favourites this time of year.'

Tor hadn't had wort beer bread since he visited his grandmother when he was a boy. He followed Jens over to the bread counter. Jens took a long, round bread with a dark brown crust from the shelf and plopped it into a paper bag. 'There you go. Do you have butter and brown cheese for that?'

'I... yes, I have.'

Jens pointed at the selection of cakes. 'We also have Christmas bakes today. Coconut macaroons and sand cakes.' He pointed at the small, pie-shaped cakes. 'Those are my favourites too. I'm partial to filling them up with whipped cream and jam myself. Or some lovely custard.'

He took one of the coconut macaroons and bit off the top. 'You don't get these better anywhere else, I swear.'

Tor couldn't help smiling. 'Fine. I'll take a few of those, but not the sand cakes. I don't like them much.'

Jens looked at him. 'Really? What's your favourite Christmas cake then? I'm sure we have it.'

Tor looked at the shelves, then shook his head. 'I'm happy with the macaroons.'

Jens wasn't about to give up so easily. 'What about a cookie man? They are a local specialty and they are really good with coffee.'

He pointed at a stack of cookie men, decorated with red food colour. 'See? Freshly baked yesterday.'

'I'll take five,' Tor said, hoping it would shut Jens up.

Jens grinned from ear to ear. 'I'm happy to see that you are getting into the holiday spirit. There's something so nice, so *koselig*, about this time of year, isn't it? No matter how old I get, I still look forward to Christmas.'

I'm not, Tor thought. Not for the last two years. But he played nice not to disappoint Jens.

'Sure. Could you give me five more yulemen and an extra paper bag?'

Tor was exhausted by the time he paid for the treats and could leave. Jens talked without taking a breath.

He even followed him outside.

'Frøy isn't with you today?'

'No, he's in a mood. I'm hoping the treats will help,' Tor said.

Jens nodded. 'Smart move.'

Tor turned and hurried up the hill, eager to get away from all the questions and the chit chat.

He didn't want to talk to anyone. How hard was that to understand?

On the way back home, he passed the fork in the road and hesitated before picking the road that led to her house. He knew it wasn't Holly's house, but he didn't know her family. He could barely remember anyone's faces these days.

But he remembered hers.

He stared at the house for a long time, then realised he would look like a complete dollop if she came outside and found him.

So he left, feeling embarrassed and foolish.

———————

After hiking for three hours, Holly was pretty sure she had seen whatever there was to see on the island. Seagulls and fish, pebbles and shrubs.

It wasn't very interesting, if she had to be honest. Especially when the sun disappeared behind the clouds. Everything was mostly grey and white, even the sea.

She sighed. It would have been better to stay in London, to go out with friends and do anything other than moping around like this.

Jack had sworn it would take her mind of all things London, but as far as she could see, it made it worse. There was nothing here to take her mind of anything.

Holly walked up to the house and discovered a small

paper bag hanging from the door handle. Curiosity got the better of her and she opened it.

Cookies. She pulled out a cookie man and looked at it. It was bigger than her hand and decorated with what she hoped was safe food colouring. Just a smiley face and buttons.

Holly sniffed it. *Vanilla,* she thought before biting off a leg. It was crunchy on the outside and surprisingly soft on the inside, and so good she had to take another bite.

Holly looked around and couldn't see anyone.

Maybe it was from Emil's parents. Or Britt, maybe? Jack had said the islanders leave things at the farm all the time. He almost stepped on a carton of eggs once.

'I'm fine with cookie men,' she said and took a new bite.

It did occur to her that if this was some kind of Nordic Noir island, somebody would more than likely have poisoned the cookies.

'Too late now,' she said, entering the house, already munching on a second cookie.

Chapter Nine

After a late breakfast, Holly caught the ferry to the mainland to see if anything could be done about her phone. Not that she had much hope, but still. Something might be salvaged. Hopefully the sim card. If the hospital had called, she wouldn't know and it was bothering her.

She was afraid they would kick her out of the programme, and she was also afraid they would let her stay. She kept flipping from hope to fear and back again. It was exhausting.

In the passenger lounge on the ferry, there was a corner with vending machines for coffee and sweets. A Christmas tree with colourful bulbs and lights lit up the drab wall behind it. Red and green garlands, with stars hanging at intervals, decorated the windows.

Surprisingly she appeared to be the only one onboard. *Rush hour was probably earlier*, she thought, smiling at the idea.

Holly went outside to the deck and leaned against the

railing. The sky was so brightly blue it almost didn't seem real. The ferry seemed to be flying across the water. The wind hit her face and droplets from the water tasted salty.

Not unpleasant. She could feel her shoulders relax. It was a strange feeling.

Holly stayed outside until the ferry passed the first island outside the town. Jack had explained there were four islands shielding the town from the North Sea.

The ferry docked at the second largest of the islands. When she had arrived five days earlier it had been so dark and windy, she couldn't remember much. Also, she had taken a taxi from the bus station and jumped on the ferry right before it sailed.

This was very different.

Holly smiled. She hadn't been a tourist anywhere for ages.

From the harbour, she walked through streets with rows of white wooden houses. Almost every window had a star or a menorah, or something else festive, she discovered.

The bridge leading from the island to the mainland was huge and old, and easy to climb. Holly stopped on the top of the bridge, looking at the town. Jack had said Haugesund wasn't big, but that they had everything you needed. She knew she wasn't pronouncing the name properly, but that was fine. Perhaps Tor could give a language class. *Now, there's an idea*, she thought. *That could be fun.*

Or maybe not. He wasn't exactly friendly. Not to mention he had the thing with those long explanations.

Across the bridge, she found the High Street easily enough. It was the one with all the shops and the Christmas decorations strung across the buildings. Mostly bells and green garlands, but also giant snowflakes lighting up the street.

Holly looked around. *Something is missing,* she thought. Why wasn't there any snow? Norway should be snowy, shouldn't it? Jack had said that the island was rainy, but still, this was the mainland, wasn't it?

She found a phone shop easily enough. Jens at the island shop had given her a note with directions.

Inside it looked like any other phone repair shop she had ever been in, including the smiling young man behind the counter.

'I dropped my phone in the slush,' Holly said, embarrassed.

He took the phone from her and looked at it. 'Did you dry it out?' he said with a Norwegian accent to his English.

Holly felt even more embarrassed. 'I put it in rice,' she admitted.

'Really? And the miracle cure didn't work?' He grinned at her, and Holly laughed.

'No, but I'm hoping it's because it hasn't been charged. I forgot my charger back home. Do you think that you can... ehm, fix it?'

'I don't know yet. How soon do you need it?' He lifted a hand. 'No, let me guess. Yesterday, right?'

'Would that be possible?'

He grinned even wider. 'Depends on the damage, I'm afraid. You're from England, right?'

'London.'

'How did you end up here and at Christmas too?' He put down the phone and wrote a note with her name.

Holly smiled. 'My brother lives on one of the islands outside of here. About an hour with the ferry. He's a chef.'

'Really? I've heard of him. Small town, people talk, you know. Everyone knows about him. Mad, isn't he? Starting a restaurant out there? You wouldn't get me on that ferry.'

'Are you afraid of the water?' Holly couldn't help laughing.

He handed her the note. 'My people are river people.'

'Pretty sure there are rivers in this country too. Far from the sea as well, I should think.' Holly couldn't help teasing him. 'Like they have tons of mountains with waterfalls, I think.'

'Yeah, but up in the mountains it's really bloody cold. Snow up to your elbows.' He shook his head. 'I'd be better off in London, I think.'

'It's cold there too and it's by the water.'

He looked at her and grinned. 'Yes, but it's a river, isn't it?'

While they talked, he had opened the phone and inspected it. Then he looked up at her. 'Listen, you might have to pray for a Christmas miracle with this one.'

'What about the sim card? Can I move that over to this phone?' Holly handed him the old phone she had been using.

He looked at it, then looked at her with an expression of disbelief. 'Seriously? That thing belongs in a museum. I can get the sim card from your phone to fit. All you need is an adapter for that, but it's probably not going to work like your own phone. At all. That thing isn't really a smart phone, is it? So I can't guarantee you can get online with it, or even get all your messages. I'm sorry.'

Holly groaned. 'Damn,' she said.

'Do you have insurance for your own phone?' He put the card back in the phone again.

'I think so. I have a phone plan for it and I have travel insurance, of course.'

'You should get in contact with the insurance company right away then. Also, it's locked to your phone plan. So, if the phone is dead, you will have a hard time finding something here. At least one that is the same as the one you have, also it will be crazy expensive. You might have to live without a connection to the world until you get back home.'

'But I won't be going back to London until after Christmas. I need a phone in the meantime. I'm expecting a really important call. Please, isn't there anything you can do?' Holly hoped she didn't sound too desperate.

He frowned. 'Okay, come back before I close, I'll see what I can do. I might be able to get you a cheaper phone you can use with the sim. I'll do my best.'

'Thank you. I'll keep my fingers crossed in the meantime.'

Holly didn't feel very confident when she ventured outside into the street. It was odd being without her own phone. Jack's phone barely had any signal and she had no idea how long it would last.

A group of carollers stood outside one of the shops, dressed in colourful down jackets, and Christmas themed bobble hats. One of them was obviously the conductor since she raised her arms and they all began to sing.

Shoppers stopped to listen. Some even joined in.

Holly listened for a moment. It was funny listening to Christmas songs in a different language. Especially when they started to sing 'Silent Night'. Different words, same melody. Holly sang the familiar words to herself, following the chorus.

Tor looked around at the street filled with holiday shoppers with utter exhaustion. He needed to buy Christmas presents for his friends and send them within a day or two, and he was miserable.

Christmas hadn't been the same the last two years. He couldn't get into the spirit of it. Mostly it just annoyed him. The idea of going inside a shop to buy anything seemed too overwhelming all off a sudden. Perhaps he should go back to the island. He could tell Henrik and Kari that all the shops were closed. Or frozen shut. Something. And then order everyone's presents online.

The idea cheered him up, and he decided to get a cup of coffee before heading for the ferry. He almost walked into Holly, trying to avoid a group of carollers. It was too late to duck away and pretend he hadn't see her.

She was singing along with the carollers, clearly enjoying herself. For a second he thought perhaps he could get away unseen, but then she turned her head and her face lit up in a huge smile.

Tor pulled himself together.

'Hi!' She came right over and touched his arm. 'You can help me. What are they singing now?'

'Oh.' Tor had to listen to the song. 'It's sort of a psalm, I think. About the nativity, is that right?'

'Of course. I loved the melody, it's very evocative, isn't it?'

Tor listened to the song and nodded. 'Yes, it is, I guess.'

The singers threw themselves into a quicker melody and Holly nudged him. 'What about this? Is that a psalm too?'

'No, not at all. It's about a barn *nisse* and a dancing rat who wants to steal his Christmas porridge.' Tor looked at her. 'But you probably don't know what a *nisse* is, do you?'

'Of course I do. It's like a brownie, only with red clothes and white beard, and a sort of insane grin,' Holly said.

'A brownie is a chocolate cake,' Tor said, slightly confused.

'Sure, but it's also the English equivalent of a *nisse*, only a bit meaner, perhaps.' Holly gave him a triumphant look. 'I bet you didn't know that.'

'I did not know that.'

For a moment neither of them said anything, they just looked at each other and it quickly became weird.

Tor tried desperately to find something to say and made a decision that surprised even himself. 'Have you had coffee yet?'

'No, I came to see if they could do anything with my phone. I was looking for a coffee shop, to be honest. Are you inviting me?' Holly's smile grew wider.

Tor nodded and waved his hand. 'I was on my way to get a coffee, and… and would like it if you joined me.'

'You sound like a waiter,' Holly said.

'I do?' *She says the oddest things,* he thought.

'Absolutely.' Holly looked around. 'Where's the coffee?'

Tor pointed again. 'A bit further ahead. Not on this street, those are bound to be full. There's a bakery a couple of streets further down with the best cakes in town. If you like soft gingerbread, that is.'

'I don't know yet,' Holly said.

'They probably have tea as well,' Tor said.

'That depends on the coffee they have on offer.'

It dawned on Tor that this was the first coffee he had shared with a woman in over two years. *Kari would love this,* he thought. Good thing he'd never tell her.

As promised, the little café was mostly empty. It was warm and friendly inside, and it smelled of vanilla and coffee.

'Oh, my god,' Holly said, staring at the cakes and savoury rolls in the display shelves. 'I'm going to sink the ferry if this goes on.'

Tor frowned. 'I hope you don't worry about that.'

'Not now, anyway. I'm on holiday, aren't I? Tell me what's good here.'

'Oh.' Tor looked at the cake display. Most cakes had been cut in individual slices, showing the fillings. 'Well. The white marzipan cake with cream and raspberry jam is always delicious, so is the chocolate cream cake. It's one of my favourites.'

'Are they Christmassy?' Holly bent down to check out the cream cakes.

'Not particularly. You can get those year round. Let me see.' He discovered what he was looking for and pointed at a display of chocolate-covered hearts. 'Those are my particular favourites and this is the only shop that sells them, and you can only get them at Christmas.'

The girl behind the counter heard him. 'I have the big ones too. They're super good today.'

Tor nodded. 'Give me two of the hearts and a bag of the smaller ones to take home. And also two of those.' He pointed at some ring-shaped cakes. 'Holly, would you like coffee or tea?'

Holly was studying the board behind the counter. 'What's a yule latte?'

'I have no idea.' He asked the girl who explained in great detail what was in the latte.

'Pepper cake crumbs, ginger and cardamom, with a sprinkle of cinnamon or cocoa. Or both,' she said in English, smiling at Holly.

'Okay. I'll have a yule latte, please,' Holly said.

Tor shook his head when the girl wanted to know if he wanted the same. 'Black coffee for me,' he said.

Holly laughed. 'That's really old school.'

'I don't like sweet or spiced-up coffee. It ruins the cake.'

The girl handed them the cakes and told them she'd bring the latte to the table.

'What about your coffee?' Holly asked when he steered towards a table by the window.

He nodded towards a side table with cups, sugar and

milk, and two large cans. 'It's self-service when you don't need a fancy barista to make your coffee.'

It took a couple of minutes to get his coffee and when he returned to the table, Holly had picked up one of the cakes. She was inspecting it with a serious expression.

'What is it? And why is it round? It looks like a churro, but I don't think that's what it is.'

'It's called *kransekake*,' he said, smiling when Holly tried to mouth the unfamiliar words. 'It means "wreath cake", but it's also called a tower cake.'

'Oh. How is it a tower?'

'It's round because you can buy or bake a whole cake with rings in different sizes and put one ring on top of the other, so you get a cone-shaped cake. And then you can decorate them. My grandmother used to make one for Christmas, and decorate them with those funny crackers, and then one for 17th of May with little flags on it. It's tradition, I guess,' he said.

'And what are they made of?' Holly broke the cake in two and smelled it.

It made him smile. 'No flour if you belong to the gluten free people. Just powdered sugar, egg whites, and ground almond. It's actually more like baked marzipan, I think.'

She took a bite and a look of delighted surprise crossed her face. 'It's chewy and crunchy.'

'I know. It's another favourite of mine. '

Holly finished both halves before the girl brought her the coffee. 'It's damned good. Do they ever put chocolate in them or something like that?'

'My gran would froth at the mouth to hear you ask that.

You don't mess with perfection. Although you can get sticks of *kransekake* where the ends are dipped in chocolate. I like them too.'

'But you wouldn't tell your grandmother that?' She was stirring her latte and laughing at him.

'Not if I wanted to taste the cake.'

Tor picked up one of the hearts and waved it at her. 'These are even better.'

The hearts were thick and covered in chocolate on the top.

He took a bite and couldn't help closing his eyes.

'This is basically a soft gingerbread cookie with chocolate,' Holly said, biting into hers.

Tor finished his in three bites. 'Too good.'

Holly took longer to enjoy her snack. 'Why do you call the gingerbread cookies pepper cookies? Is there really pepper in them?'

Tor frowned. 'Of course. There's also golden syrup, and the usual Christmas spices like cinnamon, cloves, and ginger, I think. I made the cookies when I was a kid, but I've never made the dough.'

'You made cookies?'

'It's not that difficult. We would always make one of those gingerbread houses. You sound as if you think I grew up under a rock.' Tor couldn't help smiling.

'No, it's just that you don't exactly seem very social, now do you? They call you the hermit at the shop, you know.'

She was teasing him now. Tor could see she was enjoying herself.

'I prefer my own company these days,' he said.

'You know what they say. If you keep to yourself for long enough, you might fall out of the habit of being social. Don't you miss other people?'

Holly was trying to drink the coffee and ended up with a froth moustache.

Tor tried to hide the smile. Holly frowned. 'What? It wasn't a funny question.'

'No, you have milk on you upper lip.' Tor handed her one of the paper napkins from the table.

That made her laugh as she dried her mouth. Then she looked at him again. 'Better?'

'Yes, much better.' He hoped she had forgotten her question, but of course she hadn't.

'Tell me. Don't you miss other people? You know, to see, to meet up with, to talk to.' Holly used the teaspoon to attack the coffee.

'Isn't that awfully sweet?' Tor tried to distract her again. She saw right through it.

Holly smiled. 'Really?'

'Fine. No, I don't miss people. I'm happy alone, and I have Frøy for company. I work a lot. My job is demanding and I like to focus on it. Being alone doesn't mean being lonely, you know that, right?'

He was feeling slightly uncomfortable talking about himself and he could sense that he was saying too much. He took a bite from the other *kransekake*.

Holly had finished the froth and could finally drink the coffee without making a mess. 'I can see that. I'm surrounded by people all the time, at the hospital and at my flat. My flatmate is my best friend, but she's also really sociable, so there's people over all the time. There's moments where I'm desperate for a few minutes by myself. So much so that I once invented a smoking habit.'

'A smoking habit?' Tor felt relieved she wasn't pressing him for more information. 'That sounds silly.'

'Yeah, it was, but smokers have a legitimate reason to go outside, don't they? You can't really say "I'm popping out for a bit of solitude".'

'Why not? If you need it, I mean. You have a demanding job, don't you? There must be times when you need a breather. Is that why you came to the island?' Tor could have hit himself the moment the question was out there. *Too personal*, he thought.

Holly pushed the half-empty coffee mug to the side. 'I can't drink any more of this. It's too... too much. I think I'm done with artisanal coffees for a while. A mug of Earl Grey, with just the teabag, would be better, I think.'

'Want me to get one for you? Or at least Lipton Yellow, which is the standard tea in most places, I'm afraid.' Tor was halfway out of the chair when she put her hand on his. He sat at once, staring at her hand.

Nobody had touched him for a long time. It was the strangest sensation. Tor pulled his hand back, slowly, hoping she wouldn't notice. Perhaps he really had been away from people for too long.

'No, I only meant next time we go for coffee. Then I think tea will do fine,' Holly said, her voice shaking slightly.

She's expecting there to be a next time, Tor thought. He fought the impulse to run. After all, he had started it.

He cleared his throat. 'Besides the phone, is there anything else you are here to do? In town, I mean?'

Holly shrugged. 'I'm just looking at the moment. I bought most of the Christmas presents in London with my dad because Jack said Norway is crazy expensive.'

'He's not wrong. It can be. I haven't bought any presents,' he admitted.

'Really? Do you have to buy many?'

'A few. The problem is that ideally I should buy them today, so that I can send them tomorrow, otherwise the post office can't guarantee they will get there in time,' he explained.

'For family or friends?' She had the most innocent look in the world when she asked.

'Both,' Tor said, surprising himself.

'Well, do you need any help? Or want the company? I'm really good at buying presents.'

'Are you?' Tor couldn't help smiling.

Holly nodded. 'Let's just say I'm an expert at buying stuff quickly. Now, tell me how many you need and for whom. I need to know a little about the recipients.'

Tor went along with it. It seemed like a better idea than to start rummaging around in the shops by himself.

'My mum and her partner are readers, so I'll need a few books for them. My dad is in Tromsø and his wife loves crime story box sets, so I thought I might see if I can get a hold of something they haven't seen yet. Then there's Kari and Henrik. Henrik is my friend and business partner. They have two kids who only want Lego. Doesn't matter what it is as long as it's Lego.'

'Kids are easy. I bought a stuffed sheep for Rosie, that's my brother's little girl. They have their own flock of sheep, so I think it will be a success.'

'I haven't seen any.' Tor wondered how Frøy would react to a flock of sheep.

'They're kept on a small islet off the coast of the big island. My dad and I aren't convinced they're sheep. They look like shaggy goats.'

'Must be Old Norwegians or something,' Tor said, laughing when she gaped at him. 'What? I know we have different kinds of sheep, okay. We have all sorts of farm animals in this country.'

'I would love to see them, actually. Do you know how to drive a boat?'

Tor frowned. 'Excuse me?'

'You know. One of those boats with an engine at the end. Jack has one in his boat house and so does Ninni. I think one is also a row boat.'

Tor raised his hands. 'Are you sure you want to get into a boat with me? How can you be sure we won't end up in Iceland or Shetland – or, more likely, at the bottom of the sea?'

'I thought all Norwegians could do stuff like that.' Holly looked disappointed.

'Not really. Some of us have lived in a city all our lives. Fortunately for me though, I grew up with boats.'

Holly cocked her head. 'You're joking now, right?'

'About the boat? No. It's old and not very fancy, but it's perfect for my needs.'

'Oh.' Holly looked puzzled for a second. 'Can you take me to the islet?'

'Probably, if I knew where to find it. And also, we would need permission to do so.'

'But they're my brother's animals,' Holly said. 'Of course I can go see them.'

'Have you asked him if you can go there?'

Holly frowned. 'I don't have to. He's my brother.'

Tor wasn't so sure that was enough. 'Islets like that are mostly private and you can't just walk onto private land. Also, when there's animals, there are other restrictions.'

Holly didn't look pleased. 'Yes, well, maybe I'll just take out Jack's boat and row to the islet,' she said.

Tor hid a smile. 'You can row a boat?'

'I've been in a row boat in Finsbury Park,' Holly said, on the defensive. He didn't have to know it had only happened once... during a hen party. 'I mean, how hard can it be if my brother can do it?'

'Please don't try to do something like that alone. It's dangerous,' Tor said. 'It's really difficult unless you know what you're doing, and on this coast the weather can turn quickly.'

Holly sighed. 'You can row, right?'

'I can row a boat, no problem there, but rowing about in a park pond in London, or in the Oslofjord where you always see land, is very different from here, where at some point you see nothing but water. You could get in real danger.'

Holly sighed. 'I'm sorry. If you don't want to, that's fine. It's not like I'm desperate to see the sheep-goats. Jack and

Ninni can take me. To be honest, I wanted to take a trip on the sea, not with a ferry, but with a small boat. Just to see how it is, you know?'

Tor wasn't sure where the words came from, but they flew out of his mouth before he could stop himself. 'I go out fishing most mornings. You can come out with me.'

Holly gaped. 'You have your boat here?'

'I do. It's not fancy, and you need to dress appropriately. It can get bloody cold out there. And I would pick you up at eight o'clock.'

He realised he was trying to talk her out of it. Himself too.

Holly beamed. 'Thank you! I would love to go. When?'

'Ehm, I will let you know. I don't really have a fixed time table,' Tor said, hoping she would have forgotten by then.

Chapter Ten

He was doing it again. That thing that made her laugh at him. Holly could see he wasn't sure why she was laughing, or how easy he was to read.

'I'm sorry,' she said.

'Okay.' Tor looked a bit confused.

Holly made a note not to tease him anymore, but he was too adorable. She decided to play nice. Especially to make sure he wouldn't change his mind about taking her out on the boat.

'I'm not sure if I'll manage to eat anything sweet ever again after this,' she said.

He smiled and the tension between them disappeared. 'Of course you will. That's the spirit of Christmas.'

'Pretty sure it isn't.' Holly grinned.

'It is here. Christmas in Norway is mostly about the food. You'll see.'

Holly pushed back her chair. 'I need to walk it off. Let's go find your presents. Have you made a list?'

Tor stood. 'No, why would I do that?'

'So that you remember everyone and you can jot down a few ideas on what to get them.'

'But I already told you.'

Holly linked her arm to his and strolled down the street. 'Is this whole street closed to traffic?'

'Yes, I think so. It says so right there.' Tor pointed at a sign on the wall.

'"*Gågate?*" What does it mean?'

'Directly translated it means "pedestrian street". You know, a street where you can walk.' He steered her towards a toy store. 'I can see Legos from here.'

Holly couldn't help but smile when they got inside. *Toy stores are the same everywhere*, she thought. The store was brimming with over-excited children who wanted everything they could see and exhausted parents who tried to hold them back.

'I think you'll have to fight your way through,' Holly teased.

Tor looked around. 'I'm bigger than them.'

A joke. Holly jabbed him with her elbow. 'You're bigger than everyone. You can't do that. We have to wait in line. Tell me about the kids. How old are they?'

'Nora is nine and Leah is six. Nora wants a building, doesn't matter what it is, and Leah wants an Olaf, whatever that is. I asked their parents so that they will get something they want.'

'That's thoughtful of you. Asking them, I mean.'

Tor smiled. 'How else will I know what they want, especially now that I'm here?'

'Good point. I think I see Olaf over there.' Holly handed him a box with the jolly snowman. He examined it.

'This is it?'

'You obviously haven't seen *Frozen*. There's a glitch in your social education.' *Probably not the only one*, she thought.

'Olaf it is, then.' He smiled at her. 'I'll find the building. Nora loves to build houses with Legos and her dad wants to see if she will like to build something bigger, more complicated. Like this.' He took down a box with the skyline of London. 'What do you think?'

'I want to build it. This is lovely, Tor. I'm sure she'll be thrilled.' Holly smiled at his obvious delight about the girls' gifts. It was... charming. They joined the queue.

'You're close to them, aren't you?'

'I'm their uncle. Neither of us have any siblings, and Henrik and I have been friends since kindergarten.'

Holly thought about her own brothers. 'There are times I would have loved to be an only child. Having two brothers can be exhausting for a girl.'

'What? They were horrible to you?'

'Not really. Jack is older than me and he's the responsible one. My mum passed away when I was four, so I hardly remember her. Danny is the youngest and he's a pest. A loveable pest,' she added when Tor looked concerned. 'We fought tooth and nails when we were growing up, but we're good friends now.'

'That must have been hard for you, to grow up without your mother.' The concern in his voice was sincere and Holly swallowed a surprising lump in her throat. *Oh, I should never have mentioned Mum. I talk too much,* she scolded herself.

'Not really. I was so young. I'm not even sure if I remember her or if what I remember is something Dad or Jack told me,' she said, keeping her voice steady.

She hardly ever talked about her mum. Especially not to someone who was practically a stranger. 'I think it's your turn,' she said, pointing at the cashier.

She waited at the side while Tor paid for the gifts and then followed him to the bookstore. Neither of them mentioned their families again.

It looked and smelled like every other bookstore she had ever been inside, and she perused the shelves while Tor tried to find something for his mother.

An entire table was dedicated to Christmas books. Another to troll books. She picked one up and leafed through it, fascinated by the detailed drawings, mostly in black and white.

'I'm not sure how they became a symbol of nastiness on the internet. They're really more of a force of nature and an attempt to explain nature, and why we get scared in forests,' Tor said, popping up beside her with a few books in his hand.

'Are they all in Norwegian?' Holly put down the one she was holding.

'Not usually. Tourists like them. Perhaps there's no tourists at the moment.' He smiled at her. 'Except for you.'

'Too bad.' Holly put down the book. It was far too expensive for her budget. She looked up at Tor. 'Did you find something for your mum or do you want me to help?'

'I have it. Mamma wanted this thriller, so I'm sure she hasn't read it yet. She usually gives me a list of ten titles, and I can pick two. That way she'll still be surprised and not disappointed.'

'Smart system,' Holly said.

'Smart mamma.' He waved another book. 'I also got one for her partner. He likes history and this has just arrived. I'll go pay for them.'

Holly looked around. 'Is there an English section here?'

'Over there, in the corner.'

Holly grabbed his arm. 'Come. I love looking around in bookstores. There is always something to find that surprises you. Do you read much?'

'I have attended school from an early age, and mastered the art of putting letters together in meaningful sentences,' Tor said, looking pleased with himself when she burst out laughing.

'Of course you have, but do you also read books for fun? Any particular kind?'

'Yes, I do. My house has wall to wall bookshelves.'

'You only have one bookshelf at your house,' Holly said.

'Not this house. I mean my house in Oslo. Only it's not a house, it's a flat.'

'Oh, I thought you had moved to the island. Are you here for a holiday?'

'Not really. I needed a quiet place to work for a while and I found it here.'

He seemed to be trying to avoid answering and Holly got curious. Before she had a chance to ask him again, he'd paid for the books and led her to an electronics store.

'Kari wanted something too,' he said, looking as if she had never asked him a question.

Holly decided to keep her curiosity to herself. If she tried to pry, he might do the same to her, and she didn't want that. She didn't want to talk about the hospital right now. She just wanted to have a fun day.

She tagged along while Tor roamed the electronic store before heading over to the desk where three young people looked efficient and in good moods despite the blinking reindeer headbands they were all wearing.

A short conversation with one of the reindeers, during which the only thing Holly understood was his name, ended with him producing a package from under the desk and handing it to Tor.

Tor gave Holly a triumphant smile and showed her what he had bought. 'This is perfect.'

'It's pink, with cat ears. I thought you were buying a present for the mother of the girls.' Holly wasn't sure about it.

Tor admired the bright neon pink headset. 'That's the whole idea. She almost exclusively wears black and, although she always looks good, I've hardly seen her wear anything else. So, pink it is.'

He stuck the package in his backpack and looked relieved.

'That's it. I'm done with my presents.'

'What about your friend? Don't you want a present for him?'

'I have that on the island,' he said. 'Do you know what *fenalår* is?'

Holly rolled her eyes. 'Jack produces them on the farm, from the sheep, actually. Did you buy him one of those?'

'That I did. Henrik will love it. I also got him a fly.'

Holly raised her eyebrows. 'You bought him a fly? Because a regular housefly wasn't fancy enough?'

Tor chuckled. 'Not that kind. He's an avid fly fisher. We hike in Oslomarka at least once a year.'

'What's that?' Holly had caught the word "Oslo", but not the rest.

'It's a name for the mountains and woods that surround Oslo. You can camp up there and it's really nice. And you can fish in the rivers or lakes.'

'You're really into fishing, aren't you?' Holly teased him.

'It's… nice. No stress, you know?'

Holly smiled. 'I'll take your word for it.'

They were soon outside again. The wind was picking up and it was snowing. Sort of. Holly could see that the snowflakes melted as soon as they hit the pavement.

'I have to go and get my phone,' she said.

'Okay. Don't forget that the last boat goes back to the island at six.'

'Otherwise I'll have to sleep on the pier?' Holly said.

'Yes. Or you could get a hotel room.'

She looked at him. He seemed a bit weird all of a sudden.

'You're taking that ferry too, right?'

'I am.' He looked at his watch. 'In two hours. I just have to run a few more errands first. Will you be okay?'

Holly smiled. 'I think I can manage on my own for a couple of hours.'

'Oh. Of course. That was… well, I'll see you on the ferry, then.'

He turned around, then turned back. 'Is there anywhere you want me to tell you about?'

'Like what?' Holly wasn't sure what he meant.

'Well, if you're looking for a pharmacy, it's that way. A shop for all sort of stuff, like a…' He searched for words. 'Haberydashy? Is that right?'

'Haberdashery? No, I don't need any yarn or needles,' Holly said, enjoying his efforts.

'Okay, but they have more than that in there. Toiletries and other stuff.'

Holly bit her lip, trying to stop herself from laughing. He looked right through that.

'Yes. Of course. I'm leaving,' he said.

He turned properly now and didn't look back.

Holly sighed. He was odd and also kind of hot, and far too cute. But she wasn't there to fool around with cute Norwegians.

She headed over to the phone shop and almost held her breath while she waited for Arnie to finish up with another customer. He spotted her and smiled, and Holly hoped that meant good news.

Finally he came over to her. 'Good news and bad news, I'm afraid.'

'Right.' Holly prepared herself for the worst.

'The phone is pretty much kaput. But I saved your sim card. Best I could do, I'm afraid. I have nothing as fancy as your phone here, but I have a basic one that will tide you over until you can get home. You can google on it and everything. How does that sound?'

He put both phones on the counter and Holly sighed. 'I love my phone,' she said.

'Ah, we all do. Now, do you want me to stick the sim card in the new phone?'

'How much?'

'With the new phone… 800 crowns.'

Holly did a quick calculation and tried to hide the shock. Almost 80 pounds!

Arnie frowned. 'It's as cheap as I can make it. If you go to the chain stores, they'll take even more. I promise. Tell you what, if you find it cheaper anywhere, I'll match the price.'

Holly shook her head. 'No, it's fine. I need my phone.'

'You might get it back on the travel insurance, you know. I did that once. I'll write you a proper and impressive-looking receipt so you can show them that.' Arnie looked hopeful.

'Please do.' Holly handed him her credit card.

Chapter Eleven

Tor stretched his neck, trying to spot Holly. The ferry was almost full and despite the dark skies and choppy waves, the passengers all seemed to be in high spirits.

His backpack was heavy and bulky from the presents he had bought, and it kept bumping into other people's backpacks. He took it off and carried it in his hand.

He finally spotted Holly sitting on the floor in the passengers' lounge with her back to the wall. She wasn't the only one.

Tor made his way through the other passengers, and stopped in front of her. She seemed to be engrossed in her mobile, not noticing him. He frowned. Why was she looking at a dark screen?

Holly suddenly looked up and her face lit up with a smile that almost had him stepping backward. 'You made it. I looked for you before everyone ran on board and I was worried they would leave me behind.'

She scooted over, making room for him. Tor plonked down, putting the backpack beside him.

He pointed at the screen. 'Did they fix your phone?'

'Oh, this isn't my mobile. Or it is, now, except it's not the one I lost in the snow. It'll have to do until I get back home.'

Tor frowned. 'Right. I just saw the black screen. Is this not working either?'

'No, it's fine.' She looked at him. He was so close to her that he could see her eyes were all sorts of brown.

She inhaled, then sighed. 'I'm expecting a message and it's highly likely that it's on this phone right now.'

'And you don't want to know?' Tor smiled.

'I'm not sure what I want.' Holly looked at the phone again. 'It's ridiculous, isn't it? I'm being a prat.'

'Of course not.' Tor racked his brain to try and say something sensible. 'Is this something important? Or is it bad news?'

'It's... potentially bad news,' Holly said.

'So, it's also potentially good news, isn't it?'

He was hoping to make her feel better, and she seemed to perk up. She smiled. *That's something,* he thought.

'I guess. And the third possibility is that there is no message yet. That would be good too.'

Holly pressed the button on the phone and the screen lit up. Tor sensed that she wasn't breathing. *It has to be quite the message,* he thought.

There was several beeps before Holly could punch in her code and get to the main screen. 'There's nothing,' she said, right before the screen lit up with several messages.

Holly looked at him. 'Here we go.'

She opened the message box and relaxed. 'Nothing. Well, there's old messages from when I arrived on the island, and a few from my friends and my brothers, but not the one I was expecting.'

Tor hid his curiosity. If he crossed the line, if he started asking about her life, about what seemed to scare her like that, there was no way back. And he wasn't ready for that. Not at all.

Holly laughed and stuffed the phone in her pocket. 'Sometimes I wish we didn't have these phones all the time. It can be so stressful always being available. Don't you think?'

'Yes, it is. But all you have to do is leave the phone back home or turn it off.'

'Is that what you do?' Holly looked horrified the moment she said it. 'I'm sorry. You don't have to answer that.'

'You're not asking for my bank code, Holly. Yes, I do leave it at home when I go out. I don't take pictures with it or anything like that. I'm hardly ever on social media these days and it's a huge relief.' Tor smiled when she looked aghast. 'I'm weird, I know.'

'Being aware of it is the first step.' Holly laughed again, obviously feeling better.

The ferry swerved abruptly and Holly put her hand on his thigh to steady herself. She looked pale.

'Are you feeling seasick? We can go outside if you like.' Tor thought she looked a bit green.

Holly shook her head. 'I... It wasn't like this when I arrived.'

'The weather here is unpredictable and that's being nice. You never know what you might experience. Don't worry,' he added when she paled. 'It's not even a proper breeze.'

Holly frowned. 'What about winter storms, hurricanes? That sort of thing. Do they happen often?'

'Hurricanes would be extremely rare, to be honest. But sure, we get plenty of storms because we're right on the North Sea. That's not what we're having now. This is barely a small gale.'

Holly pulled her hand back. 'If you say so. This isn't like London.'

'Far from it. If you want more reliable weather in Norway, you should come to Oslo.'

'Why? That's by the sea too, isn't it?'

'It is, but it's snuggled in at the far end of a fjord, surrounded by mountains. Even if there's a storm at sea, it usually loses most of its force by the time it hits Oslo.'

'That's where you're from, right?'

'Yes, I grew up there, but my family comes from this coast somewhere. Or from the hinterland... or maybe not. I'm not really into genealogy. All I know is that at some point, many generations ago, they migrated south.'

Holly still had that green tint on her face. 'So what made you decide to stay on the island?'

'I used Airbnb,' Tor said with a shrug.

Holly looked at him. 'I'm sorry. I'm being nosey, right?'

'No, no, that's okay.' Tor felt like an idiot. 'I needed some time off and Airbnb found the house for me. It was a lucky accident, I think.'

'Because you like it so much?' Holly closed her eyes slightly when the boat swerved again.

Tor took pity on her. 'Come on,' he said, standing up.

Holly looked confused, but she took his hand and let him pull her up on her feet. 'What's going on?'

'We need to get outside. Follow me.'

Holly had a strange feeling her feet were confused because the ground kept moving one way and her feet the other. She followed right behind Tor, and did what he did, finding support from the walls.

'Where are we going?'

Tor turned around and held out his hand again. 'Upstairs. You'll feel a lot better soon. I promise.'

Holly grabbed his hand and held on. The staircase was really steep and tall.

After what felt like a climbing a mountain, Tor pulled her up the last step and pushed open a door. A gush of wind hit her in the face, and she shuddered.

'Watch the step.' Tor pointed and she had to climb over a ridiculously high threshold.

'What's with these thresholds? Why are they so high?'

'They are made like that to stop water from coming into the ferry during really rough weather.'

He held the door open for her, and they came out on the deck. 'It's called a *slingrekant*.'

'That's not even a word,' Holly said and stopped to gasp at the view. 'Oh.'

Tor smiled. 'It means rolling guards. Or at least I think it does. Not sure. What do you think?'

'I can't even think.' Holly leaned against the railing and couldn't help smiling. All she could see was sea and sky, and a few scattered islands. 'It's stunning.'

'Yes, it is, isn't it? Are you feeling better?'

Holly mentally checked how everything was. 'Yes, actually.'

'Fresh air is the Norwegian cure for everything. If you're unwell, get some fresh air; if you can't sleep, get some fresh air; if you're feeling sad, get some fresh air. I think it comes from living too close to the sea and the mountains,' Tor said.

She looked at him. She was never quite sure if he intended to be funny or not. 'Well, fresh air is good for you, I can agree with that. I certainly feel better.'

Tor leaned against the railing next to her and looked out at the sea. 'This is the best part of living on an island. I love this.'

Holly felt his shoulder brushing against hers. 'Thank you. If you hadn't come on board, I think the chances of having an accident in the lounge would have been pretty high. That would have put a damper on the holiday spirit.'

'You're not used to being on a ferry yet?' Tor smiled when she flinched.

'No, not really. The closest I've been to this is a riverboat on the Thames and it was nothing like this,' Holly said.

She did feel a lot better now they were outside, despite the fact that the ferry swayed as bad as ever. 'How much time before we get to the island?'

Tor checked his watch. 'Another thirty minutes, I think.'

Suddenly she didn't feel so perky after all. She looked at him.

'Did you always have a beard?' She needed something to distract herself.

'No. I once was a little boy without a beard,' Tor said.

Holly narrowed her eyes. 'You're being funny, aren't you?'

'How could you guess?' Tor looked pleased with himself.

'It's okay if you don't want to tell me,' Holly said.

Tor stroked his hand over the beard. 'Shaving is boring. Frøy doesn't really care whether I shave or not, and there's only myself to worry about. So one day I didn't bother anymore.'

Holly eyed him. 'Right. You're really getting into the whole hermit thing, aren't you? Does that mean you'll stop showering and skip meals, or start to drink your meals, like out of a beer bottle?'

Tor frowned. 'Ehm. No. I haven't done any of that. I like showers and I like to eat, and I drink in moderation. Besides, Frøy is very particular about cleanliness. He would never accept it if I reeked of stale sweat. Also he loves food. He gets really mad if I don't feed him.'

'I can see that. I wouldn't want to disappoint Frøy either. He's honed that judgemental look to perfection.'

'You don't know the half of it. Sometimes he doesn't talk to me for days. He's a tyrant.'

Holly laughed. 'Perhaps you should have chosen a dog instead.'

'Oh, I didn't choose Frøy. He found me.'

'How?' Holly ignored her queasy stomach. 'I imagined that you bought him as a little black fluffball, or something.'

'No, nothing like that. I'm sure he was a cute fluffball, but I got him when he was about a year, maybe two years old. The vet isn't sure.'

'You mean Frøy was a stray?'

'Yes, Kari and the girls wanted a cat and so I came with them to the shelter. The girls found kittens and gushed all over them, while I wandered around to look. I had no intention of coming home with a cat until I almost fell over Frøy.'

'He came up to you?'

'Sort off. He was chasing another cat and bounced into me. Then he sat on my shoes and tried to climb up my trouser leg. The staff was in awe. Probably because he's heavy and I was at severe risk of getting shredded. So I picked him up and that was that.'

'Aw, he picked you. That's what cats do.'

'Personally, I think he was so much trouble the staff was eager to get rid of him. He can be a pain in the neck.'

'No, he's not. He's adorable.' Holly frowned. 'Is he home alone now?'

'He's roaming the island, killing small critters, and probably having a smoke,' Tor said.

'I hope he gets along with the other island cats,' Holly said, smiling at the exaggeration.

'He's spayed, so there's no danger of him making little Frøys, and as you know, he's the most mellow cat there is.'

'It's kind of sad, isn't it? No baby Frøys?'

'We have enough feral cats in this country, I'm afraid.

There's nothing sad about making sure there's not more cats than there already are.'

Holly turned her head. 'I know. But still, no fluffy baby Frøys is sad.'

'There's nothing romantic about feral cats,' Tor said.

Holly patted his arm. 'Right.'

Her stomach felt as if it had settled, finally. She drew a careful, deep breath, filled with cold sea air. 'Oh.'

'You feel better, yes?' Tor frowned.

'Possibly. At least the world isn't moving so wildly anymore.'

'That's because we are about to dock. See?' Tor pointed forward.

Holly lit up at the sight of the island's harbour. They could see the big sea house where Jack's restaurant would be someday.

'Oh, thank goodness. I am never taking this ferry again.'

'So, how are you going to get back to shore?' Tor was laughing at her now.

'I'll swim or hire a helicopter.' Holly liked the way he laughed. His whole demeanour changed.

'Seems like you're planning to stay here forever. Are you?'

The question took Holly by surprise. 'No, of course not. I'm going back to London. That's where my life is.'

'I know you're a doctor because you said so. Where do you work?'

Holly looked away. 'I'm supposed start as a Junior Fellow in oncology at Kings,' she said.

'What's Kings? I've never heard that before.'

'It's a hospital in London. King's College Hospital.'

Tor thought about it. 'You were supposed to, but you're not?'

'I'm not sure yet.' Holly bit her lower lip. She really didn't want to tell him about what had happened. It was too sore, too embarrassing, and she could still barely think about what had happened without feeling sick.

'That's why you're unsure about the phone,' Tor said.

'Yes, it's so important to me, and if I lose it, I could potentially be out of a career I've worked for since... since as long as I can remember,' Holly said.

'That's hard. Are you really scared you could lose it?'

'Yes, of course.' Holly turned away from him. 'They'll probably get back to me after Christmas or New Year's but I hate waiting.'

'And so you decided to come to the island for a holiday?' Tor smiled.

'My brother came to the island last year and decided to stay. He's asked me to come several times, and I haven't had time to visit until now.'

'When he's not here?' Tor smiled again.

'He'll turn up before Christmas. They're in Spain visiting Ninni's mum,' Holly said, shrugging her shoulders.

Tor fell silent. He didn't seem to mind that they didn't talk. *It's nice*, she thought. *Very nice.*

The ferry suddenly made a lot of scraping noises and Holly gasped. 'What's happening? Did we hit something?'

Tor pointed. 'Not at all. They're backing up so that they can safely dock. Just hang on for second, then we can go downstairs.'

'And be on firm ground again.' Holly couldn't hide her delight.

Tor grinned. 'You are such a *landkrabbe*.'

'A what now?' Holly grabbed the rail when the ferry seemed to make a little jump, followed by scraping noises.

'I think in English it's called a "landlubber"?'

'I'll put it on my resume. Can we leave now?'

Tor went down the staircase and Holly followed. The damn thing was so steep, she got a flash of herself falling down, dragging poor Tor with her.

Chapter Twelve

Tor turned at the end of the stairs and looked up at her. Holly could see the other passengers in the lounge were collecting their belongings and starting to walk towards them.

'You okay?' Tor touched her arm.

'Do I look that bad?' Holly grinned at him.

He frowned. 'No, you look fine, a little green around the eyes, but fine.'

'A compliment. Wow, I'm flattered.'

He got that expression on his face where he wasn't sure what she meant.

Holly shook her head. 'Don't worry. Are we there now?'

Tor opened his mouth to speak, but was interrupted by the ferry making one of those awful screechy noises again.

'Why does it do that?' Holly could see none of the other passengers batting an eye, so that probably meant everything was shipshape.

'We're landing, so to speak, and the side of the boat

131

scrapes along the pier. You need to take this ferry a lot more often so you don't get so spooked,' Tor said, laughing now.

'Easy for you to say,' Holly muttered.

A last pull from the ship almost had her toppling over, and she swore, catching her balance. Tor grabbed her arm. 'Better be careful until the doors open.'

'You seem to be saving me from falling over edges all the time,' she joked, feeling flustered and embarrassed.

'Good thing too,' he said, smiling at her.

They stood in line for the gangplank. People looked at them, some smiled while others looked away the moment she met their eyes. It struck her that both she and Tor were strangers.

She smiled at Tor. 'Are you going straight home to Frøy?'

'I... yes, except there he is.' Tor pointed at the black cat sitting by the Christmas tree. It was getting dark and the fairy lights were on, but he didn't seem to be interested in them at all.

'Oh, how sweet! He's waiting for you.' Holly touched his arm. 'I guess he's not mad at you anymore.'

'Guess not.' He seemed to like that.

When they were back on firm ground again, Tor walked over to the cat. *That's so cute*, Holly thought. *It must be so nice to have a cat or a dog.*

Frøy ran past Tor without a glance at him, and settled at Holly's feet. Holly tried to keep a straight face as she bent down to pet the cat.

'Clearly I'm still not forgiven.' Tor looked at the cat with a bemused smile.

Holly struggled, but she couldn't help it. She burst out laughing. 'He doesn't mean it,' she said.

'Oh, but he does. I have bought his favourite treats, but that's not good enough.' Tor shook his head.

Holly sat, almost falling over in the slush, and stroked the cat over his silky ears. He headbutted her hand.

'You have to be patient, don't you?' she said, looking at the cat.

'Stupid cat,' Tor said in a gentle voice, before following her lead and sitting down to stroke the cat. Frøy allowed it to happen. 'I think you're a good influence on him,' Tor said.

Their hands touched and Holly sensed something different. She couldn't look at Tor. He would see right through her.

When they stood straight again, Holly felt clumsy and awkward, not sure what to say. Tor kept his eyes on the cat.

'Are you going into the shop?' she said to break the silence.

'No, I have everything I need, I bought wrapping paper for the gifts earlier,' he said. 'Are you going? In the shop, I mean?'

Holly shook her head. 'No, I'm heading back to the house. I have a bowl of cold pasta waiting for me.'

He frowned. 'Isn't your brother a chef?'

'Yes, he is, but unfortunately it's not genetic. I am, however, brilliant with the microwave,' she said.

'Me too, I'm good at pot noodles and burgers,' Tor said, smiling again.

'And soup. Don't forget soup.' Holly smiled back at him.

'Yes, about that, it was mostly from a can, except for the fish and the bread, of course.'

'And here I was, thinking you cooked it from scratch, baked the bread, and made the cheese. I'm shocked,' she said.

Tor grinned. 'But you did like it, didn't you?'

'Very much so.'

They walked slowly, the cat running a few feet ahead. Holly looked up. She could see a few stars, but they were mostly obscured by clouds drifting across over their heads.

'It's so dark out here.' Holly pointed at the sky. 'I always pictured stars when I thought about the island.'

'Most of the time it's quite cloudy out here. But sometimes it's so clear you can see everything. It's unbelievable.'

Tor suddenly stopped and Holly realised they were at the fork in the road. 'Right. Well, thank you for your help today,' he said, a bit stiffly.

Holly nodded. 'Listen, I have more than enough pasta for both of us. Would you like to eat with me?'

He paled. She had no other word for it. *I hope he's not going to run away screaming*, she thought, preparing herself.

'Uhm, that's… that's really nice, but I have so much work waiting. I… I have deadlines,' he said.

Holly nodded. 'I see. I only wanted to reciprocate because you shared the soup. Not that my pasta would taste anywhere near as good, but still.'

Tor smiled, looking really nervous. 'Can we have a… a… something with rain,' he finally said.

'You mean a rain check?'

'Yes, that's the one. Another time, yes?'

Holly nodded and turned towards the house, but then changed her mind. Tor was already a few steps away.

'Don't forget that you promised to take me on a fishing trip,' she called after him.

When he didn't respond at once, she turned around. *God, he's annoying,* she thought.

'Holly?' He called her name with a soft lilt that it made her stomach almost flipflop.

She turned around and he was smiling at her. 'Would you like to go fishing with me the day after tomorrow?'

Holly was so surprised for a second she was speechless. Then she nodded. 'I would love to,' she said.

'Good. I'll come and get you at eight. Dress warm. It's cold out there that early.'

Holly nodded and waited for him to say something else, but he was done. He disappeared up the slope.

What am I doing? she thought, shaking her head. *Unless the fish is in a frozen box from Iceland or Tesco, I have no idea what to do with it.*

———————————

Tor muttered as he walked up the pathway. He didn't turn around. How on earth could he have been so stupid? He should have turned away when he spotted her in the street.

Now he had to take her out on the boat, and stay there for hours. What if she got bored? Or worse, what if he got bored? It was a huge risk and he berated himself for taking it. But he had invited her and he couldn't back out of it now. That would really be stupid.

He came to the turn in the path, and discovered Frøy sitting on the gatepost, his tail draped around him like a fluffy scarf.

'You're no help.'

Tor passed him and headed over to the house. He opened the door and the cat slinked in before him.

Inside, Frøy ran towards the kitchen and sat next to the refrigerator. Tor half expected him to point to his mouth, making mewing sounds.

He didn't, but he certainly had that judging cat face down pat.

'I have tuna for you and that sausage you like.'

Tor kept talking to the cat while he filled the food and water bowl. 'I shouldn't have done it, Frøy. I mean, she's a nice woman and obviously attractive and also funny, which is, you know, nice and all. But I'm not looking for anyone. I prefer to be on my own for now. You know how it was after Linn and I broke up. I thought I was over it, that that whole thing was laid to rest, and then she called me, you know? And I couldn't deal with it.'

Frøy ignored him the moment the food bowl was filled up.

Tor looked at him for a second. *I really should have gone with a dog*, he thought.

'A dog would have showed some kind of sympathy, you know,' he said to the cat.

Food, he thought. *I need to eat something*. He explored the fridge and pulled out a few different *pålegg* to put on a sandwich. While he was buttering the bread and slathering the sandwich with jam, his mind went back to Holly.

She probably doesn't eat open sandwiches, he thought.

After filling up the plate with sandwiches and the last few coconut macaroons, he brought it upstairs. When he decided to work from home – from the island, really – he had made rules for himself. No eating or drinking at the desk, shave every day, no drinks during weekdays; all sorts of rules that quickly became pointless.

As a result, he had to clear away three cups with dregs of coffee at the bottom, quite a few beer bottles and a plate from the night before.

He turned on the computer and immediately got pinged by Henrik. Or that was his first thought, until Kari waved at him from the screen.

'Just checking in to see how you're doing,' she said, with an almost angelic look on her face.

'No, you're not. You're curious. I can feel your gossip radar probing me from here,' he said, taking a bite of the jam sandwich.

'Sure, that too. But it's obvious that you haven't made much headway, have you now? You still have that god awful beard. It makes you look like one of those mucky fishermen from old paintings. Please, please, please shave it off.'

Tor stroked the offending hair. 'No, I won't. I like it. It keeps my face warm when I go outside.'

Kari rolled her eyes. 'Oh, please. You're on an island in the wettest part of the country. They practically invented rain. If anything, it must be a nuisance to keep that beard dry.'

That made him laugh. 'I'll think about it. I bought gifts for the girls today.'

She lit up. 'Can I see?'

'They're in the lounge, and I can't be bothered to go downstairs.' He explained what he had bought. 'I'll send them tomorrow, so they should be there in time for Christmas Eve.'

'They better be. What did you buy for me?'

Tor laughed again. 'I'm not telling you, am I? I'm also not telling you what I bought for Henrik.'

'You always buy him the same thing. A fly for the fishing thingy.'

'He'll love it,' Henrik said.

Kari shook her head slightly. 'Yes, he probably will.'

'Yes, he will and I had good help today, too.' Tor closed his eyes in dismay. Whatever had possessed him to say that? He was incapable of keeping his mouth shut today.

Kari bit the hook at once. 'Who helped you?'

So, he had to tell her how he had run into Holly in town.

'And she helped you?'

'Yes, she did. We had coffee and some cake, and then... then she helped me,' he said, ending the sentence lamely.

Kari tilted her head and leaned closer to the screen.

'You had coffee with her? Did she invite you or did you invite her?'

'Does it matter?' Tor nibbled on another sandwich.

'Of course. If she invited you, you probably said yes because you were surprised and didn't know what to say. If you invited her, now that's a whole new thing, isn't it? As far as I know, you haven't been with anyone since... well, before everything with Linn happened,' she said.

'I might have a whole harem thing going on out here, for all you know,' Tor said, doing his best to act mellow.

'There are what, about a hundred people living out there? And most of them are older than you. I doubt if you can get together enough females to even call it a harem, at least not one that's in the same age group as yourself. And you're not really an orgy kind of man, are you?' Kari was teasing him now.

'I can have orgies if I want to,' he said.

'Please do. Maybe it will make you feel better. Don't interrupt me, please,' she said, seeing he was about to.

Tor popped a macaroon in his mouth as she went on about how awful it was that he was still alone, and that he should get out more often. *Why is it that friends and family always think they know what's best for you,* he thought. *And then tell you about it in detail.*

He zoned out, wondering what Holly was doing.

Frøy chose that moment to jump up on his desk and give the screen a sniff before sloping across the keyboard.

Tor stroked his fur and smiled.

'Are you listening to me, Tor?'

'Not really. I don't need you to worry about me. I have my mother for that. I'm doing well out here, Kari. Right now, it's where I need to be.'

Kari rolled her eyes. 'I can see that. It would be easier if you—'

Tor interrupted her. 'If I get rid of the beard. Yes, I think someone mentioned that not too long ago.'

'Don't be a smartass.' He could see Kari taking a breath and he braced himself, knowing what was coming. 'Have you talked to Linn? About the... you know.' Kari's voice trailed.

Tor shook his head. 'Not since I talked to her in November.'

'Are you going to talk to her again? Like, to congratulate her? I know you hung up on her.'

'No. And I didn't hang up on her, I just didn't say goodbye. I have no intention of congratulating her because it's over. Linn has her new life, and I have mine. Everything is fine, and I thought we agreed to let the whole Linn drama be.' He didn't manage to keep the anger from his voice and he regretted it instantly.

'I'm sorry,' he said. 'I'm done with it. So, please. Let it go.'

Kari nodded. 'I'm sorry too. I won't bring it up again.'

'Thank you. Now, can we talk about something else?' Tor smiled.

'Are you ready for Christmas?'

Nice change of topic, he thought and played along. 'I eat Christmas cookies every day. Sometimes several times a day,' he said, showing her the macaroon.

'That's not what I mean and you know it. I hate the thought of you sitting in that old house all alone on Christmas Eve.'

'I'm not alone. Frøy is here.' Tor scratched the cat under

his chin. 'I'll even put a festive bow on him in honour of the day. He'll look very dapper.'

'That's not what I mean, and you know it.' She smiled. 'Can't you spend Christmas Eve with your new friend?'

Tor laughed out aloud and Frøy scowled at him.

'Holly's family is returning before Christmas. That's why she's here. I'm not about to crash a family Christmas, you know that. I'll be fine here.'

'But it's Christmas Eve!' Tor could see she was distressed.

'I'm not five years old and I have spent the holidays alone before. Don't fret about me. I don't like it.'

'You heard him – he doesn't like it!' Henrik sat next to his wife. 'You'll be fine, yes?'

'Yes, I will.'

'We'll hook him up to a monitor and he can sit there, watch us have a lovely Christmas.' Kari frowned. 'Or perhaps not.'

Tor laughed. 'No, thank you. That would really be depressing.'

Henrik interrupted again. 'I'm here to drag her away. The girls are wrapping your present – and Frøy's, of course – and it's not going well. I have glue and glitter in my hair.'

'You're impossible.' Kari sighed and stood. 'I'll talk to you soon, Tor. And get a Christmas tree or some flowers or *nisser* – something that reminds you of the season.'

Henrik brushed his hair with his hand and a small shower of gold-coloured glitter fell across the screen.

'Not like that,' Kari said and pulled him away. 'We'll talk

to you soon, Tor. Be nice to your neighbour, please. She sounds lovely,' she said.

'She is, and I won't.'

Tor turned off the computer and looked at Frøy.

'What do you think? Should we bother with a tree?'

Frøy rolled over on his back and offered his belly. Tor gave him a good scratch, feeling ridiculously happy that he was back in the cat's favour.

Chapter Thirteen

Holly pried open one eye when the phone alarm went off. It said seven, and she had to look twice to be sure.

Why was the alarm on this early? And then she remembered. *Oh my god*, she thought. It's the 'day after tomorrow', the day Tor was going to take her fishing. This was insane. What person in their right mind would go fishing in the middle of the night?

Even so, she got out of bed and looked out the window. All dark. Apparently night in Norway lasted half the day.

'Time to get up,' she said. 'This is what we do.'

She swung her feet out onto the floor. Thankfully the heat was on and the room was toasty.

Tor had said to dress warm. After a shower, she put on jeans and her cashmere sweater, and with Ninni's coat, she figured she'd be fine.

Also, she needed tea before she would even contemplate putting her nose outside the door. While the kettle boiled, she looked through the kitchen window. It was pitch dark, not a star or the moon in sight. It made her dizzy looking at it.

She was sipping the second cup when someone knocked on the door. She had learned from the shock of Tobbens's materialisation, and made sure to lock the door.

'Who is it?' Holly had no intention of opening unless she knew who it was. This might not be London, but bad guys lived everywhere. And she knew Scandinavia had dark currents. All the Nordic Noir had taught her that.

'It's me,' Tor said.

Holly opened the door and burst out laughing when she saw him. He had on a bright orange jacket that reached just below his bum, and it was open so she could see he was wearing trousers that went over his stomach – also bright orange, with neon green stripes around the legs and the arms.

Holly laughed. 'What are you wearing? You look like a giant lollipop lady.'

Tor smiled. 'You can laugh, but it will keep me warm and visible. And you too,' he said.

'You mean that outfit is big enough for both of us?'

That would be interesting, Holly thought, blushing at the idea.

'No, I have your gear here. We're going to be in the boat for a few hours and it gets cold. Your fancy city clothes will give you frostbite. You don't want that.'

He handed her a bundle of outerwear like his, which was surprisingly heavy and Holly staggered backwards. 'I won't be able to move in these.'

'All you have to do is sit in the boat, and trust me, you don't want to freeze.' He looked at her. 'Is that what you're wearing underneath this?'

Holly nodded. 'What's wrong with it?'

'Norwegians say there's no bad weather, only bad clothes. It rhymes in Norwegian,' he said with a lopsided smile. 'You have to dress in layers, preferably wool on wool. Do you have anything under the jeans?'

'Excuse me?' Holly dumped the outerwear on the kitchen table. Did he just ask if she had any knickers on?

'You need woollen tights, then jeans, then the overalls. And then a woollen sweater or two. That cashmere thing is nice, but you should also have a thicker sweater over it.'

Holly frowned. 'I don't have anything like that.'

'There were some sweaters in the hallway. Take one of them. Then a woollen hat, scarf, and mittens. And proper boots.'

'Are you sure we're not going on an expedition to the North Pole?'

'No, then you would have to wear two survival suits, and a polar bear hat,' he said, smiling now. 'Why don't you go and get properly dressed, and I'll make myself a coffee?'

'Fine,' Holly said, stomping up to the second floor to dig for woollen tights in Ninni's closet.

'You need woollen socks too. Bring an extra pair,' he called after her. 'And don't forget to use the bathroom. There's no bathroom on the boat.'

That almost made her change her mind, but she was committed now. She couldn't back out. It took a lot less time than she had anticipated to find what she needed as Ninni had a closet filled with winter clothes. Holly wriggled into a pair of tights, and was pleased to discover she had no problems getting her jeans over them. Perhaps all those sweets hadn't done too much damage. A quick trip to the bathroom and she was good to go.

Downstairs again, she found Tor by the table, sipping his coffee. He stood at once when she entered the kitchen, wearing the extra socks and another sweater.

'Much better. Now the overalls and the coat, and we're good to go.'

Holly pulled on the overalls and Tor fastened the clasps over her shoulders. It felt oddly intimate, despite all the layers of clothes. She held her breath until he was finished.

He frowned. 'Are you okay? Are they too tight?'

Holly shook her head, not sure if she could speak. *What the hell*, she thought.

Tor helped her into the coat. He zipped it up, then gave her a smile that made her wonder what it would be like to kiss him, and she took a step back. *Pull yourself together*, she thought.

'You look... spooked,' he said. 'Is there something wrong?'

Holly cleared her throat. 'No, not at all. I'm getting a bit too warm here, though. These clothes are different.'

Hopefully he believed that. She smiled. 'Does everyone who fishes out here dress like this? Is it mandatory?'

'No. You can freeze if you want to, but it's not recommended,' he said and hesitated. For a nerve-wracking split second Holly thought he would kiss her, and she couldn't move.

He took a step back and smiled. 'You look like a proper fisherman now. Good. Now we can go.'

Holly was still stunned from the almost kiss. The idea took her by surprise. *Or maybe it's only me*, she thought. *Maybe it's not an almost kiss, but an imaginary almost kiss.*

Her brain scrambled for something to distract her. 'What about food?'

'You don't have to worry about that. I have sandwiches and coffee, and a few other things. I've even made you a thermos of tea. We're sorted.'

Holly followed him out in the hallway. She grabbed her boots and he shook his head. 'No, they're useless. Your toes might fall off.'

'Really?' Holly looked at the boots she had been using because her own had proven so utterly useless. 'I haven't been that cold in these. I've avoided icy spots, like you said.'

'No, but when you're out on the water, it's always best to dress as warm as possible, and cold toes will ruin the trip.'

He looked around, then handed her a pair of big, furry-looking boots with colourful laces. 'Try these.'

Holly took the boots from him and inspected them. 'You're joking, right? They're pointy, like elf shoes.'

'But they're not made for elves. They are made of seal skin and are lined with proper woollen fleece, and they will keep your feet nice and toasty for hours.'

Her feet fit the shoes perfectly and she smiled at Tor.

'Maybe you're Cinderella,' he said.

'Not sure she'd wear chunky boots, even if they have

colourful laces and pointy toes.' Holly still thought they looked elvish.

'Ready?' Tor pulled a bobble hat down over his ears and Holly followed him.

Outside, Tor zipped up his coat and breathed deeply. 'Best time of the day,' he said.

Holly looked at him. 'You mean, when everyone else is asleep and you don't have to talk to anyone?'

'Something like that. I like the quiet.'

'Too bad you brought me, then,' she said, grinning at him.

'Sometimes company is nice,' he said. 'It depends on the company though, doesn't it?'

'Are you in a hurry?' Holly had trouble keeping up with him.

Tor stopped and looked back. 'Oh, sorry.' He slowed down enough for her to catch up.

'Where are we going?' Holly asked, when he took the narrow path leading down to the beach.

'My boat is by the pier below my house. This is a shortcut. It's not a road you should take by yourself in the dark, though,' he said.

'I wouldn't dream of it.' It was bloody dark and she could hardly see her feet. *Perhaps the elf shoes should have had bells on*, she thought.

The path ended in steep and narrow stone stairs. Tor turned to her and held out his hand. 'It might be slippery.'

'Thank you,' she said, feeling a lot safer with her hand in his.

She could see his house a bit higher up. The lights were on in the lounge. 'Do you keep the lights on to find your way home?'

'Not really. By the time we're back, it will be daylight,' he said. 'I like to see the lights when I go out, though.'

'That's your boat?' Holly said, when they stepped down on the wooden pier. 'I thought you meant a row boat or something.'

Tor smiled. 'This is a traditional Norwegian boat, mostly used for fishing or leisure. It's called a *snekke*. You would call it a double ender, I think. Except mine doesn't have a sail,' he said.

'Oh,' she said, studying the boat. She remembered seeing it when she woke up in his house on her first morning on the island.

It was certainly bigger than a row boat, which was a relief. It even had a roof, or half of it did, at least. It was made of wood, glossy and polished, with a half-open wheel house. There was a small door leading below deck. Along half the gunwale there was a blue tarp, like a shield. *Maybe against the winds*, she thought.

'It's beautiful,' she said, turning towards him.

Tor looked at the boat with pride and affection. 'Yes, I think so. My grandfather made it himself in the sixties, and my mum and I have taken care of it since then. As long as I look after it properly, it will last for a long time.'

Holly frowned. 'It's yours? You mean you sailed up from Oslo in this?'

He nodded. 'Of course. But not sailed. It doesn't have a sail, remember? There's a bunk in the front, and I also have camping gear in there; like a small stove and other useful things. It's roomier than it looks,' he said.

Holly walked closer to the edge of the pier. 'I've never been in a boat like this in my entire life.'

'I know.' Tor jumped into the boat and rummaged for a life vest. 'Put this on. Then you can loosen the moorings for me.'

He put on his own vest, watching her struggle with hers. 'You okay?'

She nodded. 'Peachy,' she said, feeling a sense of triumph when she managed to zip up the chunky vest.

Holly looked at the moorings. Basically it was thick rope with a loop at the end, holding the boat to the pier. 'What do I do?'

'Just pull them up and hand the ends to me,' Tor said.

Holly pulled the first and smiled. 'This is easier than the life vest, you know.'

'Good. Now, get in before the boat floats away,' he said, holding on to the edge of the pier.

'I can't jump into the boat like you did, Tor. I'm pretty sure I'll trip, then tumble overboard on the other side, and then sink like a stone to the bottom with all the clothes I'm wearing.'

He laughed. 'I'll hold the boat steady, and you can climb in. I'll help you.'

Tor held out his other hand to Holly. 'The gunwale works as a step. You'll be fine. Just be careful, it's slippery.'

She hesitated for two seconds, then stepped onto the gunwale and into the boat.

'Good girl,' he said, to make her smile again.

She sent him a triumphant look. 'How would you know?' she said.

Tor laughed. 'If you sit on the bench, I'll soon have us out.'

Holly sat on the surprisingly comfortable pillows on the bench and leaned back to watch Tor.

Tor went over to the steering wheel, pushed a button and the engine sputtered, then the relaxing sound of a well-oiled diesel engine broke the silence.

'Are you comfortable?' He looked back at her.

Holly felt a lot safer sitting down. Not that she would admit that to him.

'I'm fine, thank you.'

Also, sitting behind him like this meant she could admire him. Not his bum or anything like that – he had on far too many clothes for that to work – but even with the chunky clothes and that ridiculous bobble hat, he looked hot.

She turned around. Tor's house was already far away.

'So, where are we going?'

It was bloody dark, and she was surprised he could see anything.

'We are just going around to the next bay to check the crab pots, then we will go to the next bay over to see if there's anything in my fishing nets,' he said.

Holly laughed. 'You're like a proper fisherman, aren't you? What do you do with what you catch?'

Tor shrugged. 'I give most of it to Jens, and then he sells it in the shop. Some I use myself, and of course, there's Frøy. He's pretty demanding, you know.'

'Right.' Holly looked around. Apart from a few buckets on the deck, there was no sign of the cat. 'He's probably back at the house, snoring in front of the fireplace, isn't he?'

'Actually no.' Tor bent down and pushed open the door. 'He's snoring in here.'

Holly stood and went to see. Inside the hull, she spotted the black cat, curled up on a narrow bed, tail covering his face.

'Why does he have a life vest on?'

'Because we're on a boat, of course. Frøy is really good on board, a proper ship's cat, but if he falls overboard, the vest will keep him floating and I will be able see him,' Tor said.

Holly could see that. A black cat in the dark waters wouldn't be very visible. 'And he lets you put it on?'

'He's a sensible cat,' Tor said, completely serious.

Holly chuckled. 'I've never heard that said about a cat before.'

He had one hand on the wheel and half-sat, half-leaned on a high chair. 'Well, now you can say that you have.'

Holly didn't want to disturb the cat and closed the door carefully, leaving a gap for him to slip out if he wanted to.

'If you want tea, there's a thermos in the bag. The blue one is for you, the red one is coffee,' he said.

Holly found the thermoses and handed him the red. There were also foiled-wrapped packages and fruit, and something that looked a lot like a cake.

'Help yourself if you're hungry,' he said, opening the thermos and using the cup on the top.

'Not yet. You interrupted my morning tea.' Holly followed his example and filled up a cup.

The tea smelled of clover and cardamom, and tasted sweet and strong. 'What is this?'

'It's a Christmas blend. At least that's what the package said. My mum sends me tea. I don't know why, but I suspect she thinks it's healthy.'

'Doesn't taste healthy,' Holly said, enjoying the flavour.

'Good. We are almost there now,' he said as the boat glided into a small bay.

Holly noticed that she could see more than when they set out. Instead of pitch darkness, she could see contours of the landscape. Shadows, sort of. What she couldn't see was any kind of fishing gear.

'You have crab pots in here? How do you know where they are?'

'I look for the buoys. Mine are bright red. There should be three of them here,' Tor said, lowering the speed.

The boat almost stopped, but still glided forward. 'There's the first one,' Tor said, pointing.

Holly couldn't see anything and leaned over the gunwale.

Tor suddenly grabbed her coat by the collar and pulled her in.

'It's bloody cold water if you fall in,' he said.

'I wasn't falling.' Even so, she sat on the bench, determined to see what he was doing.

153

Frøy suddenly decided to join them. He tripped carefully around Tor, and jumped up to sit beside her.

Tor leaned out and grabbed the buoy. He pulled at it with both hands, dragging a rope out of the water, and after a short while Holly spotted something rising towards the surface.

He pulled up a contraption made with thick nets covering a metal frame. There were holes on the sides.

She leaned forward to inspect it closer. 'Where are the crabs?'

'At the bottom of the sea, I presume,' he said. 'I'll have to put more bait in it and come back in a couple of days.'

He pulled out a small bucket and opened the lid. 'Fresh mackerel,' he said. 'Crabs like fresh meat, while lobsters think the smellier, the better.'

Frøy jabbed at the bucket and Tor gave him a piece of the fish. Holly was pretty sure he didn't even chew it before swallowing. Tor tossed him another piece.

Holly looked at him. 'Lobster? You have lobsters here?'

'Oh, yes, but while we are permitted to fish crab all year round, the lobster season only lasts for two months and ended on the 31st of November. You need a license and you have to mark every lobster so buyers know they're fished legally. I didn't know that, so I missed out. And that means, if I catch a lobster by accident, I have to throw it out again.'

Holly smiled. 'And do you throw it out again?'

'Of course I do.' He looked shocked at the idea. 'Lobsters were overfished for a long time, and we have worked hard to bring them back. It's in everyone's interest to stick to the rules,' he said.

'Ethical fishing, you mean,' Holly said, quite impressed.

'Well, sometimes ethics and common sense overlap.'

He carefully placed pieces of fish inside the trap, then lowered it back into the water, gently pushing down Frøy who tried to jump up on the gunwale to see what was going on.

'Next one?' Holly watched as the trap disappeared in the water and only the colourful buoy was left.

'It should be right over there.'

They waited while the boat drifted further along, then Tor did the whole grab-a-rope thing and pulled up another trap.

'Oh my god! Look at those!' Holly couldn't keep from screaming.

Inside the trap there was at least five crabs, with russet-coloured shells and long, angry-looking claws, some big enough to bite of a finger.

Tor pulled the trap onboard, not caring about the water splashing over the deck. Frøy looked at the crabs with interest, safely on the bench.

Holly jumped back. 'You're not taking those out of there, are you?'

'Of course I am.' Tor did something to one end of the trap, and put his hand inside to pick up one of the crabs. He took it by the shell and Holly stared in fascination as he lifted it out of the trap. The legs and claws waved at him, but he didn't seem fazed.

'Give me that ruler over there,' he said, pointing at a metal ruler hanging from a hook.

Holly handed it to him. 'Why do you need a ruler?'

'If the crab is under eleven cm, back into the water it goes,' he said, measuring the crab. 'This is fourteen, so we're good.'

He opened another bucket and dropped the poor thing inside. The next two passed the test and went in the bucket with it. The other two even she could see were too small. Tor dropped them overboard.

He also removed Frøy, who found the bucket fascinating and tried to jab at the crabs waving their claws at him.

'You know, you might just have orphaned those two. They'll be at the bottom soon, wondering what the hell happened and where their parents are,' Holly said, catching a glimpse of one of the crabs as it sank.

'I don't think that's how it works,' Tor said, laughing at her.

'Are you sure?' Holly looked at him, expecting a long-winded explanation about the life and inner workings of crab colonies.

'Pretty sure. Crabs are loners. They tend to stay away from each other,' he said. 'A bit like Norwegians.'

'You're all like crabs?' Holly kept an eye on the bucket. The noises coming from it were a bit unnerving. 'You don't move sideways.'

'No, but we like our solitude. I think it's the fjords,' he said.

Holly wasn't sure if he was trying to be funny or not. 'I'll bite. Why are the fjords to blame for you lot being like crabs?'

'Because the fjords kept people apart. No roads to speak of and boats were expensive. So we lived on our islands or in the valleys, deep in the fjords, and never really saw anyone else,' he said.

Holly was shaking with laughter. 'Very funny.'

'Why do you think Vikings took off like that? They wanted to see other people, of course. I mean, they got bored, you know, and then they left. Also, they needed more people.'

'To pillage and ravage? Actually... please don't answer that.'

He didn't. Instead he put the lid on the bucket. Holly could hear scratching from inside.

The third trap was empty too. Tor put more bait in it and let it sink back into the water.

He looked behind Holly. 'I think it's time,' he said.

'Time for what?' *The ravaging? He might find himself in trouble with that,* Holly thought.

'What we came here for.' Tor started the engine again, and turned the boat around, heading for open water.

Chapter Fourteen

Holly realised it wasn't so dark anymore; there was a thin stripe of shimmer on the horizon. It wasn't blue or yellow, it was the same pink as the inside of a shell.

'The sun's coming up,' she said, turning to Tor.

Tor smiled at her delight. 'It's barely started.'

The boat chugged even further out, until there was nothing but sea between them and the rising sun.

Tor stopped the engine and let the boat float.

Holly couldn't take her eyes away. 'This is fantastic, Tor. I've never seen anything so beautiful. Do you see this every time you come out here?'

He smiled at her. 'When it's not raining. Then, the clouds get lighter, but there are no colours. You're lucky today.'

He stepped down on the deck and opened one of the coolers. 'Are you hungry?'

'Yes, I am,' Holly said.

'You sound surprised,' he said, handing her one of the foil-wrapped packages. 'I don't know what you like, so I brought a bit of everything. There's cheese and ham on those. I also have some with brown cheese and jam. Also, um, mutton sausage and cheese,' he said, taking out another two packages.

'Okay, what do you like?' Holly unwrapped the foil and looked at the sandwich – an open sandwich with cheese and ham, green paprika, and a slice of cucumber. She wasn't so sure about that.

'You can put them together, if you want to,' Tor said.

Holly smiled. 'Any with mayo?'

'The sausage, actually. It's kind of a Norwegian salami. Try it.'

She took the sandwich from him and took a bite. 'It's good,' she said.

'They used to make those with horse meat,' he said, laughing when Holly stopped chewing. 'Don't worry, these are made from mutton.'

'You shouldn't say things like that,' Holly said. 'I might go off food for good.'

'Really? I wouldn't.' Tor took a bite out of the brown cheese sandwich.

'There's nothing that would turn you away from food?'

'I'm sure there is, but I'd rather not go there, if you catch my drift,' he said.

Holly sniffed the sausage before she took the next bite. She kept her eyes on the horizon, though.

'This is lovely,' she said after a while.

Tor filled up her cup with more tea. 'Yes, it is.'

The sea was quiet, not a ripple in the water. The sun

crept slowly up, colouring the sky in all hues of pink, orange, and yellow. Holly forgot to eat. Instead she held her breath as the light filled the sky.

She looked at Tor, who sat next to her on the bench, drinking his coffee. There was no need to say anything, and it felt… good. And a bit strange. She was so used to having other people around her all the time that just sitting quietly was a novelty.

'I have brought cake,' Tor said a bit later.

'What kind?' Holly drew a long breath and could feel the knot between her shoulders ease up.

'It's a Christmas cake, with spices,' he said. 'Alma at the store sometimes puts some kind of baked goods in my groceries, and yesterday it was this beauty. This is like a poundcake, right? There's dried fruit in it and Christmas spices. No idea what they are though, I'm afraid.'

Holly broke of a piece of the slice and put it in her mouth. There were raisins in it, and she could taste cinnamon and cloves, and also something else. Not ginger. Nutmeg, maybe?

'God, that woman can bake,' she said.

'I know. She makes the most amazing wiener bread – what you would call a "Danish" – with some kind of sticky almond filling. I can't get enough,' Tor said, sharing half of the last slice with her.

'Jack said she was good but this is heavenly. Have you tasted her lemon cake? Ninni swears it's the best she's ever had.'

'It's the best I've ever had too,' Tor said.

He looked completely relaxed out here. His woollen hat was askew, and the deep frown was finally gone.

'You really enjoy this. Is it very different from your normal life in Oslo?' Holly licked her fingers to catch every last crumb of cake.

He thought about it. 'I would normally put the boat away for most of the winter and then maybe take it out on the fjord a few times if the weather is okay, but come spring, I'm out on the fjord almost every weekend. That is, if my mother isn't using the boat.'

'Do you go out with her?' Holly pulled on her mittens again. It was getting colder.

'Occasionally. But she has friends up and down the fjord, and I can't deal with that,' he said, pulling a face. 'They either talk about their grandchildren, or they know this girl who would be perfect for me, and then they look at my mum. She, of course, thinks it's hilarious.'

'You're very lucky to have such a good relationship with your mum,' Holly said.

He looked at her. 'I'm sorry. I can't imagine what it must be like for you.'

Tor had such a sweet expression on his face, Holly got a lump in her throat.

'Yes, well, I can't really miss what I never had, can I?'

'Of course you can,' he said slowly. 'You can miss what should have been there. Especially you, maybe. You were the only girl in your family.'

Holly looked at him. 'Yes, I was. My dad and brothers were wonderful, but there were definitely things I could only talk

162

about with my nanna or even my aunts, if I was desperate,' she said. 'Thankfully I had girlfriends – some of whom I've known since kindergarten – so it wasn't all doom and gloom.'

He smiled. 'You're a strong person and you have a caring family. That makes up for a lot.'

'Yes. Yes, it does.' Holly put her hand on his for a second.

'You mentioned oncology. That's your speciality?'

Holly nodded. 'Yes, well, if they will still let me practice, that is.'

'Why oncology? Is your dad a doctor?'

'No, he runs a garage with Danny. Mum never finished uni, I think. She got side-tracked and had Jack.' Holly shook her head. 'My mum died from cervical cancer. They discovered it when she was pregnant with my younger brother, Danny. She died when he was just a baby.'

Holly put her hand out for Frøy who jumped up to sit next to her.

'Do you remember anything?'

'I'm not sure. I was four, so my memories could actually be things Dad or Jack have told me about her. But obviously something stuck. As long as I can remember, I wanted to be a doctor.' She smiled at Tor. 'I wanted to save other women like her. Silly, isn't it?'

'No, not at all. You wanted to help her and couldn't, but now you can help other people. I'm sure your mother would have been proud of you.'

Holly rubbed her hands together. 'Yes, I'm sure she would have, but then, if she had lived, perhaps the need to become a doctor wouldn't have been such a driving force in my life.'

'And now you think they might take that dream away from you.'

'Yes, well, we'll see. I'm trying to not worry about it too much.'

'How can you not? When this is your dream?' Tor's voice was soft and caring.

Holly got a lump in her throat and swallowed hard. There was no way she would bawl her eyes out here... with him. 'It's a good lesson in patience,' she said, laughing lightly.

Tor didn't say anything. He filled her cup with the last of the tea and gave her some time to collect herself.

After a while she looked at him. 'What about you? You didn't mention your dad when you talked about Oslo, but you did buy presents for him.'

Tor smiled. 'That's because he lives up north, in Tromsø. I grew up with my mum. They split up when I was ten.'

'So you do know a bit about going without,' Holly said.

'Yes, but it's not the same. My dad was there if I needed him for any reason. He's married again and he's happy, I think.'

'Do you visit him often?'

'I see him once or twice a year, and when I did my military service in the north, I stayed with them whenever I had time off. He's the one who got me hooked on fly fishing.'

'That's nice. My dad taught me how fix a car and mix cocktails. Both very useful skills to have,' Holly said.

Tor laughed. 'I bet they are. Are you cold?'

Holly shook her head. 'Not really. The North Pole attire isn't too bad actually. Are we going back?'

'Not yet.' He looked up at the sky. 'See? The sun is up now. We can go and see if there's anything in the fishing nets.'

Holly leaned back on the bench. *He's a strange one*, she thought.

Then she noticed Frøy jumping up on Tor's high chair, and demanding that Tor petted him.

'I see he's forgiven you,' she said.

Tor turned to look at her, and so did Frøy. Holly fumbled for her phone, wanting to take a picture of them, and then realised it was back at the house. 'Damn,' she muttered.

There wasn't anything she could do about it now.

Holly smiled. *I'd probably drop it in the sea*, she thought.

She leaned back and enjoyed the sight of Tor driving his boat. She didn't need photographs to remember that.

Tor kept an eye on her. She seemed to be enjoying herself, and was not so sad about her mother anymore. The sunrise had made an impression, as he had expected. It did on him, every time he went out.

'Are you sure you're not cold?'

Holly nodded. 'I'm not shy. I would have let you know if I was freezing, fishes be damned.'

Odd expression, Tor thought. 'Okay. I promise we'll be back within the hour.'

When he turned into the next bay, Holly came to stand beside him. 'This is so beautiful,' she said.

He knew what Holly saw when she looked at the shore. Grey stones, brown grass, patches of snow, and the clear water. There was beauty in the contrasts, he knew that. He smiled at her.

'It looks a bit drab now, but you should really see it in the spring. Everything turns green, almost overnight. You can have snow one week, and the next week, trees have mouse ears,' he said, delighted when she laughed.

'Mouse ears? That's the name for buds?'

'Yes, but it's the very first green you can see, when the leaves are tiny and resemble ears. You have to wait a few more weeks and then you leave the house one morning and suddenly it's spring.'

'I love the imagery.' Holly held on to the back of his chair when Tor turned the boat into the bay.

She was so close that he became aware of how close she was, and he remembered that he had wanted to kiss her back at her house. Perhaps he should have, but then again, it would probably have been a mistake. He didn't want to scare her off.

'What? Have we sprung a leak? Or are we lost?' Holly nudged him with her elbow.

'No, sorry. See the buoys on each side?' He pointed at the rope. 'See that?'

'I... yes. What are you going to do with it?' Holly frowned.

He was grateful for the interruption. 'We have to lift it up and see if there are any fish in it.'

'Are you pulling it into the boat, like the crab pots?'

'No, we're just lifting it up to get to the fish. Easy,' he said.

Holly didn't look that convinced, but she didn't say anything.

Tor steadied the boat and started pulling up the net from one end. Holly watched from the high chair.

'Do you want to help?'

'Not really. I don't want to get my elves' shoes wet. You do this on your own all the time, don't you? Or does Frøy help?'

Tor chuckled. 'No, he's too lazy for that. He likes the fish, though.'

'Raw fish?' Holly wrinkled her nose. 'Not for me. I don't eat sushi.'

Tor grabbed a wriggling fish and dropped it in the bucket of saltwater standing on the deck next to him. Then another.

By the end of it, he was wet and had thrown two mackerels back into the water, but he had a couple of pollacks and cods in the bucket.

And his hands were blue from the cold water. He blew on the fingers and smiled at Holly. 'That's it. We can go home now.'

Holly hopped down from the chair and walked carefully across the wet deck. She looked into the bucket. 'Are these for Jens?'

'Yes, unless you want one?'

She laughed. 'Not in my lifetime. I wouldn't know what to do with it.'

'Then Jens it is,' he said and dropped the net back into the water.

He rinsed his hands in the water before returning to the chair. She was making herself comfortable on the bench, with Frøy sitting next to her, doing one of his fluffy cloud impressions.

She noticed that he looked at her. 'What? Did your forget a fish or something?'

'No, we're done for the day. I have to go back to the office,' he said.

'What do you do?'

'I'm an architect.'

'Fisherman by morning, architect by day. That's quite something.' She stretched her legs in front of her.

'Not really. I like what I do.' Tor hadn't started the boat yet. 'Don't you?'

Holly laughed, but it sounded a bit hollow. 'Yes, I should, shouldn't I? Sometimes things don't work out the way they are supposed to. I...' She shook her head. 'No, I'm fine. It's nothing, really.'

Tor was sure it *was* something, and wondered what could have happened at the hospital for them to send her away, but by the look on her face, it must have been something bad since she was being very evasive. He wasn't going to pressure her. If she didn't want to talk about it, she didn't want to talk about it, and it was probably better that way. He didn't want to be part of her life any more than she wanted to be part of his. And he really didn't want to talk about Linn and how he had basically run away from home. It would be embarrassing.

He smiled and started the engine. 'Let's get back, shall we?'

Holly smiled back at him, and seemed relieved that he wasn't pressing the subject. She rubbed Frøy's head and talked to him, too low for Tor to hear over the sound of the engine.

———————————

Holly hummed when she entered the house. It was warm and cosy, and despite denying it to Tor, she felt cold to the bone. How did he do that all the time?

She pulled off the outer layers of clothing and went straight up to the bathroom. Lamenting the lack of a bathtub, she hoped a hot shower would warm her up.

Her feet and the rest of her body were warm enough, but the hot water on her face and hands felt like heaven.

Afterwards, she put on sweatpants and a sweater, and went downstairs for a hot cup of tea. As she put on the kettle she became aware of an annoying sound.

On the table was the new phone, which was ringing like crazy.

Holly picked it up and realised it was chock full of messages from Jack. Pretty hysterical ones as well, she realised.

And with a lot of swearing. *Oh, my,* she thought.

He picked up the moment she called him back.

'Why haven't you answered your phone? I know you have a new one,' he said. 'Dad told me.'

'I forgot it on the kitchen table and I've been out all

morning. What's going on? Has something happened to Rosie or Ninni? Or Dad?' Holly could feel the instant worry in the pit of her stomach. 'Who is it?'

'No, of course not, everybody is fine, I promise. But I'm having a crisis and you need to help me,' he said.

Holly exhaled slowly. Everyone was okay, so that was good. 'Okay. What kind of crisis? If it's has anything to do with cooking, you know I'm useless.'

'No, there's no cooking. You know I wouldn't ask you to do anything as daft as that, surely. Do you know about the Christmas market?'

'Yes, I think Alma invited me. Sort of, anyway. Why?' Holly was on tenterhooks now. Whatever he wanted her to do, it was probably something demanding and exhausting. 'Do I have to peel potatoes for hours again? Because if that's it, then you're going to have to pay me a lot more than a Harry Potter book,' she said, remembering that one time he had asked her to do something in the restaurant.

'That old complaint again? And I gave you all the Harry Potter books and a wand, if I remember correctly.'

Holly leaned over the counter, smiling at her reflection in the window. 'Fine. What do you need?'

'Right. Well, the problem is that we can't get back in time for me to do it myself. Ninni's mum has taken ill and we've had to rebook our tickets. I'm really sorry, Holly, but I need you to take my place at the market.'

Holly burst out laughing. 'Are you off your rocker? I can't do that. I'll make a mess of it. What if anyone wants me to cook?' She vaguely remember that Alma had mentioned something about that.

'Oh, for goodness sake, Holly. I need you to run my stall. All you have to do is to sell stuff. I'm sure you can handle that.'

Holly wasn't sure at all that she could, but she could hear the urgency in his voice. 'Fine. What do I have to sell in this stall?'

'All the food and condiments is in the *stabbur*. You have to organise it and set it up nicely, and sell it to the nice people who want Christmassy things. Everything is already priced, so all you have to do is be helpful and take their money.'

'What kind of food am I selling?'

She put on the kettle while talking.

'Biscuits and jam, and, well, lots of different stuff. Everything is labelled, so it shouldn't be too hard, and Britt knows where everything is. Listen, Holly. I've put a lot of work into this, it's supposed to be like a tasting platter for the restaurant. So it's important. You can manage, right?'

He was pleading and Holly rolled her eyes, even though he couldn't see her. 'Of course I can manage. I'll talk to Britt and get it all sorted. Don't worry. I'll even send you pictures. How does that sound?'

'That sounds brilliant. I owe you.'

'Not really. I've been gorging on your food and using Ninni's winter clothes; the least I can do is be helpful. When does this thing start?'

'Saturday at ten, I think. Britt knows. Well, they all know.'

In the background Holly could hear Rosie screaming at

the top of her lungs. 'I have to go before she explodes... or someone else does,' Jack said.

Holly laughed when she put down the mobile. He was living his best life, as they say. She felt a stab of jealousy. Her life was such a mess and she had no idea how to fix it.

She brought the steaming mug of tea with her to the lounge, leaving the snacks in the kitchen for now, and patting herself mentally on the shoulder for her self-discipline.

The laptop was on the little dining table and she brought it with her to the sofa and settled in for a Google session. Perhaps Jocelyn was free to chat. *She won't believe the morning I've had*, Holly thought.

From the sofa, she discovered a biscuit box on a shelf. It was red, it had snowflakes on it, and she was willing to bet there was something yummy in there.

When she opened the box, she laughed. It was filled to the rim with allsorts, coffee creams, even some of Jack's homemade truffles. *This has to be Jack's stash*, she thought. All the goodies from home. *He hadn't become completely Norwegian just yet*, she thought with a satisfied sigh.

She popped a truffle in her mouth and it was so delicious she closed her eyes to savour it. A few allsorts later, she opened the computer and checked emails with half an eye. Nothing from the hospital.

Holly let out her breath, not sure if she should be relieved or nervous.

It was such a nightmare. She had never in a million years imagined she would end up in a situation like this. A board of strangers deciding her future. It irked her, but there was nothing to do but bite it down if she wanted to keep her future.

Another email gave her the distraction she needed. Jocelyn had sent her pictures from the hospital.

The intention was clear. Everyone who had been on duty with her was waving placards with "Come Home, Holly. We miss you!" written on them.

Jocelyn held up a different sign that said "Brian is in deep shit. He can't charm his way out of this, please don't worry".

I so hope that's true, Holly thought and took a deep breath. She felt a million light years away from home, and suddenly had the worst case of homesickness she'd experienced since she arrived on the island.

She popped another allsorts in her mouth, and wrote back to Jocelyn. Then she wrote an email to Danny, telling him all about the fishing boat and the crabs, knowing he would love that.

It didn't take long until she felt better. No matter what happened, she would soon be home again and life would be back to normal.

Chapter Fifteen

Britt was at the door before Holly had managed to
make herself a cup of tea the next day. She looked at
the clock on the wall. Barely nine in the morning. 'For fuck's
sake,' she muttered.

The knocking made her drop the teabag on the floor, and
she greeted Britt holding the bag.

'*God morgen*,' Britt said with a wide grin. 'I'm here to
help.'

'God, you people get up at the crack of dawn,' she said,
opening the door.

'Well, the crack of dawn is in half an hour, so you'll be
fine.' Britt was dressed much like Tor had been, with a
heavy coat and matching trousers.

'Jack called you, didn't he?' Holly rolled her eyes.

'Yes, of course. He thought you might need some
guidance from the wisest woman on the island.'

Britt stepped inside the hallway and closed the door

behind her. She stomped her feet, shaking off snow and rain, before taking off her boots.

'It's freezing today and I forgot my gloves.' She rubbed her hands together.

'There's about a million gloves here. I'm sure you can borrow a pair,' Holly said.

'Good. I'll do that. Do you have anything else other than that teabag?'

Holly lifted up her hand. 'Yes. There's coffee and some other types of tea, if you prefer that.'

'Coffee will do.' Britt hung up her coat and followed Holly into the kitchen. 'I see Ninni's gone berserk with the decorations again.'

'Alma said something similar. I wouldn't know,' Holly said.

'I don't bother with it much, to be honest. I'll put up lights in the window and the garden, and bring in a tree, and have tons of Christmas marzipan and cookies, of course, but that's about it,' Britt said, sinking down on one of the kitchen chairs.

Holly put on the kettle again. 'I have plenty of food, if you want breakfast.'

'Only if you have something sweet. I'd love some pastry, to be honest.'

Holly smiled. 'I'd get you some coffee creams only I polished them off last night. I have some of those cookie men, the white ones. They're different than the pepper men, right?'

Britt nodded. 'Well, there's no spices in the yulemen. If you have one, I wouldn't mind. I like those.'

Holly found the bag in the breadbox and handed it to Britt. 'I found that on the door handle the other day. I thought perhaps it was from Emil's parents. How is he?'

'Emil is living up to his name, being as annoying as possible. Which is surprisingly easy when you're nine years old,' Britt said, dipping the head of the yuleman in her coffee. 'He's sporting quite the shiner, and struts around as if it's a badge of honour.'

'Did Jack say why he called you?' Holly held up her hand. 'No, you don't have to answer that. I know. He doesn't trust me.'

Britt looked surprised. 'I wouldn't say that, but there's a lot to do. Lots of carrying and decorating and whatnot. The market is held in the town square and there will be people from town and from the hinterland coming in to sell their wares and produce. We try to outdo ourselves every year.'

'What? With, like, a theme or something? Wouldn't that just be Christmas?' Holly said.

'Sure, we're not going overboard, but people come to buy presents and goodies to take home. We have people who have been knitting all sorts of things, from baby clothes to potholders. There's also plenty of foodstuff, from me, Jack, and the few farmers we have left. The kids contribute with Christmas decorations.'

'And they sell?'

'Well, sort of. Mostly to their family members, I'm afraid, but since a lot of their family is at the market, they always sell out. The kids donate their money to a charity. I mean, we have to do something to remind them about the spirit of Christmas.' Britt looked pleased.

Holly frowned. 'Will you have one of those stalls?'

'Of course. I have a permit to sell my beer and other brews, as long as no one drinks any of it on the premises. I know Jack has made eggnog and also experimented with liqueur, but unfortunately nobody is allowed to sell stronger stuff than a light beer or cider.' Britt shook her head, then immediately brightened up. 'He actually used cherries from the tree outside this house.'

'Yeah, he's really pleased about that. Unfortunately it doesn't seem like he has left any of that here,' Holly said, smiling at Britt.

'I did taste that eggnog.' Britt wrinkled her nose. 'I prefer beer.'

'Me too, but eggnog is part of the Christmas experience, isn't it? My dad loves the stuff,' Holly said.

Britt nodded. 'We met him last summer when he was here. No eggnog then, but he did enjoy the beer.'

'I remember that. He couldn't stop talking about it.' Holly took a bite from one of the cookies.

'Nice man,' Britt said in a voice that made Holly frown.

'Yes, uhm, what are we doing today? The market is on Saturday, right?'

'It is. Most of us have been there since the start, at the weekends. This weekend's market is the last before Christmas. We have taken some of Jack's stuff with us, and there are loads of people asking for it, so you should make a killing,' Britt finished her coffee and stood. 'Time to go, I think. I have to catch the ferry in an hour and they really don't wait for anyone.'

Holly pulled on the outfit Tor had given her, and Britt

nodded in appreciation. 'You are dressed like a proper islander now. Where did you get the clothes? I can't remember Ninni wearing anything like it.'

Holly smiled. 'I got it from Tor yesterday. We went fishing on his boat, watched the sun rise, and had sort of a picnic.'

Britt looked surprised for a second, then smiled from ear to ear. 'So all we needed to get him to join the living was you. I'm not surprised. Did you have fun?'

'I did. I've never seen a cat in a life vest before.'

'Yeah, I bet that was the most interesting thing,' Britt said. 'Make sure to wear that on Saturday. It can easily be cold in town, especially since we're outside all day.'

Outside the wind whipping up a storm. Holly pulled the jacket tighter around herself regretting not using the trousers Tor had given her. 'Is it going to get worse than this?'

'Oh, it's lovely,' Britt declared when they stood on top of the pathway leading down to the farm. She closed her eyes and lifted her face.

'The wind?' Holly wasn't so sure. It was biting her face and ears. She pulled down the hat.

Britt laughed. 'This is barely a small gale. I love the weather out here. Even now, and especially when it storms properly. I go to the edge of the water when it's really bad. Makes me feel alive.'

'I'll take your word for it,' Holly said, grinning at her.

'If you stay here long enough, you'll catch it. Much like Jack did,' Britt said, grinning back.

'Catch what?' Holly said as Britt linked her arms

through hers and started walking down the rough path leading to Jack's farm.

'Island fever, of course,' Britt said.

Island fever. Holly pondered the idea. 'Well, I won't be here long enough for that. I have London fever,' she said.

Britt only smiled. 'Sometimes it doesn't take long. Although I know what you mean. I get London fever the moment I set foot on Heathrow tarmac.'

They climbed down until they stood on the farmyard.

'There's nothing in the house. Everything edible is in *stabburet*, and lucky me, I have a key.' Britt pulled out a key-chain from her pocket.

Holly looked at the building. It was odd, resting on four piles of stones and thick timber legs. Also, the top was bigger than the bottom. The roof had grass on it – dry and brittle grass, but still. It also had protruding gavels and looked ancient in her eyes.

'Why is it built like this?'

'Like what?' Britt looked at the "legs". 'Oh, that. It's to keep the food safe. *Stabburet* used to be a farm's refrigerator slash food storage building in the olden days. It was built this way to keep mice and rats from having wild food parties.'

Holly could picture rodents giving up trying to get inside, especially since the steps up to the door were high and not for people with bad knees. 'It's lovely,' she said, wondering what Tor would say about it.

Britt opened the door and pushed it open. 'Do you believe in ghosts?'

'Oh god, not you, too. No, I don't.' Holly followed Britt

inside and looked around. 'But if I did, they would haunt a place like this, wouldn't they?'

It was so dark, Holly could barely see her hands in front of her. She didn't dare move in case there was something she could trip over.

'Smell that. Isn't it fantastic?' Britt's voice seemed to exist on its own.

'It smells like food. Sausages, maybe. And plenty of dust and something burned, like logs,' Holly said, trying to get Britt to laugh and hoping the other woman wouldn't notice her voice shaking slightly.

'Voila,' Britt said and turned on the lights, which went on with a series of clicks and fluorescent shimmer.

Britt took a deep breath and smiled. 'It smells like money,' she said.

'Excuse me?'

'In the old days, when they fished for herring along the coast, they also had factories that produced herring oil. The oil would stink up the town if the wind turned east. I haven't smelled it myself, but Alma claims it smelled god awful. The fishermen would claim it smelled like money.' Britt pointed at the ceiling. 'Except these moneymakers smell delicious, of course.'

Holly looked at rows of packages wrapped in white gauze.

'That's from the sheep, isn't it?' Holly remembered Jack telling her about it.

'Oh, yes. There's a lot of work and love behind that. They are the ones already sold and will be delivered to people before Christmas. The ones that were ordered by out-of-towners, we have already sent.'

She spoke very efficiently and to the point. *This is Britt doing business*, Holly thought. She tried to nod in the right places.

'Now, all these are what we are bringing to the market.' Britt pointed at a large workbench on the side. Several cardboard boxes were set up neatly on top of it.

'Jack loves this, all this food.' Holly followed Britt to the bench.

'We are thrilled he does. Otherwise this part of the island would have been replaced by a super marina at some point.'

Holly opened a box and peered inside. 'This isn't meat,' she said.

'No, Jack has made marmalade and chutneys, I think. Also several boxes of cookies. I haven't tasted all of it, but the marmalade is to die for.' Britt took out a jar and showed it to Holly. 'This is addictive.'

Holly took the jar and looked at it. She laughed. 'He's been using my mum's recipes as a starting point. Everything has to be changed around and experimented with.'

'He said that. I think there's a few odds and bits from his grandmother's books too. She used a lot of berries; they all did. Hell, we still do. On the island you can find blueberries, juniper berries, and *krekling*,' Britt said.

'What's *krekling*?' Holly put down the jar.

'I'm not sure what it's called in English.' Britt frowned. 'Oh, yes, I do. it's crowberries, Jack told me that. They are a little bitter, but nice. Jack's grandmother, Magny, had recipes for all sorts of things. That's how they survived out here, by making use of everything that grew.'

'Is that what you do?' Holly picked through the boxes and smiled at what she found.

'I've used both *krekling* and juniper in my beer. It's not always successful, but I like experimenting.'

'As does Jack, whereas I can barely manage to get a pizza out of the box,' Holly said.

'You're not the only one who struggles. I can only cook things that come out of cans or bags, myself.'

Holly was surprised. 'But you make beer. That's cooking, isn't it? Sort of.'

Britt laughed. 'Beer is an artform. I've also started to make aquavit, but on a small scale for now. We'll see how that goes.'

'Can I come and see what you do sometime?'

'Of course. You're welcome any time. It's fun. I use it to teach the kids science and maths.'

'It really does sound like fun,' Holly said.

Britt shrugged. 'It is, but it's also about keeping the old traditions alive so it's a history lesson too. So many things are forgotten these days, left behind in the dust, that we lose so much of ourselves. Global is all well and good, and I love the internet, but I worry what will be left when everything is the same everywhere.'

Britt smiled. 'I'm sorry, I didn't mean to go on, but it's a thing with me. Perhaps it's because here on the island we're a bit off the beaten track.'

'You do have technology here, internet and phones, and

all sorts of things that needs electricity. So you're not completely off the track,' Holly said, smiling at her.

'A bit off, perhaps, but no, you're right. We don't want to go back in time, not all of us, anyway. You should hear Alma and Sigrid discuss it. According to Alma, Sigrid looks at the past through rose-coloured glasses, romanticising something that, in her opinion, is better left in the past, and then she tells her that the greatest invention ever, wasn't rockets to the moon or the car, or whatever they argue about. It was the washing machine.'

'The washing machine?' Holly could think of a few medical inventions that had been far more useful.

Britt laughed. 'Alma claims the washing machine liberated women. Washing clothes back in the day was a major operation that took days and lots of hard work. The washing machine freed women up to pursue other things. Alma loves all the new gadgets and thingamagummies.'

Holly remembered Ninni telling her the same thing. 'And what does Sigrid say in return?'

'She asks Alma for another recipe,' Britt said, laughing now.

'Clever one.' Holly couldn't help laughing herself.

'Perhaps we should get started.' Britt gestured towards the table. 'We have to carry all of this to the sea house. It's going to take more than a few trips, I'm afraid. No cars here, remember.'

'You could have a horse,' Holly said. 'And Jack said something about a donkey somewhere?'

'Yes, but he's useless at anything except throwing kids off his back. We could have taken one of the boats, but it's almost as far away. Also, if we fall overboard, we'll lose everything. Not to mention I'm rubbish at boats.'

Holly put a hand on one of the boxes, ready to lift. 'I'd rather walk, please.'

Britt burst out laughing again and Holly looked at her.

'I'm sorry, I'm teasing you. Don't worry. Tobben is picking all of this up later tonight. He will bring it to the sea house and from there we will take it on the ferry.'

Holly shook her head. 'That's a relief. I'm not big on carrying stuff for miles. Does Tobben have a horse or something?'

'Nope, he has a small three-wheeler that he claims is a tractor. It's not. But it also has a small hanger, and is very useful for things like this.' Britt laughed again. 'You should have seen your face.'

'Could you tell Jack that I carried them to the sea house? I'd love to see *his* face when he hears that,' Holly said.

'It will be my pleasure. Now, have you seen enough?' Britt looked around. 'Have I remembered everything?' she said, more to herself that time.

Holly waited, not sure what was expected of her. Britt smiled suddenly. 'Right. We usually decorate the market stalls, you know, to make it look festive and all that. I think those boxes are at the sea house.'

'Did Jack leave any instructions to you about how I should do that? Because he didn't say anything to me.' Holly wouldn't be surprised if he had.

'I have no idea. I will let you loose on whatever is there. If you want to, that is.'

'Of course I do. It will be fun,' Holly said, hoping the distraction would do her good.

'Brilliant.' Britt rubbed her hands together.

They went outside and Britt frowned when she saw it was raining. 'I keep hoping for snow. This in-between weather is annoying.'

'Do you get snow here? I haven't seen much and it doesn't seem to last for very long.'

'We do, but it needs to be really cold for it to happen, and that is rare these days.'

'I was hoping for proper snow. I've never really seen snow that is plentiful and covers everything,' Holly said with a little laugh.

'You have to go up in the mountains for that, I'm afraid. Global warming and all.'

Holly pulled up the hood over hear head and put her hands in the pockets of the thick jacket.

Britt nodded towards the house. 'Tobben said you scared the beejesus of him.'

'No, I didn't. He scared me. I was on the phone in the lounge, talking to Jack, and Tobben appeared out of nowhere. I thought he was some kind of Scandi serial killer.'

'Well, he needs to be a bit shocked once in a while. He's a salt of the earth kind of man who doesn't like surprises,' Britt said.

Holly sensed something. 'You and him, are you…?'

Britt pulled a face. 'No, we're just friends. Or friendly-ish, is perhaps a better word. Men can be so exhausting sometimes, and he's far too sensitive for me. He takes everything so seriously, you know?'

Holly smiled. 'Yes, I can see that.'

They headed up towards the pathway. Holly thought about Tor. She wasn't sure what kind of man he was, or why she couldn't stop thinking about him.

Chapter Sixteen

Tor noticed them as he came up the path after checking on the boat. He stopped in his tracks, looking around in panic for a place to hide. There was nothing. No house, no boulder appearing out of the blue, nothing. And the dry stacks were too high for him to jump over quickly.

This is becoming the most embarrassing habit I've ever had, he thought. But he still backed away.

Even so, he couldn't help watching Holly and the other woman talking and laughing. They were heading his way and there was nothing he could do about it.

Holly seems to shimmer, he thought and rolled his eyes at himself. *Yeah, I'm not going down that road.* Not now, not with a woman who will be leaving after Christmas. No matter how much he wanted her.

He wondered if he had made a mistake by taking her fishing. But she had been such a good sport about it, and he was sure she had enjoyed herself. He certainly had. More than he had in a long time, if he was honest with himself.

When they caught up with him, he would have to say hello and then there would be introductions and afterwards, every time she met him the other woman would say hi to him. And he didn't like that. He had managed to stay secluded for all these weeks, and he wanted to remain that way. He liked it that way.

The two women hadn't discovered him yet. Tor considered throwing himself on the ground, hoping they wouldn't notice him, but of course they would, and then he'd be the village idiot.

Then he saw Frøy running up behind Holly, only to stop and rub his head against her leg. She bent down and picked him up. And the damned cat let it happen. Tor was flabbergasted.

'Traitor,' he muttered.

Before he had a chance to either fall flat on his face or back away, Holly spotted him and waved.

'Damn,' he muttered.

Too late now, he thought and tried to look less like an idiot and more like a normal person.

Holly smiled at Tor who looked more and more uncomfortable as they came closer.

'Hi,' she said, putting her nose to Frøy's furry head.

Tor's eyes flicked towards Britt who smiled her best smile.

'Uhm, hi. I was just... on my way home,' he said.

'I'm Britt, the school teacher, beer brewer, and possibly aquavit producer,' Britt said, holding out her hand. 'I have seen you around, but I don't think I've had a chance to talk to you yet.'

Tor shook it. 'I'm Tor. Hi.'

Britt didn't seem fazed by his standoffishness. 'I hear you're an architect. Have you designed anything I might have seen?'

Tor glared slightly at Holly. 'I doubt it. We design mostly office buildings. You know, the soulless ones,' he said, and immediately regretted his words.

Britt laughed. 'Still, I might have seen one. How are you finding our island, Tor?' she said.

'It's... lovely.' Tor looked at Holly again, and this time she took mercy on him.

'We just wanted to say hi and return your cat,' she said, holding the fluffy traitor as if he was a teddy bear.

Frøy wriggled and she put him down after kissing him on the head.

'Frøy is something else,' Holly said, laughing at him.

'You should know that Frøy is a regular visitor to the school, Tor. The kids love him,' Britt said.

'Oh, good. I don't really know what he does or where he roams most days,' Tor said.

Holly looked at Britt whose eyes twinkled. She decided to save the poor man. He was clearly uncomfortable.

'We have to go and, uhm, prepare for Saturday,' she said. 'My brother should have been here by now, but he's been delayed, and now I have to step into his shoes.'

When Tor frowned, Britt spoke up. 'We're all attending the Christmas market in town.'

'Okay.' Tor looked confused.

'It's something the town has every year and we all become mainlanders for the day, and we sell all sorts of stuff. It's great for those last Christmas presents if you have forgotten anyone,' Britt said.

'Apparently Jack was going to manage a food stall there, but now it's been left up to me to deal with it,' Holly said, smiling at him.

'Yes, of course. Good luck,' Tor said.

'I hope we will see you there,' Britt said.

'Oh. Well, unfortunately I have conference calls most days.'

Britt smiled. 'The market is open from two o'clock until six, when the last ferry leaves for the island. If you have the time, please come by. There will be lots of good food and drinks, and no pressure to buy anything.'

Holly studied Tor. He so clearly didn't want to come, she almost felt sorry for him. But she was also a bit annoyed. 'Well, if we see you, we see you,' she said.

Tor nodded. 'Right. Yes.'

He turned around, almost stepping on Frøy, who gave him a stare that could have curdled milk, and then rushed up the partway towards his house.

Britt looked at Holly. 'He's a strange one, isn't he?'

'He really is. Are all Norwegian men like him?' Holly sighed.

'Some of them are worse, to be honest.' Britt turned towards her. 'He likes you though.'

'No, he doesn't.' Holly rolled her eyes. 'He couldn't care less about me.'

Britt laughed. 'Oh, you are too adorable. He's all hot and bothered by you. Take my word for it.'

Holly didn't want to take any word for anything, certainly not concerning Tor. Still, she couldn't help looking over her shoulder to see if Tor was still there. He wasn't and she was annoyed she had looked.

Britt pulled up the hood of her jacket. 'I have to stop by Alma's. You want to come with? Might be a piece of cake in it for you.'

Holly shook her head. 'I think I'll be heading home. I'm a bit tired.'

'Well, you better rest. See you Saturday, then. I'll come by and pick you up.'

The short walk home soothed her nerves, rain and slush and all. Holly breathed in the clean and fresh air. *They should really bottle it,* she thought.

When she opened the gate to the house, she discovered a guest.

Frøy sat on the front step, licking his paw. He headbutted her hand when Holly bent down to pet him.

'What are you doing here?' Holly looked around to see if Tor was anywhere near. 'Where's your master? Or pet, depending on your point of view, I guess. I thought you guys went home.'

Frøy rubbed his face against her leg. Holly laughed. 'Do you want to come inside? I haven't had any guests and I'm sure Jack and Ninni wouldn't mind.'

Holly opened the door and let Frøy in. He trotted inside,

sniffing all the time. But he didn't seem nervous or anything.

The first few minutes she left the door open in case he wanted to leave, but when it turned too cold, she closed it.

Somehow Frøy found his way into the kitchen and gave her a look that clearly told her treats were expected.

'I have cookies,' she said.

Frøy didn't look impressed and Holly opened the fridge to see what was there. 'I don't really have anything you can eat, Frøy. Or any kind of cat food, really. I think there's some dog food here, but you don't want that, do you?'

Frøy stood on his hindlegs, and stuck his whole head into the fridge. Holly waited patiently while he sniffed for goodies.

'Not sure jam is right for you, lovely,' she said.

Then she remembered something, left him to the sniffing and opened one of the cupboard doors. 'Right, there it is.'

Holly pulled out a tuna box and showed it to the cat. It was like finding a treasure. 'What do you think?'

Frøy dropped down on all fours and trotted over to her.

'I have no idea what it says on the label, to be honest, but I'm guessing *tunfisk* means tuna fish and also, there's a picture of what I'm guessing is a tuna on the tin. All I have to do now is to see if it's suitable for you. Tuna in oil or tomato is probably no good.' Holly took the tin over to the sink and opened it by pulling the tab, getting tuna juice all over her fingers. She sighed with relief. Tuna in water was probably okay.

Frøy made a sound and she looked at him. 'Wow, you speak.'

He kept mewing and pawing at her leg with one of his paws.

'Hang on.' Holly pulled off the rest of the lid and sat the tin down on the floor.

Frøy attacked it as if he had never eaten in his life. Holly laughed. 'Doesn't Tor feed you? I'm sure he does, you know.'

She sat at the table and checked her emails while Frøy enjoyed his treat. Still nothing. She sighed with relief, and then got mad. Why didn't they just give her the verdict so she could be done with this... this torture? Waiting like this was driving her bonkers.

Danny had sent her an email filled with fishing jokes, most of them so cheesy they were something their dad would have told. He also told her that they were doing fine and not to worry about either of them.

It lifted her spirits and reminded her she wasn't alone in the world.

A bump on her leg made her look down. She knew cats didn't smile – they weren't dogs – but Frøy had a very smug look on his furry face. Holly patted the cushion next to her on the bench. He jumped up and easily took up half the space.

'You are a funny one.' Holly put her hand on him. The purring vibrated through the soft fur. 'An after-snack nap. That's actually a good idea.'

Even so, she didn't move. How could you move when a cat decided to use you as a pillow? *It would be rude*, Holly thought.

She sent a response to Jocelyn, telling her about the

fishing trip, but this time focusing on Tor. *That would make her wonder,* she thought, smiling to herself, and then she googled Tor's name. Pictures popped up and she exclaimed in surprise.

'Tor looks even better without a beard,' she said to Frøy.

Truth be told, he looked gorgeous, especially when he was smiling. Holly enlarged the pictures. It was hard to see the resemblance between the man she had met and this smiley, happy man.

Whatever happened to him? There was nothing about his personal life that she could find and he wasn't active on any of the social media platforms, or at least she couldn't find him.

When she found his company's page, there were links, but still nothing personal. Only business.

'His friend looks nice,' she said to Frøy.

Henrik had links to his personal sites. Lots of pictures of his kids and his wife. They looked happy and lovely.

'Right. I'm so stalking now. I should be ashamed of myself,' she informed the cat.

He rolled over and flicked his tale.

But she didn't stop. She scrolled down and found pictures that Henrik had put up, pictures with Tor from the office, from parties. In one picture he had his arm around a woman. The smiles told her there had been love there at that point.

'Obviously not now, otherwise he wouldn't roam the island like some cursed sailor,' she muttered.

I'll tell you mine, if you tell me yours, she thought. She had a feeling his story would be interesting. A lot more interesting than her own story. She had already told him about her mother. That was more than she had said about her in years. Then only thing she hadn't told him was about Brian and the meltdown. It was too embarrassing.

Holly put her hand on the cat again, giving belly scratches that made Frøy purr even more. 'You are such a love bug, you silly fluffy cat.'

She looked at the screen again. Tor's happy face smiled at her. Then she felt even more like a stalker and closed the computer.

Would he come to the market, she wondered? Probably not.

Her hand touched Frøy's collar and she smiled. Well, she wasn't about to give up that easily.

While Frøy napped, she put together a few things and made a little pouch. Then she wrote a short message, rolled it together and put that in the pouch too.

When she was finished, she found Frøy sitting by the door, ready to go home.

———————

Frøy was howling outside the door when Tor came downstairs to let him in.

'Why aren't you using the window?' Tor said and opened the door. 'It's open so that I don't have to run downstairs and risk breaking my neck.'

Frøy trotted inside, ignoring Tor's look. He plonked himself down on in front of the fireplace in the lounge and Tor discovered he had something around his neck.

'What have to brought with you now? Is this why you didn't jump up to the windowsill? And why am I always asking you stuff when I know you can't talk back?' Tor managed to untie the small pouch Frøy had in his collar.

It looked like a small Christmas present, jolly paper and all.

Tor looked at Frøy. He was no help. Besides he already knew it had to be from Holly. No one else on the island would do anything like this.

He opened the pouch an shook out the content. Two wrapped sweets and a small note.

I hope to see you at the market. I'll be there all day. Frøy ate a tin of tuna at my house.

Tor looked at the cat. 'You know, fluffy fur can only hide so much.'

He unwrapped one of the sweets and popped it in his mouth. Some kind of chocolatey coffee flavour. 'Good,' he said, feeling ridiculously happy that she had sent him a gift.

'Maybe I'll send you to visit her more often. You can be my ambassador,' Tor said.

Frøy crept closer to the fire.

Chapter Seventeen

The first cup of tea on the day of the market tasted like heaven, filled up with milk and sugar. It felt good to have a purpose, even if it meant working in a market stall all day.

Too much holiday is not healthy, she thought. *Especially not for me. Too much thinking, too much in my own head. Not good. Not good at all.* She hadn't heard or seen Tor since the fishing trip. Perhaps Frøy had lost the note or Tor just didn't want to spend more time with her. She hoped that wasn't the case.

She sipped the tea and pondered what to make for breakfast.

Or perhaps she should skip it. With all the crisps and sweets she had been living on, she'd risk more than losing her medical license. *Nope*, she thought. *Not going there.*

'Something healthy then,' she said to the grinning brownie in the corner of the kitchen. 'I wish I could put all of you in a closet. Like Chuckie or those creature puppets that turned into monsters when they get wet.'

She turned away from the doll, and searched for food. She ended up with an apple and a cookie. *At least it's semi-healthy*, she thought. After finishing the tea, she took the apple with her out in the hallway.

Lesson learned from the boating trip with Tor, she put on tights before jeans, sweater and everything else. He had left her the overalls and coat, so she was prepared for a day outside. Before she had time to put on all the outerwear though, Britt knocked on the door.

Holly opened with one elfish boot on, and the other in her hand. She also had the cookie in her mouth.

'My kind of breakfast,' Britt said, leaving the door open behind her.

Holly managed to pull on the other boot and took the cookie from her mouth. 'I have an apple in my pocket,' she said, and took another bite of the cookie.

'Yes, it's very useful to bring an apple, but you don't have to worry about that, actually. We will be fed. I can guarantee you that. Personally I think Alma's motto is to feed us until we all look like bulky snowmen.' Britt turned her head. 'Our ride is here.'

Holly discovered a small vehicle of sorts stopping on the gravel road outside the house. Tobben sat on top of it. He lifted a hand and waved at her.

'He's giving us a lift to the harbour,' Britt said.

'The sea house is like what, 300-400 feet away?'

Britt laughed. 'I know, but it's fun. Come on. You can choose between sitting next to Tobben or in the hanger. If you sit next to Tobben you will have the pleasure of his dazzling small talk, mostly about the winter storms and how one day the ferry will stop coming, and the prize of food, or you can sit in the back and enjoy the view.'

Holly frowned. 'I'll take the view, if you don't mind.'

'I don't mind at all, I'm already dazzling,' Britt said, flashing a smile at Tobben who didn't look too impressed.

Holly scooted into the little wagon and held on to the edges with both hands.

'All aboard?' Tobben called, before Britt rolled her eyes at Holly to make her smile.

The little tractor, or whatever it was, rolled along the pathway. Holly dangled her legs and enjoyed the scenery. There was a cold wind from the sea, and she could hear seagulls screaming in the distance.

Behind her, Tobben and Britt talked in Norwegian. It was obvious that they were comfortable with each other, as she could hear the friendliness in their voices. She wondered again if there was something going on between them. *None of your business*, she reminded herself.

At the hospital gossip and rumours were part of the daily routine, and mostly it was friendly and amusing… until it wasn't. But she didn't want to dwell on that today.

When they came to the fork in the road, Holly stretched her neck, trying to see if Tor was anywhere in sight.

Not a glimpse of man nor cat.

I shouldn't be thinking about him, she told herself. *He's a hermit, for goodness sake.* And after the way he had disappeared after meeting her and Britt on the path, she was sure he didn't spend a minute of his day thinking about her. Somehow that annoyed her.

They arrived at the harbour and Tobben stopped outside of the sea house. 'Here we go, ladies,' he said with a broad smile.

Britt jumped off and stretched her back. Holly followed. The harbour was quiet and the only boat was a large row boat with no sail or engine, as far as Holly could see. She walked over to the edge and looked down. The water was choppy and grey, but she could still see the seaweed floating just below the surface. The smell of the sea, salty and fresh, made her feel as if she breathed easier.

Britt grabbed Holly's arm. 'Let's go inside. I'm in the mood for breakfast, to be honest.'

She pulled up the heavy door and for a moment Holly couldn't see. She blinked a few times until her eyes got used to the light inside.

'Wow,' she said. 'This is huge.'

'Is this your first time in here?' Britt looked at her.

'Yes, actually. I know Jack plans to turn it into a restaurant. It sounded crazy at first.' Holly stepped inside. 'Still does, to be honest.'

Everything was made of wood, and not painted or polished but rough wood, with windows a bit high up, and a solid floor. There was a second floor, she knew that. But it seemed to be really high up. At one end of the building she caught a glimpse of a gleaming kitchen, and at the other, two large doors.

'Where do they lead?' She looked at Britt.

'Right out to a small pier, and the wide open sea,' Britt

said. 'It's where the herring boats would stop to unload their catch of the day.'

On one side, a huge fireplace dominated the wall, and there was a long wooden table standing in front of it.

'Of course it's crazy, but he seems to have good plans. We're all in on it, poor man. Your brother is patient, I can tell you that.'

Holly smiled. 'He put up with Danny and me, so I'm not surprised. This looks a lot better than I had imagined, you know.'

Britt put her hands on her hips. 'It's getting there. And when we're done with the market, Christmas can start. We'll have a proper Christmas Eve dinner with food and drinks to look forward to, and I'm curious to see what you think of my beer.'

'That sounds lovely,' Holly said. 'Jack sings its praises.'

'Yeah, it will be on the menu in the restaurant next year. After Christmas Eve we'll have the New Year's Eve party to look forward too. If the weather is nice, we'll have that outside.'

'A beach party? In December?' Holly couldn't quite see it.

'Sure, but like I said, it's not until New Year's Eve.' Britt laughed again. 'You should see your face. It's a way to say goodbye to the old and hello to the new, and of course, an excuse to get sloshed. How else can we keep warm out here?'

Holly laughed. 'I love that.'

'But, sadly, for now we have to work,' Britt said.

She waved at the boxes standing next to the door. 'All

this will be brought to town, and to our market stalls. And then we have a damn exhausting day to get through.'

'There's no need for that kind of language,' a stern voice said behind them.

Holly looked over her shoulder and discovered Alma coming in with a basket on her arm.

'Sometimes that's just what is needed. Is that coffee you have there?' Britt said.

'Yes, of course.' Alma put the basket on the table, and started to take things out and put them on the table. 'Holly, there's paper cups and plates in the kitchen. Right on the counter. Can you bring them?'

Holly was curious to see the kitchen. She opened the door and switched on the lights. 'Wow,' she said.

It was top tech all the way, gleaming steel and shiny surfaces. *This is Jack's dream come true*, she thought, unable to stifle a giggle.

She found the plates and cups, and returned to the big room just as Tobben arrived and took a pepper cookie from Alma who scowled at him.

'It's impressive, isn't it?' he said when Holly came back.

'It looks like it's been designed by NASA,' Holly said.

Alma took the plates from her. 'I think it looks very nice, very professional,' she said.

'Like a mad scientist's laboratory,' Britt said, joining them. 'What have you brought us?'

'Sandwiches, of course. Here, drink some coffee. It might clear your mind,' Alma said, opening a large thermos.

'What, no cookies or anything lovely?' Britt plunked herself down next to Holly.

The aroma of coffee filled Holly's nose and she held out her cup. 'Is there any milk in the kitchen? Shall I bring it?'

Alma frowned. 'Not sure there is. Most of us drink our coffee black, like normal people. I can get tea for you, if you prefer that?'

Holly shook her head. 'No, coffee is fine.'

'We have coffee cream, if that'll do you,' Britt said, stretching over to the counter and then placing a small carton on the table in front of her. 'Alma thinks we all drink our coffee black, but we don't. Some of us, including Jens, don't mind a few drops of the white stuff to take the edge of the acidity.'

Alma snorted slightly. 'Only children need cream in their coffee.'

'Children shouldn't drink coffee,' Britt said, winking at Holly.

Alma ignored her and smiled at Holly. 'Help yourself, Holly. There are all sorts of *pålegg*, as you can see. It's always good to eat properly before we got to work.'

Holly looked at the table. There were two baskets with different types of bread and rolls, all brown, and several plates of different toppings for your sandwich.

'Not sure she knows about *pålegg*, Alma,' Britt said, grinning at Holly.

'No idea what that means,' Holly said. If Tor had been there, he would have given her a long explanation.

'It means anything you can put on a sandwich,' Britt said.

'Thank you.' Holly followed the others lead and made

her first open sandwich for herself with cheese. *Cheese is safe*, she thought.

'Try this,' Britt said, and put a plate of different slices of meat in front of her. 'It's all made of pork.'

'What kind of ham is this?' Holly said, studying the plate.

'The square one is called *sylte*, and it's like pressed ham, with some cloves and whatnot in it.'

'Honestly, Britt. You know better than that. It's pressed meat from the pigs head, mixed with ground spices like clover, allspice, and ginger. I use an old recipe from the island,' Alma said, sending Britt a glowering look.

Britt laughed. 'It's very tasty. The other one is made of rolled rib meat. I'm sure you can take a small piece and try it first.'

She didn't wait for Holly's response, but put a few slices of different *pålegg* on her plate. Holly put the roll on her sandwich and took a bite. The taste was salty and fragrant. 'Delicious. You really made this?' she said to Alma.

'Of course. Ready-made isn't the same,' Alma said, clearly pleased with Holly's reaction.

Britt looked at Alma. 'You really haven't brought any sweet bakes or something? Even a waffle will do right now.'

'I have brought a nice *kringle* today. I hope you like it, Holly.'

Holly smiled. 'I won't even try to pronounce that.'

She watched as Alma took out another foil-wrapped package. It was a pretzel-shaped cake, decorated with pearl sugar and flaked almonds, thin stripes of white icing, and smelling of cardamom.

'I think my stomach just woke up,' Holly said. 'It looks delicious.'

Britt leaned over. 'Did you put *sukat* in this thing?'

Alma cut a large piece, put it on a plate and handed it to Holly before turning to Britt.

'No, I didn't. This one has a lovely almond filling. No raisins and no *sukat*. I can't stand watching you pick out every tiny piece of *sukat* and building a little mountain on the plate as if you were five years old.'

'What's *sukat*?' Holly took another bite of the sandwich.

'It's simply candied citrus peel,' Alma said, turning to Britt again. 'You're too old to complain about that.'

'No, I'm not. *Sukat* is gross.' Britt accepted the plate Alma handed her. 'You make the best *kringle* in the world. Why would you ruin such scrumptiousness with things that look like square pieces of snot?'

Alma shot her a furious look, then looked at Holly. 'I think you call it "succade", Holly. It's not gross and it's not snot.'

Holly smiled. 'I'm glad it isn't.'

She took a bite of the cake and closed her eyes. The cake was light and fluffy, and tasted of sweet almonds and butter with just a hint of cardamom. 'Oh my god, this is to die for.'

'Thank you. It's my mother's recipe.'

Holly was too busy to enjoy the cake to mind much when the two women shifted to Norwegian when Tobben and Jens came in with more boxes.

The breakfast ended an hour later, when the last of the *kringle* was devoured by Jens and someone said the ferry would come at any minute.

Jens smiled at Holly. 'I'm sorry Jack and Ninni have been delayed. I hope everything is fine with Ninni's mother.'

'Jack didn't say anything about her last time I talked to him, so I presume she's fine,' Holly said.

'She's always fine. My guess is she has made up some grievances to keep them there longer,' Alma said.

Holly could sense there was more to the story about Ninni's mother. All she knew about her was what Jack had told her. 'She lives in Spain permanently, doesn't she?'

'That she does. The island was never enough for her, and Bergen was too rainy and cold,' Alma said. 'But I'll say this for her, she loves Rosie. I can't hold that against her. Even if she makes up some outrageous story to keep them there for longer.'

'Well, you never know. The law of averages says she has to be ill at least once,' Jens said, laughing at his own joke.

Alma scowled at him. 'There's no need for gossip. I don't want Holly to think that we have no manners and that we backtalk people.'

Jens raised his eyebrows. 'You brought it up, my dear.'

Alma said something sharp in Norwegian and Holly wondered if it was a swear word. It might be, as Britt had to stifle a laugh.

'I think we should leave now,' Alma said. 'We should have everything lined on the pier before the ferry gets here.'

At Alma's command, they all stood and everyone took

their plates and cups over to a rubbish bin while Alma packed the food into the basket again.

The streets teemed with people, obviously with money to spend, when Tor came up the steep hill from the harbour. The sun was setting, and Christmas lights lit up the whole street.

He had chosen to take his own boat instead of the ferry, knowing that it would be filled with islanders. He wasn't quite ready to be stuck on a boat with people he had managed to avoid for most of his stay, even if Holly would be there.

Someone had decorated a statue of two fishermen with scarves. It made them look at bit silly, *which was probably the intention*, he thought.

When he finally stood in the street, right below the red brick church and the old post office building, he realised that he didn't know where to look for the islanders. He knew that the main street was fairly long and he had no idea where the market was.

There were kids everywhere, holding sticky sweets and most wearing some kind of Christmassy outfit: red hats, bright red dots on their faces, and colourful scarves.

He remembered the excitement of that age. The thrill of going out when it was dark to see all the Christmas lights and getting a taste of what was to come.

He discovered that most people were heading in the

same direction. *Most likely to the market*, he thought and followed them down the street.

A few minutes later he found himself in front of the Christmas market. It was placed on the town square below the town hall.

The pink one, he thought and smiled. There was something so silly about an Italian style building, brightly pink, in the middle of a west coast Norwegian town.

At the market, there seemed to be endless rows of stalls, filled with everything anyone could imagine they needed for Christmas.

Tor ventured into the crowd, hoping that if he just walked around, he'd find Holly.

The smell of food permeated the air – that, and cheerful Christmas music coming from loudspeakers, strategically placed everywhere.

Tor walked past all sorts of arts and crafts; both traditional and modern by the look of it, everything from knitwear and decorations carved in wood, to honey wax candles, to all sorts of teas and coffees, and mass produced Christmas decorations and toys. He stopped by a stall selling trolls. They made him smile and he couldn't resist buying one for Holly. The troll seller pointed vaguely in the opposite direction when he asked if she knew where the islanders were.

Tor stuffed the troll in his pocket, feeling stupid at once. But it reminded him of Holly and hopefully she'd like it.

Or maybe she would be insulted, he wasn't too sure.

Holly rubbed her hands together. She couldn't use the thick mittens when she wrapped items or handled money, and it felt as if her fingers were about to fall off. Unfortunately, the heat lamp Tobben had put up in her stall made absolutely no difference.

Holly blew on her fingers again. Nobody else seemed bothered by the cold. What were these people made off? Did they have no sense of temperature? Alma stood a few stalls down from her, selling knitwear and Christmas cakes. She recognised them from the coffee shop Tor had taken her to. They were the ones made almost completely of marzipan, baked in rings, and put on top of each other. And they were very popular, from what she could see.

Britt was on the other side of her, together with Tobben. They were selling meat from the *stabbur*, and of course Britt's beer, and people were waiting in a long queue. Britt had said that most of the meat had already been ordered and were just there to be picked up by buyers.

Holly had made several pyramids of Jack's products on the table, and kept replacing them with new items all the time. Bitter orange marmalade, lingonberry and crowberry jam, Jack's special mustard and a whole stack of all of his biscuits, packed in lovely, Christmassy paper.

There had been plenty of people stopping by her stall. She had sold almost all the mustard and the cookies already. Jack would be pleased.

'I brought you this,' Britt popped inside the stall, holding two paper cups with some kind of steaming brew.

Britt handed her a cup. 'It'll warm you right up. I could hear your teeth chattering from my stall.'

'Doesn't Tobben need your help?'

'He can manage for a minute. Besides, he's more effective this way. People are scared to say no to him. Now drink.'

The cup was blissfully warm and Holly folded her fingers around it. It smelled of spices and she could see raisins in it. Holly frowned. 'Mulled wine?'

Britt pulled a face. 'We call it *gløgg*. No alcohol in it, I'm afraid. It's not permitted at these things.'

The *gløgg* was a lot sweeter than she expected and Holly wasn't sure what to make of it. Mostly she was grateful it was warm.

Britt laughed. 'Oh, you should see your face. What you have there is the baby friendly version; made with a – oh I don't know how to explain this – it's a sort of squash with berries, some apple juice, spices, mostly cinnamon, and raisins. Normally we use red wine.'

'It smells good,' Holly said, taking another sip.

'That it does. You might want to try Alma's hot cocoa as well. That's to die for.' Britt pointed at Alma's stall. Jens was busy filling cups from a large pot, handing them out to red-faced children.

Holly put down the not-wine. 'Maybe I'll try that later.'

Britt looked over her shoulder, and could see Tobben in what looked like a heated argument with a costumer. 'I have to go back before he does something stupid. You're doing really well, Holly.'

Holly was ridiculously happy with the praise. Most people, after realising she didn't speak a word of Norwegian, happily chatted in English.

She checked the stock behind the desk. She had already sold so much, she was worried she would run out soon.

'Oh, hi. You must be Holly,' a chirpy woman said, smiling broadly at her.

'Yes, I guess I must be. Hi.' Holly had no idea who she was.

The woman had long, blonde hair, braided into messy plaits and had one kid in each hand. Both kids were dressed in the same red woollen hat and red vest, the same kind of overalls Holly was wearing, and boots.

She spoke sharply when one of them, the smallest one, tried to pull loose. She was having none of that.

'I have to drop these two over there with the choir. They're on soon.' The woman pointed over to a group of children standing by a huge Christmas tree. 'They're only going to sing two songs, so I'll be back afterwards to help you,' she said.

'Right. And you must be?' Holly didn't want to let her behind the stall without knowing who she was.

'Oh, of course. I'm Sigrid, this is Ole and Anja. We have a smallholding on the other side of the island. Jack and my Olav work together.' She nodded at her children. 'They have talked about you ever since you took care of Emil's eye.'

'I was happy to help, but I hope they are more careful with snowballs now,' Holly said.

Sigrid laughed. 'I wouldn't bet on it, but I did have a stern talking to Ole about not throwing snowballs in people's faces.'

The girl, nine or ten, Holly guessed, grinned widely at her and said something she didn't understand.

Sigrid looked at her. 'You can say that in English, Anja. Go ahead.'

'Are you Jack's sister?' Anja said, and immediately had the giggles.

Holly smiled at the little girl. 'Yes, I am.'

Anja frowned, clearly trying to formulate new words. 'Hi, Jack's sister,' she finally said.

Sigrid smiled at her. 'A bit of stage fright, I'm afraid.'

'No, that's really good. Thank you, Anja. It's nice to meet you too.'

Ole interrupted, not wanting to be outshined by his sister. 'Hi, Jack's sister,' he piped up.

'Hi Ole,' Holly said. It came out as "Ollie", but he didn't seem to mind.

Sigrid rolled her eyes. 'This could go on for ever. I'll be right back, I promise.'

She hauled the kids with her towards the Christmas tree.

Holly couldn't help laughing. *She's something else*, she thought. She rubbed her hands together again. The *gløgg* was finished and so was the heat. She blew hot air on her fingers yet again, and turned back towards the Christmas tree.

Tor was standing there, looking at her. He had come! Holly lifted her hand and waved at him, but he turned around and disappeared.

What on earth was he doing? What was wrong with him? Holly gaped. Why would he come and then run away when he saw her? Because that's what it looked like.

She was distracted by a few costumers, and then Jens came over to the stall and grinned at her. He held out a cup. 'Britt told me to give you this.'

'Thank you.' Holly looked at the cup. There was a large dollop of whipped cream on it, with a sprinkle of what looked like cinnamon. A spoon stuck out of the yumminess.

'I made that,' Jens said, beaming at her.

She took a sip and knew she had cream all over her lip. 'This is absolutely delicious, Jens.'

'That's because I add a bit of coffee for the adults. Just a hint, mind you, and also there's real vanilla in it. It's my own recipe.'

Holly could see why Jack liked him so much. He reminded her of an overexcited Santa, especially since he had on a red bobble hat.

'Are you sure you haven't put anything else in this?' she teased to make him smile.

'No, that would be naughty and also against the law, sadly.' His eyes twinkled. 'Well, I will see you later. It seems I am needed.'

Holly turned her head and discovered Alma waving at him.

No booze anywhere. *Seems a bit overly strict,* Holly thought. Right now a drink would have been perfect. She finished the cocoa, then dropped the cup in the bin, together with the cup of *gløgg. It's not an attractive name,* she thought. Whenever she tried to say it out aloud, it sounded more like "gluggs", like something you pulled out of a swamp.

The music from the loudspeakers stopped and everyone

looked at the Christmas tree. The little choir had assembled in some semblance of order in front of it.

Holly leaned on the counter, smiling when Anja waved at her.

Then she was busy with more customers and had to concentrate.

Chapter Eighteen

Tor hesitated before approaching Holly again. He heard the kids singing – out of tune, but their enthusiasm made up for it.

He could still turn around and leave.

The clapping started and he got startled. *Make a decision, idiot*, he scolded himself.

Holly had already seen him. If he didn't go to her now, she would likely never speak to him again.

And suddenly that became important to him.

He squared his shoulders and headed towards Holly's stall before he gave himself another reason to go home. He stopped in front of the stall and pretended to look at the jars of marmalade while Holly talked to a woman.

She didn't look at him, and so he could study her. She looked happy and a bit flushed. Her hands waved a bit and she was smiling and laughing.

Tor almost dropped the jar he was holding when she

turned towards him. She did not look happy now. 'Did you change your mind?'

'Uhm, sorry?' Tor wasn't sure what she was talking about.

'I saw you, I even waved at you, and then you ran off,' she said.

'Ah, that. No, that was something else. Here. I got you these,' he said and handed her what he had bought.

Holly frowned, but she took the present. The seller had no more Christmas wrapping left, so she had put them in a small brown paper bag.

'Why on earth would you... Oh.' Holly held up the gloves he had bought. They were brightly striped, in several colours, but most importantly, they were fingerless.

'I hope they fit. I saw that you kept blowing on your hands. These will keep your hands warmer. Or at least warm*ish*,' he added quickly.

A huge beam of a smile almost had him backing away for the third time.

Holly quickly pulled the gloves on and wriggled her fingers. 'They are lovely, Tor. I love them. Thank you. I can't believe you bought these for me.'

Tor wasn't sure what to say. Or do. He wondered if he should give her the troll too, but had no idea how to do it without making it really awkward.

Holly pointed at the goods she was selling. 'Do you like marmalade? On me, of course. I mean, not on me, you know, but as a thank you gift.'

Tor had a sudden vision of Holly covered in marmalade. He cleared his voice. 'For what?'

'Isn't it obvious? You've saved me on more than one occasion now,' she said. 'This is a lifesaver too.'

'A jar of marmalade for a life? Seems like a fair exchange,' he said, only to see her beam at him again.

'You better believe it. This is my brother's homemade marmalade with lemons and Seville bitter oranges – all organic – and if Jack is to believed, it was bloody hard to get hold of them.' Holly spoke so fast, she almost didn't breathe. 'He said they don't know what bitter oranges are here.'

'I've never tasted bitter oranges,' he said.

'Try it.' Holly took a teaspoon and dipped it into an open glass. She put the dollop on a small cracker and handed to him. 'Here.'

Tor put the cracker in his mouth and chewed slowly. The smell of orange was intense. It was good. Bitter and sweet at the same time, and with a strong taste of citrus. 'This is delicious,' he said.

Holly looked pleased. 'It's Jack's own recipe. He loves the stuff.'

'And you don't?' Tor smiled at her.

She seemed taken aback by that. 'Uhm, I don't hate it, I'm just more of a cherry jam person.'

'I'll keep that in mind.' Tor looked at the pyramid of different glasses she had made, which sat alongside homemade biscuits. 'What else is good here?'

'Probably everything. Jack is very good at what he does. It turns out that people love homemade mustard and marmalade. Not together, I'm guessing.'

Tor wracked his mind to find something more he could

say, something that didn't make him feel as if he was fifteen again and had a major crush on a girl. *Don't even go there*, he warned himself.

'The mustard probably goes well with *gravlaks*,' he said, and almost groaned.

'With what? Is that like smoked *laks*?' Holly handed a jar of mustard to another customer.

'No, different processes. You don't smoke *gravlaks*, you cure it. It's good, though. With mustard sauce,' Tor said, knowing he was babbling.

'I like cured salmon,' Holly said, pulling her hat over her ears.

'Someone is probably selling it here,' he said, nodding at the other stalls, all teeming with eager customers.

'I'll ask Alma for a taste.' Holly handed a box of biscuits to a man who looked well pleased with it.

'You don't have to. I make my own,' Tor said before he managed to stop himself. 'I mean, *gravlaks* for Christmas is an absolute necessity, and my grandfather taught me how to make it.'

Holly cocked her head, smiling at him. 'Are you inviting me for a *gravlaks* taste?'

'I might,' he said, in a defensive voice.

'And what if I don't like mustard?'

'Not obligatory. You can have it without the sauce.'

Holly laughed. He liked to see her laugh.

'Fine. What more will you be serving at your feast?'

'I don't know yet, and I have to warn you I'm not much of a chef. I mean, *gravlaks* is as advanced as it gets.'

'Maybe we can do a potluck thing. I can bring

something too. God knows Jack has made enough food to last a lifetime.'

He was enjoying himself now. 'No, you don't have to bring anything. We can discover what kind of Norwegian food you like or dislike.'

'You're going to feed me weird food? Like scorched sheep's head? Yes, Jack told me about that.' Holly shuddered at the thought. 'Danny keeps trying to convince me to eat it. I think he has a bet with Dad.'

'I'm not insane. No sheep's heads for me.' He shook his head with emphasis. 'I don't like my food looking back at me.'

'Good to know.' Holly served another costumer. Jars of marmalade and mustard disappeared and Tor waited patiently while she worked. From where he was standing he could see that the market was fading.

'How long does this thing last?' he said.

'I had hoped it would be over by now, to be honest. My feet are killing me and it's been a long day already. But we're all returning home on the last ferry, so even if the market stays open longer, we're not.'

Holly stretched her neck and looked around. 'One of the others was supposed to help me, but I think she's disappeared. Damn it, I could really use a trip to the bathroom.'

'You need a break? Let me help.'

Holly smiled. 'Really? You don't have to. I'm guessing you came here to do some shopping, taste some beer or whatever is here. Not to be used as free help.'

'I came to see you,' he said and then regretted his words at once. *Keep your cool*, he thought and made an attempt to say something that made sense. 'I mean, you did send me that note with Frøy. It would have been rude not to come, you know.'

She was laughing now. 'I see. Well, do you mind stepping inside the stall for a moment? There's a door at the back.'

'Not at all.' Tor walked around and Holly let him in.

'I have a price list.' Holly showed him a piece of paper. 'All you have to do is follow it.'

She smiled at him and for a horrifying moment he thought she might hug him. He had no idea how to react to that.

She didn't. Instead she pointed at a Christmas tin under the counter. 'The cash is in there. And there's also the card reader thingy. Took me a while to figure that out.'

'I have been known to handle small machinery,' he said, taking it away from her. 'Architecture isn't always about building skyscrapers, you know.'

'Brilliant. I'll just find the loo and be right back, I promise. Please don't drop anything.'

Tor watched her leave, then a customer approached him. One dressed in a festive hat and a nose that was a bit more red than it should be.

Holly found the toilets without any difficulty. Portable toilets weren't exactly the best things in the world, but when she had to go, she had to go.

When she got out, rubbing her hands with the wipes provided, she bumped into Britt.

'I was wondering where you were off to,' she said with a huge smile.

'Call of nature,' Holly said.

Britt looked at her with perfect innocence. 'I just saw Sigrid with the kids, so who's watching your stall?'

Holly looked at her for a second, then rolled her eyes.

'Oh, please. You know Tor is there, helping me out.'

Britt shrugged. 'I may have spotted him. Did you ask him to come?'

Holly faltered. 'Sort off. I did remind him we would be here.'

'And he came.' Britt smiled. 'That might be as romantic as a Norwegian man can get, you know.'

'No, it's not like that. And there really isn't anything romantic about selling mustard and Christmas cookies,' Holly said.

'Never underestimate the sexiness of a man who steps up. He came all the way from the island to help you, didn't he?'

Holly was not having that conversation. 'Actually, I think Tor wanted to see the market. It's Christmas soon and this is a great place to fill up on presents, as you said yourself.'

'Of course,' Britt said, trying to hide her laughter.

Holly smiled. 'I hope you didn't scare him off, by the way.'

'I would never.' Britt pretended to look offended. 'I

223

didn't even go over to say hello. He's a bit skittish, you know.'

I can't argue with that, Holly thought. 'I'm sure he wouldn't have been scared off. He came over to say hi and then I asked him to help.'

'He's a nice boy.' Britt looked pleased when she was next in line. 'My turn. Finally.'

Holly hurried back to the stall and could see that there was several people talking to him, before leaving with a jar or a box.

'Hi,' she said, ducking into the stall.

Tor turned and smiled at her. 'Hi. I had people asking about the restaurant and if it's open during Christmas.'

Holly suddenly became very aware of how small the stall was.

'I have no idea. Jack never said anything about it.' Holly tried to take a step back, to get some space between her and Tor, but gave up when she bumped into the wall.

'Well, if he wants to open, I think he would have plenty of customers.'

'I'll tell him.' Holly pulled herself together and smiled at another customer.

Tor handed the customer a biscuit tin, and proceeded to handle the card machine like a pro.

'Are you hungry?' he asked when the customer left.

'Not really. We had breakfast at the restaurant before we left. A massive breakfast with cake. I'm surprised you're not all waddling like chubby ducks if you eat like that every day.'

'There's everyday breakfast and then there's Christmas breakfast. Huge difference,' Tor said.

'What's everyday breakfast?' Holly knew he was aching to tell her.

'Two pieces of brown bread, one with yellow cheese and one with salami or liver pâté, or the classic mackerel in tomato sauce. And if you're really lucky, you'll get a piece of fruit.'

'Very Spartan sounding,' Holly said.

'Oh, yes. Especially since you'll get the same thing for lunch, because you make your own *matpakke*.'

Holly knit her brow. 'Which is?'

'Your packed lunch.' Tor smiled and something about him made Holly look at him. He was different somehow.

'Ah, the famous Norwegian packed lunch. Does everyone do that?'

'Yes, it starts in kindergarten and continues until we retire. Some of us have a cafeteria at work, but, as we also only have half an hour for lunch, standing in line for food is wasting good coffee and eating time.'

'Seriously Spartan,' Holly said. Half an hour for lunch would barely be enough time for her to get down to the coffee shop.

'Are you hungry? I mean, there's plenty of food everywhere if you want something,' Holly said, trying not to hit him in the face when she brought up a new tin. 'And nobody sells sandwiches, I promise.'

Tor leaned against the counter. 'Just around here, they are roasting sausages that give off a very interesting fragrance. Something with rosemary, I think.'

Holly narrowed her eyes. 'Good thing I'm not that hungry.'

Tor looked at her. 'Are you sure? You've been her a long time today, haven't you? I mean, long enough for you to need a bathroom break.'

He smiled ever so slowly, and Holly couldn't believe the way she reacted to him. *Oh my*, she thought. *This is not good. Not good at all.*

For some reason she could hardly breathe. There really wasn't much space inside the stall. *That's probably it*, she thought.

A cheerful voice interrupted the moment. 'I'm so sorry I'm so late, Holly.' Sigrid gave her a pained look. 'Olav was late and I can't let the kids loose on their own. They'd be wrecking the place if I did that.' She suddenly realised Tor was there. 'Oh, are you helping her?'

'Only because I had to go to the bathroom,' Holly said.

Sigrid smiled. 'Good. Well, I'm guessing neither of you have had a chance to look around, so perhaps you two should leave this to me?'

Holly hesitated, then berated herself for hesitating, and then nodded. 'Thank you. I would like to take a look, actually.'

The stall was too small for all three of them, so Tor and Holly stepped outside.

'Are you sure it's okay to just leave everything to Sigrid like that? I feel as if I'm taking advantage of her.'

'It's called *dugnad*,' Tor said.

'What?' Holly pulled up the zipper on her coat.

'*Dugnad*. It's what Norwegians call it when there's a

group or community that needs help and everyone participates. Everyone on the island always steps in to help one of their own. Like she's doing now,' he said, nodding towards Sigrid who was about to sell a jar of Jack's best chutney to a woman.

'I think Jack told me about it. Almost like the Amish when they raise a barn or something, and everyone chips in.'

'Well, I don't think I've ever heard of anyone building a barn. It's more like helping each other when the lawns need cutting or garbage needs cleaning. Smaller than a barn stuff,' he said.

'Okay. Can we eat now?' Holly looked around. All the delicious smells made her hungry.

He took her hand. 'Follow me. I am starving,' he said.

Holly waved at Sigrid before they turned a corner and the lovely aroma of roasting food almost made her swoon.

Tor stopped in front of a huge grill, where there were more sausages in one place than Holly had ever seen.

'What would you like, Holly?' he asked.

Holly smiled at the man who was in charge of the grill. 'I'm not sure what to choose, to be honest.'

He lit up. 'Everything here is good. We have the spicy stuff and the sort of healthy stuff, and we have fish if you like that. Smoked pork is delicious, of course, but our speciality are the grilled sausages. Do you like chilli or a bit milder? There's also cheese.'

Holly decided to throw caution to the wind. *How many times in my life will I eat something like this*, she thought.

'Give me spicy, please.'

The man grinned. 'Wise choice. It's my own recipe, so it comes with a guarantee.'

'You mean she'll get her money back if she doesn't like it?' Tor said.

'No, I mean I can guarantee that she will like it,' the man said, winking at Holly. 'But to be sure, you can have a small taste, yes? I don't want you to take a bite of my handmade sausage, hate it, and then throw it away. It's bad for business and also it will break my heart. Okay?'

Holly tried to repress the giggles, and only managed the smallest of nods.

He had a plate next to the grill with samples and handed one of them to Holly. 'What do you think?'

Holly chewed carefully, not sure what to expect. 'It's hot and really, really good. I'll have one of those.'

'See? I told you so and I'm never wrong'

He put buns on the grill to warm them up, all the time talking about the spices and how difficult it was to get it just right.

Holly watched as the buns got nice, grilled stripes on them, then the vendor put the sausage in the middle and looked like he expected her to say something. Holly had no idea what though.

When she didn't respond at once, he pointed at a table filled with condiments. 'What's your choice? We have raw and crisp onion, pickled red beets, shrimp salad, ketchup and mustard, of course, but also remoulade and mayonnaise, and finally my wife's favourite: pickled relish. She makes it herself.'

'I'll have the relish and the mustard, please.'

He loaded it on top of the sausage and handed it to her. 'Good appetite,' he said.

'Uhm, thank you,' Holly said.

The vendor made Tor his choice and handed the sausage to him.

Holly looked at his food. 'What are you eating?'

'This is bacon sausage with shrimp salad and ketchup. It's freaking delicious.' Tor took a huge bite.

Holly couldn't help laughing. 'You have shrimps in your beard.'

He was chewing and looking like a chipmunk, and he really did have small pink shrimps in his beard.

Tor stared cross-eyed down his nose. 'Where?'

Holly took the serviette the vendor had given her and tried to help him. 'Are you sure you don't have birds in here? Something is holding on to that shrimp,' she said to make him laugh.

'Please don't lose that thing in there. Frøy will tear the beard off my face when I get home,' he said.

'Stand still.' Holly rubbed his cheek.

'If you spit on that thing…' he said.

Holly laughed. 'I would never. Do you have any idea how unhygienic that is?'

'Yes, I do.' Tor took a step back and put his hand around her fingers when he took the serviette from her. 'You're going to rub away my beard,' he said.

Holly pulled her hand away and suddenly it was all awkward again. *I'm behaving like a bloody fourteen-year-old,* she thought.

Tor threw the serviette in one of the many bins, and looked at her. 'What? Are there more shrimps?'

Holly breathed out slowly. 'No, not at all. You look... a lot better.'

He smiled. 'A lot better than what?'

'Than a man with shrimp cocktail in his beard. I can't believe you would put that on a sausage, by the way.'

Before he answered, he gobbled up the rest of the food. 'It's one of those rare experiences of perfect taste,' he said, laughing at her.

To hide her fluttering breath, Holly took another bite of her sausage.

Tor watched her. 'Good?'

Holly nodded before finishing the rest. 'Really good.'

'Let's see what else we can get ourself entangled in, shall we?'

He took her hand and almost pulled her with him.

'Where are you taking me?'

'I think we need dessert, don't you? If there's anything my people can make, it's sweet stuff.' He scanned the market stalls and grinned. 'That one. You'll like this, I hope.'

Holly could smell cinnamon as they got closer. 'You're not feeding me more waffles, are you? Because I've had lots of those already.'

'No, this is different. This is proper old fashion yummies. I bet the Vikings made this, although most likely without the cinnamon,' he said.

When they approached the market stall, they saw lots of people in front of it. Holly stretched her neck to see what they were looking at, and Tor pulled her in so she could watch.

It looks like a cooking show, she thought. Two women, both with colourful headscarves, were having a great time showing off their skills.

The centrepiece was a large cooking plate. One of the women was using a huge rolling pin to roll out a thin dough, while the other stood by the heat and picked it up on a long, thinner rolling pin.

'Is it a pancake?' Holly asked Tor.

He shook his head. 'Not even close,' he said.

The woman folded the not-really-a-pancake gently out on the plate, then she just as gently flipped the sides and lifted it up, putting it on a cloth next to her.

All the while she was talking to the audience.

'What is she saying?' Holly looked up at Tor.

'She's explaining the process. These are called *lefser*, and there are variations all over the country. You can use them with savoury food or as cakes, depending on what you put on them. What she's making is used with *kling*, which is basically a spread made of butter, cream, sour cream, and sugar.'

He laughed when he saw the expression on her face. 'This is what we do at Christmas. All year round it's all about healthy and moderation, and at Christmas it's upside down world.'

'Do you eat them hot?' Holly couldn't see that the women were handing out the fresh *lefse*.

'No, I don't think so.' Tor pointed at the end of the

counter where there were several plates of square cakes. 'These are the ones we want.'

He elbowed his way to the counter and bought a few pieces. When he got back to her, he had a lopsided grin on his face and two paper bags in his hands.

'Here. I had to buy a few potato *lefser* too. They are good with smoked salmon or *gravlaks*,' he said.

He opened one bag and showed it to her. 'Take one. If you don't like it, you don't have to eat it.'

Holly was game. She took one of the *lefser* and eyed it. It was rectangular, not round, and there were layers in it, and when she took a bite, there was the taste of creamy, buttery sugar and cinnamon that just melted on her tongue.

'Oh my god, this is… wow.' Holly took another bite.

'Good, right?' Tor looked delighted when she tried to take his from him. 'No, that's mine. Here, take another one.'

Holly took another *lefse* and bit into it, expecting the same, creamy buttery taste. She frowned. 'Why is this different?'

'I don't know. I thought they were all the same.' Tor took it from her and sniffed it. His face lit up. 'There's brown cheese on this. You don't like that?'

'Not really, and I think this cheese is different from the one Alma gave me on the waffles. I didn't really like that either.'

'This is real brown cheese. Made with goat milk.' Tor smiled at her. 'I'll give you mine if you'll give me yours.'

'Yours first,' she said.

'What? You don't trust me?' Tor feigned insult.

Holly shook her head. 'I do not like goat milk, white goat's cheese or your brown version.'

Tor held out both his hands, open towards her. She snapped the good *lefse* and handed him the other.

'Does your brother like the cheese?' Tor ate his with every sign of enjoyment.

'Yes, he can't get enough of it. That and Old Cheese, whatever that is.'

Tor frowned. 'That's... that's awful. I can't eat it.'

'Good. Then you won't try to get me to eat it, will you?'

After dessert was over Tor looked at her. 'Now what will we do?'

'Well, I probably have to go back to the stall. Poor Sigrid has her kids to look after.'

Tor looked disappointed, but nodded. 'Of course.'

'Would you like to help me? We'll finish in an hour or so, and then take the ferry back.'

'I... would love to stay.'

Holly raised her eyebrows. 'Are you sure? Because it's fine if you don't want to. It's not very interesting, so if you have anything else you rather be doing, that's fine.'

Tor smiled. 'This is what I'd rather be doing.'

Holly opened her mouth to answer, then got completely flustered and knew she was blushing like a whole crop of tomatoes.

'Uhm, thank you.'

He laughed. 'This is fun.'

'Really? I can't imagine why,' Holly said, getting herself together. 'It's a lot talking to people for another hours. Won't that ruin the whole hermit thing for you?'

He took her hand again, and Holly's heart skipped more than just a few beats. 'Maybe it's time to stop being the hermit? And if I leave now, who's going to tell you about the pink city hall behind us?'

Holly looked up. The huge building was indeed pink. Proper pink too, like a four-year-old's princess pink. 'I didn't notice that!'

'It's great isn't it?' Tor smiled, looking at the building.

'Sure. Why is it pink?' Holly was fascinated now.

'Honestly? I don't know.' Tor laughed when she pretended to box his shoulder. 'But does it matter? It's the perfect colour. I know the architects were heavily inspired by Italian architecture and they must have liked pink.'

'Lame answer, but okay. Are there any other pink city halls in Norway?'

'No, only this one. Makes it all the more special, I think. And here we are,' he said, stopping in front of her stall.

Sigrid looked relived when she noticed them.

'There have been so many people here,' she said. 'It's a good thing the two of you are back.'

It certainly is, Holly thought, when Sigrid had left and Tor took up half the room in the stall.

They didn't talk much, but she was so aware of his presence. It was impossible not to touch or bump into each other, exchanging smiles and jokes, and Holly didn't notice the time until Britt knocked on their counter.

'Guys, we'd better pack up if we want to catch the last ferry. Do you need any help?'

Holly smiled at her. 'I think we'll manage. There's barely a full box left, to be honest.'

'Good for you. Tobben and I will help Alma, but we have a lot of stuff to carry back, we could really use your help too.'

Tor looked at her once they'd put the last of the items in the box. 'I had a good time today,' he said.

'Me too.' Holly smiled at him while closing the doors to the stall.

With the doors closed, it became dark, and suddenly his proximity was almost too much. Holly couldn't breathe, he was so close.

'Are you... are you taking the ferry with us?'

'No, I took my boat today. I would ask you to come, but they obviously need you.'

'Yes, they do.' Holly looked at him. 'I'm sorry.'

Tor touched her cheek. 'Don't be. I'll see you on the island, right?'

'Right.' Holly wasn't sure what that meant. Tonight, tomorrow? What?

She was about to ask him when he leaned in. The intention was clear and she had no problem with it when he kissed her.

No problem at all.

Chapter Nineteen

The phone beeped again. She had just arrived from the market and Holly folded her arms over her chest and leaned against the kitchen counter, not ready to check her messages yet.

What if they had made a decision? And she was out?

The idea that she was finished as a doctor felt like a stab in the belly. She turned away. Tea first, and *then* she would look at the phone.

On the counter was the box with the rest of Jack's produce. She picked up the last of the biscuit tins and opened it. Stuffing a jammie dodger in her mouth felt like heaven. While she waited for the kettle, she gobbled up another. God, he was good at baking.

The kettle took forever, so she quickly checked the message, and breathed a sigh of relief when she saw it was from Jack. She sent a text back. While she waited for him to respond, she snooped in the fridge, looking for something to snack on.

Holly opened one of the foil packages and whistled when she realised it was some kind of chocolate cake. She took the cake over to the table, then sent Jack a new text.

You're really getting the hang of the biscuits. We sold almost all of the boxes and most of the marmalade and mustard.

It took some time before he responded, giving her ample time to make the tea. She even had time to put milk and sugar in it.

I didn't make most of them. Ninni did, he responded.

Impressive, Holly thought, feeling a tiny stab of envy. *I would love to be that together*, she thought.

When are you coming? It's almost Christmas. I want to see Rosie before I have to go back home.

This time he answered right away.

We're leaving tomorrow, pretty late, I'm afraid. We'll stay in Bergen for one night, then come straight to the island.

Holly smiled.

Okay. You better not be delayed again. I really don't want to spend Christmas alone here.

The islanders would never let you spend Christmas alone. But I promise we'll be there. In the meantime, you have plenty of time to clean the house.

Ha, ha, very funny. Give Rosie a kiss from me.

Holly put down the phone and looked around. How rude, and that reminded her of Tor and his weird last name: Ruud.

She wondered how Tor was doing after their kiss. It had certainly been passionate. Who knows what could have happened if they had stayed in that stall for much longer. Unfortunately, Britt had come back and pounded on the wall.

She didn't regret it. But the timing was so off. She only had a short time left on the island, then she would have to go home and that would be it.

But she really wanted to sleep with him, so much she could barely think about anything else.

The phone pinged again. Holly looked at it with half an eye.

It was a text from Ninni:

Who's the we?

Holly laughed. She picked up the phone and called her. Ninni picked up at once. 'I thought you were doing the Christmas market thing alone,' she said.

'No, I had help. From the local hermit.' Holly leaned back.

'Really? Because I heard that he hates people and that he looks like an old fisherman with a scruffy beard. Is he old?'

'You know perfectly well that he's not. Nor does he hate people or look like an old fisherman. He's lovely, actually.'

'That sounds intriguing. Tell me everything.'

Holly could hear Rosie yelling something in the background. 'Do you have to go?'

'No, she's yelling at Jack for not taking her to the pool. Not sure how we're going to get her out of there when we go home. Tell me about him.'

Holly pulled her feet under her on the bench. 'But you know about him. Tor was here before you two left.'

'Yes, but I never talked to him. He was just this man who brushed past you when you went into the shop. I said hello to his cat more than him.'

'He's not like that, not now.' Holly detailed how Tor had been the day before. 'We were closing the stall, and it was kind of dark and then he kissed me. Or I kissed him. I'm not sure who was first, to be honest.'

'That must have been romantic,' Ninni said, laughing when Holly squealed.

'It wasn't romantic at all. It was awkward and too hot in there, and there were so many people outside, and it was… oh, who am I kidding. It was a great kiss.'

Now Ninni was squealing. 'Oh, I love that. Are you going to kiss him again?'

Holly certainly hoped so. 'I don't know,' she said.

'Why not? He must like you. Why wouldn't you kiss him again?'

'He might not want to kiss me again,' Holly said and was rewarded with Ninni snorting.

'If he doesn't want to kiss you again, he's either gay or he's a total idiot.'

Holly laughed. 'I'm sure he's an idiot,' she said.

She could hear Jack in the background.

'None of your concern, Jack,' Ninni said. 'And stop feeding Rosie chocolate. Unless you are really keen to change her diaper.'

Holly pulled the foil away from the cake and stabbed her teaspoon in it.

'What's that noise?' Ninni asked.

'I'm attacking a chocolate cake I found in your fridge.' Holly popped the teaspoon in her mouth. The chocolate melted, and when she chewed it, there was a strong taste of something else coming through. 'Why is there liquorice in this cake?'

'Oh, you found the Delfia cake. Careful with that. It's really rich. There's all sorts of goodies in it. Soft sweet liquorice shaped like boats, marzipan, strawberry marshmallow Santas, Non-Stop – that's our take on Smarties – and the Norwegian equivalent of jelly babies, called "sticky men".'

'Sticky men? That just sounds weird,' Holly said, trying to get a better look at the sweet.

'Well, they're shaped like stick figure men. I love those.'

'It's like a giant truffle,' Holly said, taking another spoon, this time with a piece of marzipan and another sticky man. 'God, it's good!'

'It's a house speciality. Enjoy it, but don't eat it all at once. You'll make yourself sick. When are you going to see him again?'

'I... don't know. Tomorrow, presumably. Why?'

'I think you should kiss him again and see where it

leads. It makes for a good distraction. Jack said you haven't heard from the hospital yet.'

'Are you telling me to shag him so that I don't think about that?' Holly almost choked on a piece of liquorice when she laughed.

'Yes, of course I am! Have some fun while you're there. The island is all about healing and fun. You know that.'

Holly found one of the marshmallow Santas. It was chewy and sweet, and tasted slightly of strawberries.

'You're bad. Oh, and you can tell Jack I ate his jaffa cakes. He needs to bring more.'

Ninni giggled. 'They're my jaffa cakes. I love them and you can buy more in most shops where you are, but only the orange flavour, I'm afraid.'

'I didn't know that! I'll get you a new package tomorrow.'

Jack was on the phone. 'Who are you kissing? I hope it's not Tobben,' he said.

'I'll have you know that Tobben is a perfectly nice man, but it's not me he wants to kiss.'

'Then who is it?'

Holly grinned. 'I think he fancies Britt, actually. I've seen him looking at her, you know.'

'No, idiot. Who are you kissing?'

'You don't know him. And stop harassing me. It's none of your business who I kiss,' Holly said.

When she hung up the phone a few minutes later, she felt better. It was silly to take everything so seriously. There was no need to, really.

Holly took another spoonful of cake, and this time

crunchie Non-Stops followed. *Insanely good*, she thought. *Perhaps I should go out for a while, before I eat all the cake and make myself sick. That would be bad.*

Something wet was in his ear. Something a bit raspy. Tor tried to wave it away, but it came back.

He opened his eyes and was jabbed by a huge, furry paw.

'What are you doing, you maniac?'

Frøy sat on his chest, paws primly placed in front of him. He blinked several times.

Tor looked at him. 'What?'

Frøy didn't roll his eyes, but it was close, Tor was sure.

He reached for his phone to see what time it was. About ten minutes past cat dinner time. 'Do you know that delayed gratification is a sign of mental strength? I'm sorry my nap ruined your dinner time.'

Frøy jumped off his chest and off the sofa, and strolled over to the open door. He waited to make sure Tor followed.

'I'm coming, I'm coming.' Tor put his feet on the floor, pulling a face at the cold. He had come back from town a bit later than expected and completely knackered, and had crashed on the sofa.

He had also forgot to put on the heaters, apparently.

Frøy disappeared out the door.

It was freezing. Tor grabbed a woollen sweater and pulled it on.

He walked into the kitchen and found Frøy sitting next to his bowl, patiently waiting for food.

'Dry kibble today, buddy, how's that for breakfast? I'll get you some fresh fish tomorrow.'

Frøy watched the bowl fill up, then dove in as if he hadn't eaten in ages.

Tor made a cup of coffee and walked over to the window.

'It's grey out there, Frøy. We might be in for a spell of snow.' He looked at the cat who had inhaled his food and was now busy cleaning his whiskers.

Tor sighed. 'Why did she kiss me? Or rather, why did I kiss her? It was dumb, that's what it was. I just couldn't help myself.'

Frøy looked up, then right down again.

Tor snorted. 'You're no help, are you?'

He shook his head. It was a kiss. A very nice kiss, but still. Just a kiss. So why couldn't he forget it?

It made him wonder about Holly. Did she think about it?

Probably not.

Outside the snow started to fall in large flakes. He looked at the clock on the wall. There was no meetings waiting for him, nothing scheduled. And he really didn't want to go fishing in this weather. But he did need to take a walk, to clear his head, and perhaps get his mind off of... other things.

Changing into winter gear didn't take long and he was lacing up his booths when Frøy decided that his after dinner nap was over.

'Good thing you have thick fur,' Tor said and opened the door.

The wind hit him, cold and icy, and he lifted his face for a moment, enjoying the fresh smell from the sea.

'I think our fishing trip has to wait until the wind settles, Frøy,' he said, following the cat outside.

The snow was heaping up. *A proper snowstorm*, he thought.

Frøy dived into the snow with cat glee, coming out of the snowdrifts covered in white dust. He shook his fur clean, then dived in again.

'You must be the weirdest cat in the world,' Tor said.

The pathway was covered in snow by now, and he walked carefully. Falling on his bum and breaking something was not part of the plan.

When he eventually came down to the pathway along the cliffs he walked over to the edge Holly almost fell over. From there he could see almost to the mainland. Or imagine that he could.

It was stunning. White everywhere he looked reflected the moonlight, and then the grey-blue waters surrounding the island.

The air was crisp and he took a deep breath, enjoying the feeling.

'Do you know that there's a really long drop from there?' Holly said behind him.

Tor almost stepped forward in shock. Instead he turned carefully around and looked at her. She was dressed as if she was heading on an expedition to the North Pole.

'Yes, I do, actually and I almost experienced it right now.

You really should make some noise when you sneak up on a person,' he said, stepping away from the edge.

'Must be the snow.' Holly lit up in a huge smile. 'I've never seen anything like it.'

Tor smiled. 'It's something else, isn't it? You should see it on the mountains when the sun is shining. It's stunning.'

'I'd love that.' Holly looked up at the dark skies. 'Will it continue, do you think?'

'No idea. Looks like it, but there's a lot of wind out here. It's probably going towards the sea,' he said. 'And most likely it will be gone by tomorrow, anyway.'

Holly looked at him. 'You have no idea, do you?'

Tor shook his head. 'I'm a city boy, remember?'

They fell silent and Tor found it excruciatingly awkward. He searched his brain for something to say, something that didn't sound like he was a babbling idiot. 'Uhm. I thought you had gone home,' he finally said.

'Same here.' Holly looked out on the sea. 'I needed some fresh air. Standing outside on the ferry wasn't enough, apparently.'

'Yes, I took a nap when I came home, and Frøy actually sat on me, demanding dinner,' he said.

'He did?' Holly looked up and smiled, then looked down again.

'Yes, he does that when he thinks I've neglected my duties as his butler, I think.'

'So you're not his master, then?'

'Not even close.' The awkwardness was rattling his brain powers. 'Ehm, are you all right?' he said after another few seconds.

Holly shrugged. 'Of course. Why wouldn't I be?'

'I don't know. I… ehm…' He had no idea what to say.

'You're not sure?' Holly had a little smile on her face.

Tor frowned. Was she making fun of him? 'Not really,' he said.

'It was only a kiss,' Holly said, smiling wider now. 'No need to tie yourself in knots.'

'Is that what I'm doing?' Tor couldn't help smiling back at her.

'Looks like it,' Holly said.

Tor drew a sharp breath. *Time to not be an idiot*, he thought. Maybe this was the time to channel his inner Viking? *Thor* would have seized the moment. 'I'd like to do it again, actually. Kiss you, I mean.'

'Really?' Holly was teasing him now. Even he could see that.

'Yes. I'll understand if you say no, but please don't.'

Holly took a step closer, then stopped. 'What will you do if I say no? Jump off the cliff?'

'Uhm, no. I'm not that dramatic,' he said, grinning now.

'Good. Because it's an awful long way down and heights make me dizzy. I wouldn't be able to climb down and save you.'

'Really? I thought you were Wonder Woman,' Tor said, enjoying himself.

'Of course I am, but that doesn't mean I can fly.'

Tor held out his hand and pulled her close.

The embarrassment disappeared. So did the cold.

Tor held one of her hands. 'Now what?' he said.

'I've heard it's like riding a bicycle,' Holly said.

He could feel his ears turn red and the look on her face suggested she found that endearing.

'Well, not here, obviously. We don't want to risk frostbite in more sensitive places,' he said.

It made them both laugh and the tension between them eased.

'Are we doing this? I mean, you're leaving soon, presumably after New Year, and I really have to think about returning home myself.'

While he was talking, he pulled the mitten off her hand, and knit her fingers with his.

'It's called a holiday fling, Tor. It's not that complicated.'

He nodded. 'Okay. I can deal with that.'

Holly looked at him as if she was expecting something and Tor wondered how on earth she managed to make him feel like a complete dollop just by looking at him. He searched his brain for something sensible to say. 'I... I am lost for words,' he finally said.

It made her laugh. *That has to be a good sign*, he thought.

Holly stopped laughing then and looked so serious he almost forgot to breathe. 'So am I,' she said.

He had no idea what to say next, so he pulled her close and kissed her again.

Then, still holding her hand, he brought her back to the house.

Chapter Twenty

Tor slept like a bear and was just as warm, though Holly was grateful for the additional two duvets anyway.

The room was freezing and she discovered that the window was open, letting in the wind. Outside it was dark and she could hear the water thrashing against the pier.

She realised that the snoring that had woken her up wasn't coming from Tor and when she looked around, she found Frøy laying across them both in the bed. The snoring was him purring.

For a second she considered waking Tor up, but she had to pee. *Nature's call first,* she thought. She got out of bed and almost yelped when her feet hit the floor. In a hurry, she pulled on her socks and pulled Tor's sweatshirt over her head. *Much better,* she thought.

By the door, she turned to look back at him. He rolled over and slept on. She smiled and gathered the rest of her clothes before leaving the room.

Holly decided that a trip to the bathroom was more important than putting on the rest of her clothes in the hallway. Frøy watched her with interest. 'Are you judging me, fluffy?'

I'm not doing the walk of shame in front of a cat, she thought, tapping him on the head as she climbed down the stairs.

The cat thumped down next to her, trying to get in the way.

'Are you trying to stop me from leaving?'

Holly opened the kitchen door, and smiled when she realised the heat was on in there. She dropped the rest of her clothes on the floor before hurrying to the bathroom, making sure not to squash Frøy when she closed the door.

When she came back into the kitchen, Frøy had curled up on the pile of her clothes. 'You are not right in the head, my friend,' she said. Trying to wriggle her clothes from under a huge lump of a cat was a lot harder than she had anticipated.

'Will you get off my pants and my bra, Frøy?' she said.

Frøy thought it was hilarious, that much was clear. He sprawled out all four legs and waved his tail in her face.

I'm not going to be bested by a cat, she thought. Holly flipped him over and grabbed her clothes.

Frøy jumped up and gave her a proper judgemental cat look before strolling away to sit in front of his dish. There was food in it, probably from the day before, but he ignored that.

'I'm so not giving you tuna. I don't even know if Tor has

anything like that.' Holly looked behind her when she heard the familiar sound of her phone.

'Now what,' she muttered. She found the phone in the back pocket of her jeans.

It was Jack. Holly read the message and then looked at the time. *Bollocks*, she thought. *They're on their way home now and the house is such a mess!*

Suddenly all of her calm disappeared. She started putting on the rest of her clothes, and looked around for something to write on, so she could leave a note for Tor.

By the time she had written the note, put it on his coffee maker, and was ready to leave, Frøy had disappeared.

Holly figured he had returned to Tor and opened the door to the lounge carefully. Tor was still sleeping upstairs and she didn't have the heart to wake him.

The wind wasn't too bad outside and she pulled down her woollen hat and headed towards the road.

———

By the time she arrived at the house, Holly knew she was too late. All the lights were on and she could see smoke curling up from the chimney.

Damn, damn, damn, she thought. How on earth did they manage to get to the island already? She knew the ferry didn't run this early.

The moment she put her hand on the door handle, a dog started barking like a maniac from inside.

Frikk, Holly thought. She had never met Ninni's dog, and judging from the level of barking, he hated her already.

'Shut up, you stupid mutt,' she heard her brother shouting.

Holly hesitated to open the door. It would be a really bad holiday if the dog mauled her right before Christmas.

'Jack, it's me! Will Frikk attack me if I come in?'

The door cracked open and a bleary-eyed Jack looked at her.

'Ah, look at you, my sister who wasn't here to greet us,' he said, grinning from ear to ear.

'Don't be a bastard,' Holly said. 'Can I come in? Or do I have to sleep in the *stabbur*?'

'Look at you! Picking up all the Norwegian culture,' he teased her.

'Will you let her in before you let all the heat out?' Ninni called from inside the house.

Jack nodded. 'Okay, come in, Holly. Heating is very important in these parts.'

As soon as she was inside and the door locked, he lifted her up in a bear hug. 'I'm so happy to see you!'

Holly squealed and tried to wriggle loose. 'Will you stop it, you madman! I'm not five years old anymore.'

Jack put her down. 'You will always be my snotty baby sister, so get over it. Take off your coat and boots and get inside. Where did you get that gear, by the way?'

'Wouldn't you like to know. What about Frikk?' Holly took of the boots and coat, stuffing the woollen hat and mittens in the pockets.

'Frikk is with Ninni. He's guarding his house and his flock, but once he understands you're part of the family, he'll be fine.'

'Where has he been? I forgot to ask you if you had brought him to Spain with you,' Holly said.

Jack rolled his eyes. 'He's been with Petter, Ninni's dad. We went to Bergen first, picked up Frikk and then took the night bus. A friend of Petters ferried us to the island in his boat. God, travelling is exhausting.'

Holly could hear Frikk growling from the lounge. 'How is he with cats?'

'Cats? Where?' Ninni came out from the kitchen with Rosie on her hip. Rosie was chewing on a sweet bun.

'Not here, obviously, but I have been in contact with a cat lately,' Holly said.

'He loves cats.' Ninni smiled before giving Holly a hug. 'Welcome. I'm so happy you are here!'

Rosie became part of the hug and giggled. Holly looked at her.

'She's grown so much since I saw her last. Hi, Rosie.'

The baby grinned and offered her the now soggy bun. Holly pretended to take a huge bite, which made Rosie giggle even more.

'You have no idea,' Jack said and took Rosie from Ninni. 'Watch this.'

He put Rosie down on the floor and she ran off. She stretched up to reach the handle to the lounge door.

'Flikk out,' she said, and pushed the door open.

The dog stopped growling and licked Rosie on the cheek. She pointed at him with a tiny finger. 'Flikk, sit,' she said.

Holly gaped as Frikk sat and was rewarded with the bun.

Rosie patted him on the head.

Ninni laughed. 'You should see your face, Holly.'

'When did she start to walk? And talk like that? Dad didn't say anything.'

'She does this more and more now. I can barely keep up.' Jack's voice brimmed with pride.

Holly looked at Ninni. 'I'm so sorry about the mess. I had plans to clean and hoover, but I got distracted by the market and… and everything.'

She hadn't noticed that Frikk was sniffing her leg. Holly held out her hand and he graciously gave it a small sniff and then wagged his tail. 'You're beautiful, aren't you?' Holly said.

'Flikk!' Rosie said, holding onto her other leg.

'Right. Frikk.'

Ninni saved her. 'Are you up for breakfast? As you know, thanks to Jack we have plenty of what he calls proper tea, and we also have coffee. What's your favourite?'

'Tea would be heaven. I didn't really get much sleep last night.' The moment the words left her mouth, she groaned inside.

Jack burst out laughing, followed by Ninni and a few seconds later, Rosie joined in.

Holly bent down and picked her up. 'Laughing at your poor aunt already? That's not nice.'

Rosie giggled and said something intelligible.

'I totally agree,' Holly said.

Jack steered her towards one of the chairs in the kitchen. 'Sit down, tell us all about the cat and the not sleeping. Does this have anything to do with the hermit you kissed?'

Holly rolled her eyes. 'You sound exactly like Dad. Poor Rosie when she becomes a teenager.'

'First of all, that was mean. Second, Rosie will be sensible. Not wild like you,' he said.

'That… that's ridiculous.' Holly took the cup of tea Ninni handed her. 'Thank you. I can't discuss things with Jack before tea and breakfast.'

Jack picked up Rosie and put her in the high chair. Then he handed her a piece of toast. Rosie threw the toast away, and Frikk caught it before it touched the floor.

'No more toast for you, silly,' Jack said.

'You gave her the bun. I told you not to,' Ninni said, handing Jack his cup and sitting down with a coffee for herself. 'I mean, would you eat a dry toast when you know there are yummies in the house?'

'Yummy,' Rosie declared and looked at her father. 'Yummy!'

'Oh my god, I've created a monster,' Jack muttered. 'There are no more buns, baby, because you ate them all.'

Holly smiled. 'No buns, but there is *lefse*, if she likes that. I brought it from the market.'

Jack lit up. 'Is there more than one?'

'Yes, you can go see for yourself. It's in the fridge.'

Jack brought back the paper bag and made a show of it for Rosie who clapped her hands in anticipation.

'There's cinnamon and that sticky cheese,' Holly said.

'Brown cheese? We love that, don't we, Rosie?' Jack broke one of the *lefser* in half and then again, and handed Rosie a quarter.

'Enjoy.'

Rosie grabbed it with both hands and jammed it in her mouth. She was clearly enjoying herself.

Ninni split a cinnamon *lefse* with Holly. 'Did Alma make these?'

'No, two women at the market did. It was like watching a very cold version of *The Great British Bake Off*,' Holly said.

Jack looked at her, his eyes shining. 'So, tell us about the hermit. Or the not-so-hermit anymore, if you're staying with him.'

'He's not totally lonely. He has a cat, you know,' Ninni said.

Holly nodded. 'A huge, black cat. He's gorgeous, all fluffy and massive.'

Jack raised his eyebrows. 'Please tell me you're still talking about the cat.'

'Of course it's the cat, silly. Tor isn't fluffy,' she said, watching her brother almost choke on his tea.

Ninni laughed so hard she lost her breath. 'Oh my god, we have to meet him,' she said when she finally managed to breathe normally again.

'You'll meet him at some point,' Holly said, a bit hesitant.

'I'm so happy to be home. I'm exhausted from spending too much time with my mum,' Ninni said. 'We get on a lot better with shorter visits.'

'She wanted us to stay over Christmas,' Jack said, smiling at Ninni.

'Yes, like that was ever going to happen. She knows that. I want to celebrate Christmas in my own house, and she doesn't want to come to the island.' Ninni shook her head.

Jack and Holly exchanged looks, but didn't say anything.

'But Rosie and *mormor* had a great time together, didn't you, sweetie?' Ninni stroked Rosie's curls.

'Yes, they did.' Jack smiled. 'It was lovely to see. The connection between them, it was instant.'

Ninni smiled. 'And she almost managed to not comment on how much Rosie looks like "our side of the family".'

Jack scrunched his face. 'Can we go back to talking about Holly's sexcapades? You know, with the massive, not so fluffy hermit?'

Holly offered up the requested distraction. 'Tor is... nice and sweet, and really hot, so you better be nice to him.'

Jack lifted his hands. 'I will treat him like royalty.'

'Good, because he's a bit out of practice with socialising, so be really nice.'

'What does he do? And why is he here on the island?' Ninni handed Rosie a sippy cup.

'He's an architect, actually, working from home. Why he's here, I don't really know, to be honest.' Holly shrugged. 'I haven't asked him.'

'I bet he's done something dodgy, and now he's in hiding. Like, he stole the cat and someone wants it back.'

Holly gaped at Jack. 'No, that's not it at all. He came from a shelter and he's not some expensive breed. The cat, I mean.'

Jack chuckled. 'I hope not. But maybe it's not the cat. Maybe he's not an architect, but an actual, bona fide fisherman.'

'Again, so much no. He's an architect and I know that

because I checked him out on social media. So there. Also, are you trying to tell me that being a fisherman is dodgy? Because I really don't think so.' Holly scowled at him.

Ninni shook her head. 'Please don't stick out your tongue, Holly. You'll be a bad example to Rosie. She's copying everything these days. Which reminds me, if she starts swearing in English, I'll know who to blame.'

'Harsh,' Holly said, tickling one of Rosie's chubby hands.

'Halsh,' Rosie said with glee.

Ninni smiled. 'Point proven.'

Holly looked at her brother. 'See? You better watch your mouth, Daddy.'

'I didn't say anything. You did.' Jack pulled a face at her and laughed when Rosie tried to copy him.

Ninni rolled her eyes. 'She's like a little parrot.'

Jack looked at his watch. 'I have to meet Tobbén and Olav. We're setting up the fire pit for New Year's Eve. How cool is that?' He looked thrilled at the idea. 'Want to come with me, Holly?

Holly shook her head. 'I don't think so.'

Ninni handed Rosie a toy. 'I think I will put this one down for a nap and then maybe take a nap myself before I have to even imagine being social. Travelling from Costa Blanca to this island is a long trip and I don't feel human yet.'

Jack looked at Holly. 'Are you sure? We're going to dig a fire pit, maybe two, on our beach. Might be fun.'

'No, it sounds like hard work. I'm tired,' Holly said.

'Ah, that kind of night,' Jack said. 'Better not tell Dad then.'

'Please don't. He's going to give me the sex talk again. He loves doing that.'

Ninni leaned over. 'What is the sex talk?'

Jack looked at Holly. 'Dad has this theory, and it started with me, of course, that if he explained sex as embarrassingly as possible, none of us would get ourselves into trouble. And now that I think we've proved that to him, he does it because he's mean.'

Holly rolled her eyes. 'The first time he told me, I was fifteen and ready to go on my very first date. There were graphs and explanations and long stories about how to not do things and also to always wear protection. He does this whole presentation with drawings and quotes from Health and Safety.'

Ninni was shaking with laughter. 'That sounds like Paul, yes.'

'He claims it's his fatherly bonus to torture his children.' Jack tickled Rosie under her cheek. 'And it's a proud tradition I will continue with my children. You have so much to look forward to, Rosie.'

Rosie put a sticky hand on his face and then threw her toy on the floor.

'And that's the cue for us to leave. Jack, I will see you later. Holly, will you be fine?'

'Of course I will. I'll take a quick shower and then I'll go see Tor.'

'Tor? You mean Thor, right?' Jack looked confused.

'Please don't call him that. He absolutely hates being called Thor.'

'What is wrong with Thor? He's awesome,' Jack said.

'No Norwegian Tor would spell their name with "th". I'm with Holly's Tor on this one,' Ninni said, lifting Rosie out of the high chair. 'Remember the first time someone called you "yak"?' she said to Jack. 'You hated that.'

He cringed. 'I'm not a bloody ox,' he said.

Holly waved her finger at him. 'See? That's the exact same reaction Tor had.'

'That's hilarious,' Ninni said.

She bent down and kissed Jack, making Rosie squeal with laughter.

'I'll see you later, Holly,' Ninni said, before going upstairs. They could hear her talking to Rosie as they climbed the stairs.

Jack turned to Holly. 'How have you been here these last few days? I'm guessing you've done things other than just... frolicking... with the architect slash fisherman?'

'Frolicking? Really?'

'Yes, you know what I mean. How have you been doing here alone?'

Holly leaned back in the chair. 'I've hiked on the island a few times. I'm sorry to have to tell you this, but it's not very interesting, at least not in the winter. It's mostly grey stones and grey sea and grey sky, total Nordic Noir. I also went fishing on Tor's boat. We caught crabs and fish,' she said, when he looked like he was about to interrupt her with his nosiness. 'It was gorgeous. We drank coffee and watched the sun rise.'

'Sounds like a proper holiday romance,' Jack said and pulled a face.

Holly ignored him. 'And after that I slaved at the market for my forgetful and ungrateful brother. Oh, and I also helped Emil when Ole threw a snowball in his face.'

'You *have* been busy.' Jack filled up their cups. 'Have you managed to relax a little? Dad doesn't want to ask you too much, in case you don't want to talk about it. I have no such reservations. Tell me. Have you heard from the hospital?'

Holly shook her head. 'Not yet. Drives me bonkers, as you can well understand.'

'Are you worried they won't let you come back?' Jack looked concerned now.

Just hearing it said out aloud made Holly cringe. 'Of course I am,' she said. 'I don't know what I'll do with myself if they don't. I've worked so hard for what feels like forever and to lose it now when I'm finally nearly there, is terrifying.'

'That's how I felt when I lost my job in London. All those years felt completely wasted. And now look at me.' Jack looked around the kitchen and picked up one of the brownie-*nisser* and grinned. 'Now I live in a house filled with psycho dolls.'

Holly laughed. 'They are so creepy. Like giant elves on shelves. First time I came in the door, I wasn't sure what to think. Luckily Alma insisted on following me inside.'

Jack smiled at her. 'You look better. Happier. These last few years all I've ever seen from you are worries about exams and high stress. No wonder you flipped.'

'I did not flip,' Holly said, on the defence at once. 'I... had a small breakdown.'

'You flipped. A complete 180 degree flip of the century,' Jack said. 'Dad said he had to come and pick you up and then you stayed in bed for a week. I've never seen him so scared.'

Holly looked down at her fingers. 'He told me. I'm sorry I did that to him.'

'Well, he did the right thing sending you here to be un-flipped.'

'It was your idea. But you're right. He probably did. I do feel a lot better. I can see why you love this place so much,' Holly said.

Jack laughed. 'Yeah, I'm crazy about it. Have you seen the restaurant yet?'

'I have. It's fantastic, but I still don't know how you can have a restaurant in the middle of the North Sea like that. Who will come and eat? How will you have enough guests?'

'That's the beauty of it. It turns out that in the summer, the "boat people" love restaurants like ours.'

'The boat people?'

'Apparently there are loads of Norwegians who own boats, and they like to use them during the summer, to travel up and down the coast. And hordes of them stop at this island. We had a great summer this year even if we weren't officially open yet. People came from town too. And we even had a few Christmas office parties out here before we left for Spain.'

'That's really wonderful, Jack. So, you're making money on this adventure of yours?'

'Well, it has cost quite a bit to turn the old building into a restaurant, and I can tell you that Norwegians take regulations seriously. God, we had a nightmare getting all the permits. And the building is listed, so we couldn't do any changes without applying first. But we got there. Thankfully I had loads of help.'

'You really love it here, don't you, Jack?' Holly couldn't help smiling at his delight.

'Yes, I do. I feel at home here.' Jack chuckled. 'I never thought I could live away from London, to be honest.'

Holly finished her tea. 'It sounds so easy, you know. Just picking up all your roots and planting them in a new place.'

'You know how it was for me, Holly. I never fitted in with Dad's family like you and Danny. I always felt like an outsider. Here, I'm one of the islanders. It feels good, you know?'

Holly nodded. 'I'm glad you feel that way. I really do. I just miss you in London. I mean, since you left, I haven't had a decent meal. No special lunches or dinners at all. I can't cook and neither can anyone else I know. Maybe that's the reason I flipped? Which I didn't.'

He laughed again. 'Probably. I'll make up for it while you're here. You'll love the food, I promise.'

'Thank you, I appreciate that. And no weird Norwegian food, if you please.'

'Would I ever?' Jack stood and cleaned the table before she managed to get out of the chair.

'You're such a catch,' she said, teasing him.

'Take your shower and run back to your beau.'

'My beau? What are you, ninety years old?' Holly grinned.

'No, but we would very much like to meet him.'

Holly smiled. 'I'll have to prepare him first. He doesn't even know you lot are back yet.'

'Tell him we're lovely people and we mean no harm. That would work.'

'I'll do my best.'

Jack watched her. 'Will you come back here later? Or will you stay with the hermit?'

Holly blushed. 'I don't know yet. You don't mind, do you? After all, you're not supposed to be here yet.'

Jack shook his head. 'No, not at all. Let me know if you're not coming back, that's all. Oh, and tomorrow there's this thing at Sigrid and Olav's, bring your beau with you.'

'What thing is that?'

'A Christmas thing. Food, fun. You'll like it.'

'What kind of food? I'm warning you. I don't want anything weird.'

'It's not weird.' Jack whistled and Frikk popped up from under the table. Holly hadn't noticed him there.

She waited until Jack and Frikk had gone outside, locked the door behind them and headed upstairs for a shower.

Chapter Twenty-One

The water was choppy by the time Tor had finished checking the nets and the crab traps. He looked at Frøy who was busy trying to jab the crabs.

'You're tempting fate. One of these days the crab will bite your paw, you know.'

The cat ignored him.

Tor turned the boat around and headed home. He wasn't in any hurry to get there, he needed to clear his head.

He hadn't been sure what to expect when he woke up. Certainly not that Holly had left.

He had gone downstairs looking for her and found her note on the kitchen counter. 'My brother and his family are on their way home. I have to clean the house. See you later.'

And then she had signed it with two x's.

What did that mean? He had no idea. Who wrote x's on a note?

It kept puzzling him, even as he went out to sea.

The sun was up by the time he arrived at the first trap and Tor pulled out the note and read it again. Nope, still didn't make sense. *Maybe it means x-tra good*, he thought, grinning.

Frøy jumped up on the deck, nudging Tor with his head.

Tory stroked him. 'You've had your snack. You're not a void that needs to be filled up constantly, you know.'

Frøy flicked his tale and decided to ignore him. He stepped over the gunwale and walked primly on the outside of the wheelhouse, until he found his favourite spot in the front.

'Could you move over, please. You're blocking the view,' Tor called out.

The cat didn't turn around at his voice, but he did shuffle a few centimetres to one side.

'Much appreciated,' Tor said, shaking his head.

He steered the boat towards home, planning a late breakfast and trying to think what Holly might have meant with her note.

Holly hesitated when she came down the narrow path to the pier. There was no sign of Tor's boat, so perhaps he was out checking the nets and traps. She looked at her phone. It was past two. He should be back by now.

She decided to wait and sat on the pier. It was mostly dry and the sun was doing its best impression of shining, creating sparkles on the water's surface.

When she squinted her eyes, she imagined seeing all the

way to Shetland. According to Tor, they were at almost the same latitude.

Holly took a picture to send to her dad. *He would love this*, she thought.

But then she put away the phone again. There was something about sitting on a pier, feet dangling above the water and listening to the waves crashing against the pier posts that made her feel good. Or perhaps it was the night she had spent with Tor.

Jack's right about the air out here, she thought. There was something so fresh and crisp about it and it felt as if every shadowy corner of her brain had cleared up.

The island was such a good place to get grounded again. It felt as if anything could happen, and that would be fine with her, especially as so much already had.

She heard the sound of Tor's boat before she could see it. Holly shielded her eyes, and tried to locate the boat, and smiled when it showed up behind the headland.

The smile turned to laughter when she spotted the cat sitting on the foredeck, clearly enjoying the wind in his face. *He looks like a fluffy figurehead*, she thought.

Tor guided the boat to gently glide alongside the pier. The engine stopped and he smiled at her. 'Fancy seeing you here,' he said.

'Sorry I left this morning.' Holly grabbed the rope he threw to her and looped it around the posts.

'See? You're getting the hang of this,' Tor said, while putting the crab bucket on the pier before climbing out of the boat.

Frøy did it with a lot more elegance, then strutted over

to Holly and rubbed his head against her outstretched hand.

'You know, he likes you better than me.' Tor shook his head.

Holly petted the cat's silky head. 'He's a clever cat.'

Tor grabbed one of the bench pillows and used it to sit on , then he made her sit next to him. 'Is something wrong?'

Suddenly it felt embarrassing to tell him. Holly looked at the sea again. 'When I got home this morning, Jack and Ninni had arrived before me. It was a bit... awkward.'

'Oh.' Tor frowned. 'Is this because your brother minds that you didn't sleep in your own bed, or is it because you did something you now regret?'

'I don't regret it for a minute.' Holly looked up at him. 'Do you?'

His smile was slow and utterly stomach pinching. 'That would be stupid, so no. I don't regret it at all.'

'Right, because that would be stupid. And it's not Jack's business who I sleep with. He would like to meet you, though.'

Tor frowned. 'Yes, I imagine so.'

Holly bumped her shoulder against his. 'Jack is one of the best people I know. I'm a bit more concerned about you, to be honest.'

'Me? Why? I'll be nice to him.' He looked genuinely surprised.

'I know you have been seeing more of the people on this island since you became... friendly with me, and I also realise that meeting my family might not be something you're altogether comfortable with.'

He didn't say anything for a little while as Holly petted Frøy who had taken up residence partly on her lap. He was too big for anything else.

'When I came here to the island, I was in bad shape. I just wanted to be left alone and I worked very hard to stay that way. The only one I talked too was Jens, and that was mostly to arrange things.'

'Why would you do that? It's not healthy, you know.'

Tor shrugged. 'Because if I talked to people, especially in a small place like this, they would ask questions about who I was, why I was on the island, what I do for a living, all that stuff.'

'It sounds pretty normal, Tor. People are friendly. It's not a bad thing,' Holly said, unable to stop herself laughing at him.

'Maybe, but I didn't want any part of it. I was busy being miserable and didn't want to have to pretend to anyone.'

'You managed that. Some of them didn't even know your name. They call you the hermit.' Holly laughed when he looked at her. 'You didn't know?'

'No, how could I? I never talk to anyone.' He laughed when she laughed.

'Oh, you're too much. Does that mean that all the socialising you've done lately, is because of me?' Holly suddenly wondered if she had bullied him out of his lair.

Tor shook his head. 'I wanted to be with you. And that means meeting the others, too. Including your family. I've been moping around long enough. It's time to stop being miserable.'

Holly looked down at the cat. 'Why did you become a hermit, Tor? I mean, you're hardly the kind who lives in a cage and never uses hot water and soap, but still. Staying away from everybody, that's not healthy.'

Tor shrugged. 'I keep in contact with Henrik and his wife, and with my mother. If I didn't they would all be here in a minute. When I arrived, I didn't want company. I didn't need it.'

She noticed he still hadn't told her the why. And she was curious, she had to admit that.

'I was in a relationship,' Tor said slowly. 'It didn't end well.'

'I'm sorry,' Holly said. 'What happened?'

'My partner at the time got pregnant and we lost the baby about six months into the pregnancy.'

Holly was lost for words for a second. 'It must have been so hard for you.'

'It was. Mostly because I felt so guilty, you know. I didn't want to be a father, not then, and I handled it badly. She didn't really feel as if I supported her, not at first and not when we lost the baby.' He looked so sad, Holly ached for him.

'The truth is that before she told me, I was going to break up with her, and then I stayed because I felt trapped. When Linn lost the baby, my instant reaction was relief, and I think Linn sensed that. It didn't matter that I felt such a loss when it sank in that the baby was gone. We never talked about it, and I couldn't even admit it to myself. We went our separate ways soon after. So, in the end, I was free, except by then I wanted the baby and Linn. Does that make sense?'

Holly took his hand. 'I'm sorry, Tor.'

'Life took a different turn. The strange thing was that as time passed, it became this feeling of loss that I didn't think I would feel. I mean, it wasn't as if we had lost a baby after it was born, but I grieved even so.' Tor shook his head. 'And then about two months ago, Linn called me to let me know that she had had a baby and sounded so happy. She didn't want to tell me before because she didn't want me to be sad.'

Tor looked at Holly. 'I can't remember what I said, but I remember hanging up the phone, opening my computer and finding this house. I couldn't stay in Oslo a minute longer.'

'I don't know much about grief, Tor. Not of losing a child, anyway, but my dad spoke about his grief sometimes. He said that he could be fine for months, years even, and then, out of the blue, it hits him. It never really goes away. So, maybe it caught up with you.'

He smiled. 'Maybe. I feel better now, though. Perhaps meeting you helped, or perhaps I've achieved some perspective on what happened.'

'I'm glad you feel better.' Holly leaned her head against his shoulder. Sitting like this, on the pier, felt so good.

He rested his cheek on her head. 'And you. What happened to you?'

Holly frowned. 'It's nothing compared to your loss, and I can't really blame anyone but myself. Even if I want to.'

'Tell me.' Tor smiled when she looked up at him. 'Please.'

Holly drew a deep breath. 'Some months back I had a short relationship with another doctor. It was one of those things that happens, and it wasn't serious for either of us, so we ended it and went our merry ways. Everything was fine.'

Holly stared at the sea, too embarrassed to look at Tor anymore.

'Did he harass you or something like that? Because that's serious.'

'No, it was nothing like that. But a few weeks ago we had different opinions on a patient, and Brian became more and more angry because I refused to agree with him. It escalated, with him calling me a man-eating bitch and all sorts of really nasty personal stuff. And the angrier he got, the more I stood my ground. We were standing in a corridor when it happened, with patients and nurses all around us.'

She fell silent. It didn't exactly put her in a favourable light.

'What did you do?' Tor still held her hand.

Holly pulled a face. 'I lost my temper and lifted my fists. Before I could hit him Brian stumbled backwards, fell over a chair, and went down like a potato sack. The patients found it hilarious. My boss, not so much. And Brian filed a formal complaint the next day. He wants them to fire me because I refused to follow his orders, and because I yelled back at him.'

Holly could still feel the anger and made fists of her hands.

'Sounds to me like he deserved it,' Tor said.

'He did, but I shouldn't have screamed at him, and especially not in front of patients. I was suspended for a month on the spot, or until they decide what to do with me,' she said.

Tor frowned. 'And because of this you could lose your job?'

'Yes. I made a spectacle of myself and now I have to face the consequences.'

'So, what will happen to you? If you lose your job, I mean.'

'Like I said, I was supposed to start my specialist training in oncology in January, but if they decide against me, that will be lost. I might not even be able to work as a doctor, especially if it goes on my record. Which it probably will. Nobody wants a doctor who has had a screaming fight with a colleague.' Holly put her head in her hands. 'God, I can't believe I did that. I mean, I wouldn't want to work with someone like me.'

'Wouldn't they have to take into consideration that you didn't actually hit him? And that you were seriously provoked?'

'That's what I'm hoping for, but there are no guarantees. All I can do, really, is to wait for the hospital's decision.'

'That's bad. I mean, it's Christmas and you have to wait for how long?'

'I might still hear something before Christmas Day, but if I don't it will probably not be until next year.' Holly looked at him. 'There's very little I can do about it.'

Tor put his arm around her shoulder. 'Personally I

would hire you in a second. You stood to a bully and to hell with him.'

'You're sweet. Thank you.' Holly patted her hand on his chest. 'Sorry. I'm not supposed to say thank you, am I?'

She could feel him laughing through her hand. It made her breathe easier and suddenly nothing was that bad anymore.

'So, what happens to Brian? I'm assuming he's suspended too?'

'No, he filed the complaint, and nothing will happen to him unless they decide in favour of me. Then, maybe... I don't know. This is my first disciplinary case.'

Tor thought about it for a second. 'What about the patient? Who was right, you or Brian?'

Holly sighed. 'Brian, unfortunately. It would probably work in my favour if I had been right, but Brian was. He thought it was gallstones, I was sure it was appendicitis.'

Tor nodded. 'I'm sorry. I hope they reinstate you.'

'Me too, but I wouldn't mind if they waited until next year now,' Holly said. 'I don't want to fret over it the rest of this holiday. My bum is wet.'

Tor chuckled. 'So is mine. This pillow isn't waterproof. Which it should be, since it says so on the label.'

He stood and pulled her up after him.

'I think we need to get inside and warm up.'

Holly nodded. 'Let's do that, please.'

Much later they were sitting on the floor in the lounge, in front of the fireplace, eating weird Norwegian food.

Tor handed her a piece of rolled potato *lefse*. 'Okay, this is *gravlaks*, with mustard sauce.'

Holly let him feed her. Tor watched her chew the small nibble, then lit up when she groaned in delight. 'Oh, that's better than smoked salmon. Did you buy that on the market?'

'No, I told you, I made that myself, and then a very lovely woman gave me a jar of mustard sauce.'

'Can I have some more?'

Tor handed her the rest of the lefse. 'I also have some of the island's famous *fenalår* that your brother makes. Have you tasted it?'

'Not yet.' Holly was enjoying the sight of him.

Tor was sitting on the floor in his boxers with a blanket across his shoulders, while Holly was wearing one of his sweatshirts that was so long it was practically a dress.

'Then you are in for a treat.' He gave her a plate with some kind of very thin crispy bread, with a thin slice of meat.

Holly dutifully took a mouthful. 'Soft and salty, and even a bit sweet. No wonder people stood in line for these. I can't believe Jack actually makes this,' she said, taking the plate out of his reach. 'No, all mine.'

'I have to ask you something,' Tor said while they polished off the rest of the food.

'Please do,' Holly said, feeling happy and content.

'Remember the note you wrote me this morning?'

'Yes, it's not really a long time ago, Tor,' Holly said, amused at his serious face.

'What the heck do the x's mean? I've wondered about that all day,' he said with a huge grin.

Holly laughed. 'Really? You don't know?'

'I wouldn't have asked otherwise,' Tor said.

'That's funny. Well, it means kisses. It's something we Brits put at the end of a text or an email or something like that. What do you do?'

Tor thought about it. 'If it's informal, smiley faces.'

'Ha, that's nice too, I think.' Holly looked at him. 'Are you still hungry?'

'Are you?'

'Not so much, but I brought a cake. It's in my bag in the hallway. I hope it's been keeping cold.'

'What kind of cake?' Tor asked as he stood to go fetch it.

'We need two spoons too,' she said. 'It's that kind of cake.'

He returned with her bag and two spoons. 'I didn't want to snoop through your stuff,' he said, sitting down again.

Holly smiled, then opened the bag and found the foil-wrapped package.

'This is insanely good. I'm sure you know all about it, but it turns out Ninni made this.'

'Did you steal it?'

'No, silly. I asked nicely first,' she said, opening the foil and showing it to him. 'Here, what do you think?'

Tor's face lit up with a huge grin. 'Delfia cake. This is my absolute favourite Christmas cake. Well, depending on what they put in it. Do you know what's in it?'

'Let me see, there are liquorice boats, marzipan, sticky men, Santa-shaped marshmallows that taste like strawberries, and Norwegian Smarties. It's like a giant truffle with extras,' Holly said.

'That's the best. When I was little, they had dried figs and biscuits in it, and nothing else. I would pick that out. Then my mother started adding sweets instead.' He took a scoop and put the spoon in his mouth. 'She's put a bit of coffee in it too, and I think there's a drop or two of cognac. To die for.'

'Yes, I know.' Holly took a bite and looked at him while the chocolate melted in her mouth.

Tor frowned. 'What? Do I have chocolate in my beard? Or a marshmallow Santa?'

'Even with that beard, you are so lovely,' she said.

'Is that a compliment?' Tor laughed.

'Oh, absolutely.' Holly dropped the spoon and leaned over to kiss him.

Who cares if the cake melts, she thought, losing herself in his kiss.

Chapter Twenty-Two

Ninni had found a bright red toboggan and placed Rosie on it.

'Hold tight, baby. Daddy will push you.'

Rosie held onto the edges and grinned so wide, it was contagious. Behind her, Jack was pushing the toboggan gently forward. Frikk was far ahead, sniffing at the undergrowth.

Holly looked at Rosie. She was such a perfect picture of delight. She pulled out her phone and took a picture of her and Jack, then sent it to her dad.

'What are you doing?' Jack came up from behind the toboggan.

'Taking a pic for Dad,' she said.

'He must have thousands by now,' Jack said.

'I should think so. Do you know that he has them all printed?' She laughed at Jack's surprised look. 'Oh, yes. They're in photo books, even the blurry ones. It's for Rosie, he says, because in these time, no one bothers to print out

279

pics and when the "interweb" will be turned off, then what happens?'

'So his plan for the apocalypse is to make paper copies?' Jack rolled his eyes. 'You sound just like him, you know.'

'I've practised. Now, what is this thing we're going to?'

'It's tradition, apparently, to eat hot porridge on Little Christmas Eve,' Jack said.

'And why do they call it Little Christmas Eve?' Holly found it perplexing.

Ninni overheard them. 'Because tomorrow is Christmas Eve, of course.'

'Okay, do you also have Little New Year's Eve, then?'

Ninni thought about it. 'No, that's not really a thing. That's just the day before.'

'Makes absolutely no sense,' Holly said.

'And all your traditions make sense, of course.' Ninni smiled at her.

'She's got you there, baby sis,' Jack said.

'I concede. There are some dodgy traditions on our side too. But to get back to my original question. I'm not very keen on porridge, to be honest. Do I have to eat it?'

The question was aimed at Jack who shook his head. 'You don't have to eat it, but you have to try it on toast.'

Holly narrowed her eyes. 'Did you just quote yourself?'

'What does that mean?' Ninni looked at them.

'He used to say that all the time when we were growing up. He would usually cook supper for us, and I was a fussy eater. But he would make me a piece of toast if I put some dinner on it.'

'I had to. You couldn't live on toast alone! Dad was

working and it was my job to make us all our tea. Danny would eat my fingers if I wasn't quick enough. He was like a hoover. You, on the other hand, were a right little madam,' Jack said.

'I was... picky,' Holly said.

'Don't even try. She would hold her breath if she didn't want to eat. I was thirteen and fed up with the whole tantrum thing, and that's when I made up the rule.'

Holly smiled at Ninni. 'And because of him, I tasted all kinds of food. I would put a thin layer of whatever he made for supper on the toast and eat it in small bites, trying to demonstrate for Jack how much I hated it. But he made loads of lovely food, so I didn't convince anyone.'

'She still wants mac & cheese on toast.' Jack laughed when Holly slapped his arm.

Ninni was keeping a sharp eye on Rosie who was by now laying flat forward on the toboggan, singing to herself. Her bobble hat was askew on her head and her bright red boots dragged in the road on either side.

Frikk suddenly barked, but it wasn't an angry tone.

'What are you barking at, you daft mutt,' Jack called out.

Ninni burst out laughing. 'Look at the fence post.'

Holly gaped when she saw Frøy sitting on top of the post, his front paws close together and the fluffy tail around him. Did that mean Tor was close? She hoped so.

'Is your boyfriend here?' Jack came up behind her.

'Might be. Tor is taking the boat to the farm, he has to check on the nets or something. Sometimes he takes Frøy with him, and other times Frøy roams the island pretty much on his own. And don't call him my boyfriend,' she said.

'Not sure what else I should call him,' Jack said.

'You can call him Tor, like everyone else.' Holly didn't really want to discuss Tor with Jack. Not even for fun.

'Fine, don't tell me, then,' Jack said.

'Tell you what?' Holly stopped and looked at him. 'What?'

'Well, what are you going to do with him?'

Holly frowned. 'Well, Jack, I have every intention of having as much sex with him as I can possibly cram in during this whole Christmas thing. Are you happy now?'

'Sex!'

They both looked down at Rosie who smiled like a little angel.

Jack drew a sharp breath. 'Now see what you've done.'

'I didn't do anything!'

Ninni came over to them. 'What's going on?'

'Sex!' Rosie yelled, clearly enjoying the effect it had.

Ninni picked her up from the toboggan. 'You are so clever,' she said.

Jack and Holly exchanged looks. 'Excuse me?' Jack said.

'You should know this by now, Jack.' Ninni turned towards Holly. 'The word for six in Norwegian is *seks*. It's pronounced the same way, so Rosie is so clever because she can count, aren't you, lovely?' She kissed Rosie until the little girl shrieked with laughter.

'Still your fault,' Holly muttered.

'Shut up,' Jack said under his breath.

Ninni looked at them. 'See Rosie. This is what you can expect when you have siblings. Won't that be fun?'

Rosie waved one arm. 'Pus!'

Holly looked at the gatepost. Frøy was still sitting there like some unmovable guardian of Valhalla.

She walked over to him and put a hand on his fur. 'Are you here alone? Where's Tor?'

Frøy sniffed her hand, then rubbed his head against her chin.

'Nice. Your fur is full of snow, silly.'

When she opened the gate to let Ninni and Jack through – Jack now with Rosie on his shoulders – Frikk shot ahead and Frøy jumped down to follow by her side.

Holly stopped to look at the farmhouse. There was smoke coming from the chimney, and there was a distinct smell of burning wood in the air. Behind the white house, she could see a red barn and a few outbuildings. It seemed bigger than Jack's place. There was a large paddock at one side, and on the other side there was a stunning view to the sea.

'That's where they had the beach party when I first came,' Jack said. 'It's something else, isn't it?'

Holly nodded. 'Yes, it is. Is this where you picked mussels?'

'No, that's a different bay.'

They walked a bit further and Holly could see there was a pier and small boathouses there. 'Tor's boat is here,' she said, pointing it out to Jack.

'That's a nice boat,' he said.

Holly nodded. 'It is. His grandfather actually built it and he sailed it up here from Oslo.'

'Don't worry, I won't call him the b-word,' Jack teased, putting his arm around her shoulder.

'Thank you. Much appreciated.'

'Maybe I'll just call him your Viking smoochie,' Jack said, laughing when she tried to hit him.

The door to the house slammed open and Ole scrambled to get out before his sister. He stepped on the wet ground, remembered he didn't have any shoes on and jumped back on the steps, narrowly missing his sister.

Anja turned around and yelled something.

Ninni put the toboggan up against the wall and heaved Rosie up, pretending to throw her at Anja.

The inside of the house was almost as decorated as Ninni and Jack's house. Holly noticed a few of the creepy *nisse*-brownie dolls, but mostly everything was decorated with what mostly looked homemade decorations.

There was a Christmas tree in the lounge, with a lot of toilet roll Santas, heaps of shiny, coloured paper hearts and cotton balls. And lights, so many coloured lights it was hard to see the tree.

Holly smiled at Sigrid. 'Thanks for having me.'

Sigrid gave her a big hug. 'The kids haven't talked about anything else since the market. We have a few more kids here today. As you can probably hear.'

Holly could hear the sounds of stomping feet coming from the next floor and a lot of giggling.

'Yes, I can. Ninni says this is a Norwegian tradition of sorts?'

Sigrid giggled. 'Yes, it's a tradition of eating until you're stuffed, really. Now, I know Jack loves it, but I don't expect you to. So if you don't like it, I have backup food for you.'

'Really?' Holly smiled. 'You didn't have to do that. I'm sure I'm going to love it, whatever *it* is.'

'Good. Then come with me. We are eating in the kitchen. There isn't enough space for a dining room, I'm afraid.'

'I know the feeling, I used to share an apartment with five other people,' Holly said. 'There wasn't space for anything. Your house is wonderful, by the way.'

Sigrid laughed. 'I would say it's a work in progress, but I'm happy as long as it's warm and comfortable.'

'Sounds good to me.'

Inside the kitchen Tor was talking to a young woman, who clearly found him attractive. She was batting her eyelashes, giggling and twirling her hair, and Holly hated her on sight.

A tall man stood by the cooker, stirring a large pot. He waved at Holly. 'Hi. I'm Olav. I missed you at the market. Welcome. I would offer you a handshake, but if this burns, I'm dead.'

'Best not to let that happen,' Holly said. 'Nice to meet you.'

Tor spotted her at once and pulled out the chair next to him. The young woman stood to shake Holly's hand. 'I'm Guro, Sigrid's sister.'

'Hi, pleased to meet you,' Holly said, smiling back.

'I came yesterday for Christmas, you know. My boyfriend is coming later in the week,' Guro said.

Okay, perhaps not hating her, but still a bit weary. Oh, god,

I'm jealous, Holly thought. *That's ridiculous*, was her next thought.

Holly sat next to Tor and looked at him. 'I wasn't sure if you'd be here yet.'

'It didn't take that long,' he said. 'I'm looking forward to this.'

Holly smiled. 'It's the food, isn't it?'

'No, this is all about you.' Tor leaned closer, kissing her lightly on the lips. 'I have been here for half an hour.'

'Rosie had an accident right as we were leaving, and with all the layers of clothes they put on her, it took some time to get her sorted.'

Tor nodded. 'That's what I thought.'

The table was set with colourful Christmas napkins and spoons, and in the middle stood several sugar bowls, shakers with cinnamon, and plates with butter. Holly frowned.

'Why is there butter?' she whispered to Tor. 'Do you eat bread with this?'

He looked at the plates with butter. 'No, it's there because melted butter is delicious in porridge,' he said.

Holly wasn't so sure about that. It seemed odd. 'Okay,' she said.

Ninni and Jack came in with Rosie. Holly took Tor's hand.

'My brother and his partner Ninni. And Rosie, of course. Guys, say hello to Tor.'

Jack smiled and came over to shake Tor's hand. 'It's nice to finally meet the hermit,' he said.

'Don't be rude. We're really happy to meet you properly, Tor,' Ninni said.

'It was about time to come out of the cave for Christmas,' Tor said.

'Well said.' Ninni gave him an approving look before sitting down with Rosie on her lap. Jack pulled up a chair next to her. He made faces to keep Rosie entertained.

Tor put his hand on the back of Holly's chair. *It feels nice,* she thought. For a moment she felt as if she too belonged in this strange place.

A small gaggle of children came running inside, and Sigrid hushed them. 'You're not horses,' she scolded. 'Sit down and behave yourself.'

Holly recognised Emil with the remains of his black eye. He grinned at Holly and pointed at his face. Holly nodded. 'All better,' she said.

'Yes,' he said.

Anja plonked herself next to him and he said something to her.

'His mamma likes you,' Anja said slowly.

'Thank you. I'm happy Emil's eye is all better,' Holly said.

Anja translated and Emil nodded several times.

'He speaks English too, but he's shy,' Anja explained.

When every chair was occupied, and everyone had settled down, the serving started.

Stacks of earthenware bowls lined the cooker. Sigrid put porridge in each one and Olav put them on the table, one for each person.

Holly looked at the bowl when he put it down in front of her.

'It's only half full, so you can taste it first.'

'Thank you.' Holly smiled at him.

She looked at the bowl. The porridge was steaming hot. It was white and creamy, and smelled faintly of vanilla. Not at all what she had expected. Not a steel-cut oat in sight.

She watched Tor and the others. Sugar and cinnamon in generous amounts, and everyone put a dollop of butter in the middle of the bowl.

Melted butter? Why would they do that?

Holly put sugar and cinnamon on the porridge and picked up a spoon. *It smells good*, she thought.

When she put the spoon in her mouth, she became aware that everyone was staring at her.

Holly tasted silky cream and soft rice, with hints of vanilla, a touch of salt and that warming cinnamon flavour.

'This is so good,' she exclaimed. 'I mean, really, really good. Like cinnamon cream.'

Tor leaned into her. 'You don't have to eat if you don't want to,' he whispered.

'I love it, and you have porridge in your beard,' Holly said, smiling sweetly at him.

'Whatever you do, don't wipe it off,' he said, but with a smile.

He took the napkin she offered him and rubbed his cheek. 'Better?'

'Much better.' *He would look good if he put his whole face in the bowl*, Holly thought.

'Do I have more? Holly?' Tor nudged her.

'No, no, you're fine,' Holly said, a bit flustered.

She discovered that Jack was keeping an eye on her, and pulled a face at him. He grinned back, then continued to help Rosie eat as she decided that slapping her hand in the porridge bowl was hilarious. It got the attention she wanted though and she was smiling from ear to ear.

Ninni looked at Jack. 'I thought you were supervising her,' she said.

'I was, but she's too fast. She's like Superwoman in a tiny, chubby package,' he said, rescuing the bowl from a new attack. 'Don't do that, Rosie. No.'

Rosie screwed up her face and emitted a wail that had everyone turn their heads. Ninni picked Rosie up and turned her around. 'What are you screaming about?'

'Diaper bag is in the hall,' Jack said, getting up from the table.

They disappeared together with Rosie screaming all the way.

Sigrid stood from her chair. 'Anyone for seconds?'

A lot of bowls were lifted from the table. Sigrid caught Holly's look. 'Are you up for it?'

'Yes, please. It's delicious.'

She looked at Tor's bowl, where the butter was melting nicely in the middle. 'Can I try that?'

He pushed the bowl closer to her. 'Help yourself.'

Holly felt all eyes on her again when she filled the spoon with porridge and dipped it slightly in the butter puddle.

Then she put it in her mouth. She frowned, then shook her head.

'No, that's... no. I'll have mine without the butter, please.'

Holly realised she was full about halfway through the second bowl. It was too rich.

She turned to Tor who had finished his second serving.

'Did Jens get in touch with you?'

He looked surprised for a moment, then nodded. 'Yes, he did.'

'Are you coming tomorrow, then?'

Tor nodded. 'Absolutely.'

Holly smiled at him. 'Good. That's really good.'

She didn't say anything after that. It was enough to sit in a cosy kitchen, listen to children laughing and Rosie babbling, and know that she had nothing to worry about.

Chapter Twenty-Three

Christmas Eve

Rosie sat on Jack's shoulders again, slapping her hands on his head. She had thrown his hat away before they left the house. It was now protruding from his back pocket.

The weather was grey and the skies heavy. 'Maybe we'll get some proper snow tonight,' Ninni had said with delight.

Holly didn't mind. If it got colder now, she'd crawl under the duvet with Tor, and not come out until spring.

'Where are the two of you off too?' Holly looked up at her brother.

'We are just going to burn off some energy, so that Rosie can take a nap before we go to dinner. Because if she doesn't, she'll be cranky when Santa comes. Isn't that right, Rosie?'

Rosie paid no attention to either of them. She was too busy enjoying herself pulling Jack's ears.

'You two are so adorable together,' Holly said, touching Rosie's boot.

'Yes, we are. Rosie wins, of course. It's hard to compete with a toddler.' Jack smiled at Holly. 'Even if she is sticky and snotty right now.'

'She's so much like you, Jack. I know she doesn't look like you, but she acts so much like you. She's a lucky girl,' Holly said. 'I mean, you raised me, and look how amazingly amazing I turned out.'

'True. I take full credit for that, of course. And that has a lot to do with this, you know. I got to practice on you and Danny, and that made it easy for me to take on Rosie.'

Rosie leaned forward and drooled on his head. 'Also, I would miss out on things like this,' he said, lifting Rosie down from his shoulders and handing her to Holly.

'No!' Rosie said, squirming in Holly' arm.

'A little help, please. It's like holding a slippery ball,' Holly said.

Jack wiped his head before putting the woollen hat back on. 'You can put her down, but don't let go of her. She's a sprinter, that one.'

'I know that!' Holly put Rosie down, and held on to the back of her winter suit while Rosie struggled to get away.

'Will you bring Tor to our house first, or go straight to Alma's?' Jack asked, while keeping an eye on Rosie.

'I'll go to Tor's and change there,' she said. 'Then we'll come to you first.'

Jack nodded at the bag she was carrying. 'Is that why you took your dress with you?'

'Sure, I don't want to give him an excuse to change his mind. He can't say no if I'm all dressed up, now can he?'

'Not if he has half a brain. Don't be late. Norwegians, especially Alma, do not approve of tardiness, I'm afraid.'

Rosie threw a tantrum by throwing herself forward, making Holly lose the grip on her suit. She hit the slushy ground, kicking her legs.

Jack shook his head. 'She's got great lungs. I'd better take her for that walk and then go home.'

Holly nodded. 'See you then.'

She headed for the pathway leading to Tor's house, then stopped to look back at Jack and Rosie. They were walking now, holding hands, the tantrum obviously forgotten.

They looked so sweet together. She loved that Jack was so happy. *I hope I find someone that makes me half that happy,* she thought. Tor... Tor was special, but it wasn't like that. It was a holiday romance, not a happily ever after romance.

Maybe some other time, she thought and started to walk to Tor's house. *Christmas Eve would certainly be different this year...*

After the porridge party, she had no idea what to expect, but it was going to be some sort of dinner, apparently. Alma was cooking with Jack's help, Sigrid, Olav, and their kids would be there, as would Britt and Guro. Tobben was with his sister on the mainland.

When she climbed the last hill up to the edge, where she had almost fallen off, she met Frøy.

'Hi Frøy. What are you wearing?'

The cat sat and looked up. He had a bright, fire-truck red

bow around his neck. 'You look very elegant,' she said and stroked his head.

She couldn't see Tor anywhere, so she had to brave the pathway down to the house by herself.

When she came to the door, she could see he had decorated. There was a wreath on the door and Christmas lights in the windows.

Holly opened the door and peaked inside. 'Tor? Are you here?'

He popped his head out the kitchen door. 'Did you see Frøy out there?'

'Yes, he looks very festive,' she said.

'Do you know how hard I had to work to get that bow on him?'

'I can only imagine.' Holly held up her bag. 'Can I put this anywhere?'

'Sure. What is it?'

'It's my dress. I thought I could change here and then we could go to this thing together.' Holly looked at him.

Tor frowned. 'You weren't sure I would come, were you?'

'I figured you might change your mind.' Holly wondered if that had been stupid. *What if she came across as clingy or needy? That would be awful.*

He came all the way over to her and put a warm hand against her cheek. 'I said I would, didn't I?'

'Yes, you did. But still. I need you there.'

Holly got up on her toes and kissed him.

'Why would you need me?' Tor let his hand rest on the back of her head.

'I need you to translate the culture. Like you did yesterday.' She leaned against him. He felt as solid as a rock. 'Christmas Eve at home is spent drinking wine, wrapping last minute presents, stuffing our faces with Ferrero Rocher or some kind of chocolate truffles. Or we go out to a bar, have some drinks and have fun. Jack says it's a big deal here. He says it's the most important dinner of the year. Which is odd, since he's not cooking any of his own creations.'

Tor laughed. 'As with everything else in life, some people take it serious, others not so much. It's a semi big deal. We dress up, eat for an entire evening, and then sleep off the food coma the next day. You do that in England too?'

'Of course we do, but there's hardly any dressing up. Not like this.'

Tor grinned. 'And I'll be wearing my best suit. Well, my only suit, as it stands.'

'An actual suit?' Holly laughed.

'Damn straight and with shoes to match.'

Holly hesitated. 'Let me see if I understand this correctly. You travel to this island in your little boat and with polar bear clothes, determined to avoid people at all costs, but you also bring a suit?'

Tor nodded. 'I never know when I have to look smart, so I always pack a suit. There might be meetings with people who always dress up in suits, and I can't sit there in a sweatshirt and jeans. Honestly, I've done a fair amount of meetings from the house, and I have then worn my shirt, tie and jacket… but with pyjama bottoms.'

While he was talking, he helped her take off the boots and the coat, then he pulled her with him into the kitchen.

Holly giggled. 'That must have been a lovely sight if you stood to get a cup of coffee or something.'

'Which is why I wear the pyjama bottoms. I care about my presentation, you know.'

'You do look good in pyjama bottoms,' Holly said.

'I know,' he said, looking very pleased with himself.

Holly realised the kitchen smelled good. 'What are you doing?'

'I was about to eat something. Are you hungry?'

'Not really.' Holly smiled at him. 'Not for food, anyway.'

Tor touched her face again. He smiled, and she felt almost dizzy.

'I think we can come up with something to... you know, keep us busy for... how much time do we have?'

'We're supposed to be there at six and Jack said we can absolutely not be late,' Holly said,

'Oh, so plenty of time.' Tor kissed her and Holly was almost lifted off the floor. 'But not in the kitchen,' he said.

He took her hand and was about to climb up the stairs.

'Too far.' Holly pulled him into the lounge.

They fell over each other onto the couch and ignored the cat who returned to the kitchen and flopped down in front of the heater.

Holly looked up at Tor. 'We can't sleep,' she said. 'We can't be late. Look, it's dark outside already.'

'It's barely four o'clock. We have plenty of time,' Tor said, smiling at her nervous face. She was adorable. 'I would offer you something to eat, but you need to be hungry for later.'

'God, you're heavy,' Holly said, trying to get up from the sofa.

'I'd be insulted if you weren't right.' Tor didn't want her to leave. She was warm and soft, and he loved the way she looked right now.

'You're awfully fit, you know,' she said, putting her hand on his chest.

'Must be the fishing and the hiking.' Tor played with her hair.

'No, well, that too, but I meant you're awfully good looking. Even with all that scraggly beard,' she said.

He smiled. 'You don't like my beard?'

'It has it's uses,' Holly said, shrieking when he rubbed the beard on her face. 'Don't do that! I'm going to look as if I've been scratched by Frøy.'

'Do you want me to get rid of it?' He asked with his face close to hers.

'Nope, I wouldn't do that. It's your beard, and it must have taken you ages to grow it,' she teased.

Then she kissed him and rolled away. 'I need to shower and then get dressed.'

'Will it take two hours?' Tor held out his hands to pull her back, and she pulled away.

'No, don't do that. Don't distract me.'

'I could watch you forever,' he said, suddenly becoming serious.

Holly blushed and he realised he loved watching that.

'Really? Well, we don't have forever, now do we?' she said, looking away.

'You're right. Go, take your shower,' Tor said, waving at her. 'I'll wait here.'

'Please don't fall asleep. I don't want to be late,' she said from the door.

'I'm getting up,' he called after her, then he fell back on the sofa.

He missed her already. He sighed. Better get dressed. Christmas Eve was a big deal and he wanted Holly to enjoy herself.

Tor put on his pants and caught a glimpse of his face in the hallway mirror. He stroked his beard and then smiled. It was time.

———————

Holly put on her dress, and examined herself in the mirror.

Not too bad, she thought. *Good thing it's not a tight fit.*

The red dress looked festive enough, with not too much cleavage on show. Looking good was fine, but looking sexy seemed inappropriate for a family party. She put up her hair in a loose bun and finished the look with pearl stud earrings.

Downstairs the sofa was empty, and so was the kitchen, except for Frøy who rolled around when she came in.

'Where's Tor?' She asked, scratching his head.

Frøy jumped up and seemed to wonder the same. Holly

straightened his bow. 'Now we can't have you losing this, can we?'

Tor came through the door dressed in jeans and boots, carrying wood from outside.

'How are you not freezing to death?' Holly gaped at him.

'I'm always hot.' Tor dropped the wood into the basket next to the fireplace. 'But not as hot as you. Wow, Holly, you look great,' he said.

Holly enjoyed the look he gave her, but raised her hands when he took a step towards her. 'No, don't mess up my make-up. I can see what you're up to.'

Still, he pulled her close and Holly shrieked when he let his icy fingers run along the neckline of her dress.

'That's cruel,' she whispered before he kissed her. He smelled of outdoors and fire and something that was only him. 'You have snow in your beard.'

'More like rain, I'm afraid.' He let go of her. 'I'll just take a quick shower myself and then we can go.'

Holly went into the lounge again, picking up her phone. Jocelyn answered on the first ring.

'Are you snowed in yet?' Jocelyn said.

'No, not really. I'm sitting in a lovely lounge, in my shiny new Christmas frock, waiting for Tor to get ready.'

'In his lounge, you say? Did you sleep with him on Christmas Eve?'

Holly giggled. 'Does it matter what day it is?'

'God, no, of course not. I'm thrilled and really jealous that you're having a proper Viking holiday. Are there any other sexy Vikings on that island?'

'Not really. As far as I know, all the Vikings are on their way to Christmas dinner, or they're cooking it. If you want to go Viking hunting, you have to come in the summer.'

'I could live on a Norwegian island for a week or two,' Jocelyn said. 'I mean, they have Wi-Fi and hot water, right?'

Holly could just picture it. Jocelyn stomping along on high heels and in the tightest swimsuit available. 'Yes, they do. You'd be a sight, though,' she said.

'Aren't I always? Listen, rumour has it that Brian is out. I'm not sure if that's good news for you, or if, you know, they're going to be hard on both of you. I really hope it's good news. Have you heard anything?'

'Nope, not a word. I've decided not to worry about it though. They won't let me know now until after Boxing Day, anyway. I'm happy Brian is having a crappy Christmas though.'

'Good for you. I hope you have a lovely evening. I'm certainly going to,' Jocelyn said.

'What are you up to?' Holly could picture her in the apartment, getting ready for a night out.

'I'm on my way out, as you well know. We're hitting a club and then, well, you know...' Jocelyn said, giggling again. 'I miss you! When are you coming home? I mean, whatever happens with the hospital, you're still coming home , aren't you? Or are you doing a Jack?'

Holly laughed. 'I'm definitely not doing what Jack has done. I couldn't even if I wanted to, which I don't. Pretty sure Norway has plenty of doctors, and they would all be licensed, which I'm not. Not at the moment, anyway.'

'Oh. Are you sure you can leave your Viking that easily?'

Jocelyn meant to joke, but it hit a nerve with Holly. 'I... please don't ruin my holiday romance with your sensible questions. Go out, have fun, and I'll talk to you tomorrow,' she said.

'Fine, no too early, mind you. I'm planning on a having a hangover and a lie-in. I'm not due back in the hospital until Boxing Day, and I'm going to make the most of my days off. If you know what I mean.' Jocelyn giggled.

'Yes, I do. Okay, I'm going to leave you to it. Be careful.'

'You sound like my mother.'

Holly put away the phone. Christmas Eve would have been so different if she had been home. She smiled. So different. No Tor for starters, and he was worth more than what she was missing out on.

'So, how do I look?'

She turned around and gasped.

'Holly?' Tor laughed when she stared at him as if she had never seen him before. 'Please don't faint on me.'

Holly found her voice. 'What did you do?'

He touched his chin, a bit self-conscious. 'I realised it had been going on long enough. I'm not a hermit anymore, am I?'

'I like it.' Holly walked closer and put her fingers on his chin. 'I'm glad you didn't take off all of it. It suits you like this.'

'Really?' He looked pleased. 'Good. And the suit?'

Holly hadn't really noticed the suit. He looked so different from the gruff fisherman she was used to. The suit was navy blue, with a white shirt and a bright red tie with green spots. On closer inspection, the spots turned out to be miniature Christmas trees.

'Oh, I like that. That's a nice touch. You look too good for words. You clean up nicely, I have to say.'

Tor stroked his hand over the tie. 'Thank you. So, shall we go?'

'Please. I don't want to arrive after Jack and Ninni.'

When they were ready to leave, Tor shook his head. 'I almost forgot the most important thing. Hang on a second.'

Holly stepped outside. Being fully dressed in winter clothes in a warm house, was too much. She had the bag with the party shoes slung over her shoulder.

It took about a second to understand why she had seen so few Norwegian women in skirts. 'Bloody hell,' she muttered to herself when the wind attacked her legs.

Tor turned up in the doorway, carrying a large bag filled with colourful presents. 'What's wrong?'

'I just remembered why the overalls are such a useful piece of clothing.'

He looked at her legs. 'Right. Do you have any tights with you?'

'No, they're at Ninni's. I'll be fine. It's not that far.'

Frøy decided it was time to leave then and the red bow bobbed up and down as he ran up the path.

Chapter Twenty-Four

Tor and Holly followed Frøy, fingers entwined. Holly glanced at the bag he was carrying. 'Do you have Christmas presents for everyone?'

'Of course I have. My mother would die of shame if I didn't bring presents on Christmas Eve.'

'She's celebrating Christmas with her partner, right?'

'Yes. He has two kids and three grandchildren, and his family owns a cabin up in the mountains. If you want to have proper snow these days, that's where you have to be.'

Holly squeezed his hand. 'And that's where you should have been, isn't it?'

'No, not really. I'm terrible at skiing, and I prefer to stay by the coast.'

Holly sensed a sore spot. 'You don't get along with them?'

Tor shrugged. 'There's nothing wrong with any of them, they're nice people, but I don't fit in. They moved in together after I left for university, so it's not like I grew up with any them. There's not a strong bond or anything like that.'

'That sounds sad. Jack always felt left out of our wider family, and he was a part of it from when he was five years old.' Holly shook her head. 'And he was right, too. They always made sure he wasn't treated like Danny and me.'

'Because his father was Norwegian?'

'No, because my father treated him as if he was his. The rest of the family took offence. It's nice to see him so happy now,' Holly said.

'It was different for me. My dad was always there and Mum's partner was never a dad to me. He's a good man and he makes my mum happy. That's good enough for me.'

'But you still don't want to spend Christmas with them?'

'Not really. It's too… stiff, too formal, you know? I don't feel comfortable.'

'Meaning you don't take Christmas that seriously?'

'Let's put it this way. If it wasn't for you, I would have spent Christmas alone in the house with Frøy. And I would have been perfectly content with that.'

'Good thing I rescued you from a lonely, sad Christmas, then,' Holly said.

Tor chuckled. 'Yes, I'm very lucky.'

They walked down towards the fork in the road, where they could see the school and Britt's house. Holly pointed at the little white building behind the school. 'Do you know what that is?'

'Yes, it's an old prayer house. It's not like church or a chapel, it's more like a meeting place for believers. You will find places like this in the valleys and on the islands, everywhere that's a bit isolated from the bigger places.'

'So, it used to be a church?'

'Not an actual church. People would have services there, arranged by themselves or some of the many mission organisations that use to exist in this country. When people needed a minister, he would come from the mainland. Or at least, I think that's how it worked. I've never actually been in a prayer house,' Tor said, smiling at her.

Holly looked at the little house. 'It's a lovely building, isn't it?'

'Yes, you will find houses in the same style all along the coast. They are all built in more or less the same way, and they are all white.'

'If they don't use it as a prayer house now, then what is it for?'

'I wouldn't know. Not an islander, remember?' Tor teased her.

Holly raised her eyebrows. 'And here I thought you knew everything.'

'Whatever gave you that impression?' Tor said.

Holly laughed. 'That's funny.'

'I'm glad you're enjoying yourself.' He lifted her hand and kissed it. 'You should always be happy.'

'Nobody is always happy, Tor. That would be exhausting, I think.'

'Yes, but you know what I mean.'

She could see the roof of Ninni and Jack's house when they stopped again. Further out, she spotted the harbour.

'It must have been daunting to live here year round, back before mobile phones and electricity,' she said.

'How?' Tor pulled her away from a puddle in the road.

'Alma said that they would be cut off during storms. No contact with the mainland. Nowadays that wouldn't happen as you can always get in touch with someone, but when people lived here before, there must have been times when they felt as if the rest of the world didn't exist.'

Tor frowned. 'That's very dark, Holly. I think you have a touch of *Åsgårdsreia*,' he said.

'The what now?'

'"The Wild Hunt", I think is the proper translation. It was the belief that on Christmas Eve, the souls of the dead, together with goblins, witches and demons – the underground people is what we call them – would fly through the night, chasing each other. And everyone caught outside would be captured and brought to the underworld. It was a tradition that everyone on the farm would sleep on the floor in the main house, and keep the lights going all night.'

'You guys have some ghoulish stories, Tor.'

'It's the darkness,' he said, grinning at her. 'People had to entertain themselves during the long winters, and scary stories have always been a hit.'

Holly became aware of the darkness engulfing them as clouds rolled in, hiding the stars and making it even darker. From the little prayer house, bells suddenly rang out. It was such a surprising sound. She looked at Tor.

'It's five o'clock,' Tor said. 'They're ringing in Christmas, or is it chiming? Not sure what the right word is, I'm afraid.

Anyway, it's time for Christmas peace. Everything is closed now, more or less, all over the country, and people have retreated into their houses. If you were in any of our towns or villages now, you would be hard pressed to see anyone.'

Holly laughed. 'Sounds to me you're all still wary of the Wild Hunt. I'm not even going to try to say that in Norwegian.'

'Maybe. Or we're just trying to keep the dark at bay. Look.'

He was pointing at the lights in the windows of the houses, the fairy lights over the door and windows at the big sea house, and also the lights where people had decorated garden fences, front doors, and even brushes.

'See? We don't curse the darkness, we put up lights. It's peaceful and cosy, and it makes us feel safe.'

'It's the *hygge* thing again, isn't it?'

'Yes, but we don't call it that. We say cosy or *koselig*.'

'Isn't that the same?'

Tor nodded. 'I guess so. We use *koselig* the way the Danish use *hygge*. I'm not sure the Danes ever use the word *koselig*. I never thought about that,' he said.

Holly leaned her head against his shoulder. 'I like it.'

When they approached Ninni and Jack's house, the door swung open. Frøy kept close to Holly, his yellow eyes glowing in the dark.

Jack poked his head outside. 'Ah, there you are. Ehm, I need some help with a few things. Tor, can you carry stuff?'

'Yes, of course I can.' Tor lifted the bag he was holding, as if to demonstrate his carrying abilities. 'What do you need?'

Jack disappeared inside and came out with what looked like the entire inside of the house. 'Here's the Christmas presents. I'll take the food and Ninni will take Rosie.'

Holly looked at the bags. 'All of these are presents?'

'No, not all. We're leaving everything from our side here to be opened tomorrow. You know, so we can have a proper Christmas,' Jack said, grinning at her. 'Ninni also brought your presents from your room. Only the gifts for the islanders, and of course some of ours. You might want to help him, you know. The poor man might buckle under the strain.'

Holly took a few of the bags. 'This is a proper party, isn't it?'

'You haven't seen anything yet,' Jack said, looking so pleased with himself that Holly had to swallow a lump in her throat.

Frikk came bouncing out of the house, barely sniffed Frøy, then took off ahead of them. Finally they were all outside. Ninni had Rosie on her hip, the little girl waving at everyone.

'Have we remembered everything?' Ninni said.

Jack smiled. 'If we haven't it's not really that far to go back and get it.'

'You're right. Of course it isn't.' Ninni smiled at Holly. 'I hope you'll enjoy it, though.'

'I'm sure I will.'

Holly had a small feeling of trepidation in the pit of her stomach when they walked towards the shop. They didn't go in, of course – it was closed, as Tor had said – instead they walked around to the back, to the entrance to the attached house.

'Oh, that's nice,' Holly said.

Torches had been put into the ground all the way up to the door that was decorated with a huge wreath, complete with colourful bows and lights. It made her smile.

Ninni knocked on the door and someone immediately opened it.

'You're just in time for the kitchen drama. Jack, we need you.' Britt pulled him inside. 'The rest of you can sort yourself out, right?'

Ninni rolled her eyes. 'Go, go. We'll be fine. Just leave us enough room to get inside, will you?'

Somehow they managed to take off all the wintery clothes and enter the rest of the house dressed for the fancy part of the evening. Holly smiled when Ninni took the snow suit off Rosie. The dress she was wearing was one she had bought her niece for her birthday.

'I can't believe it still fits her,' she said, delighted.

Ninni straightened the bow she had put in Rosie's curls. 'Of course it does. In a few months, not so much, I'm afraid. It's so lovely, Holly.'

It was green and sparkly, and had a teddy bear on the front. Rosie pointed at it and said something not so clear. 'Yes, it's your *bjørn*. Come on, baby. Let's find Jens,' Ninni said.

The house smelled... interesting. 'That's definitely not roast or turkey,' Holly whispered to Tor.

'Stick meat,' he said, laughing when she frowned at him. 'It's smoked lambs rib. Trust me, you're going to love it.'

They followed Ninni and Rosie into the lounge, where Jens was sitting in a deep chair with Ole on his knee. Ninni put Rosie down on the floor and she headed for Jens with one of her happy squeals.

'There's my girl,' he said and put her up on his other knee.

Tor found places for them on the sofa, and pulled her down next to him, while Ninni went to check on what was happening in the kitchen.

'This is lovely,' Holly said.

She looked around. There was a fire in a huge fireplace, which Frøy had curled up in front of while Frikk snuck under the table. In one part of the room a Christmas tree almost reached the ceiling, decorated with long, thin strips of silver tinsel along with bulbs in all sorts of colours. *Some look really old*, Holly thought. The lights were different to what she was used to. Instead of the tiny LED lights, they looked like white candle lights, giving the tree an old-fashioned look. A sparkly star in the top completed the look.

Holly caught Jens looking at her. 'The tree is so lovely,' she said.

'We like a good Christmas tree, Alma and I.' He pointed at the table. 'Help yourself to the goodies. But not too many. We're having dinner soon. And god help us all if we don't eat,' he said, with a huge smile on his face.

On the table there were all sorts of bowls and plates, almost spilling over with cakes, cookies, and sweets. A big box of confectionery chocolate stood in the middle.

Tor leaned over and helped himself to a cookie covered

in sugar and almond shavings. 'Good,' he said. 'I mean, really good.'

Holly looked at him. 'What is it?'

'I'm not sure, actually. I've never had these before,' Tor said. He looked at Jens.

Jens smiled. 'They are called Jewish cakes. It's an old recipe and very common here on the west coast. Try it, Holly. Unless you're allergic to almonds?'

'She's not,' Tor said, breaking the cake in half, and handing it to Holly. 'She had the *kransekake* in town and marzipan yesterday, remember?'

Holly took a bite and nodded. 'Really good. Almost like shortbread.'

'According to tradition there has to be seven different types of Christmas bakes,' Jens said. 'Alma likes to bake, so we always have more. Hence the assortment.'

He was interrupted by Rosie showing him her bow. 'Yes, my sweet. It's lovely and looks a lot better on you than it will on me.'

Rosie waved her hand and Holly picked up a small doughnut, and handed it to her.

She took one for herself and sniffed it before taking a bite. 'These are insanely good. Alma made these too?'

'Oh, yes. She starts in the beginning of December and so it goes on. It's a wonder I'm not as big as this house,' Jens said.

Holly caught Ole staring at the tree – not at the decorations, but at the piles of presents underneath it. Ole said something to Jens and pointed at the tree.

Holly turned to Tor. 'He's asking when *Nissen* is

coming,' he said. 'Santa, I mean, and Jens is reminding him he won't come until after dinner.'

'Santa is coming here?' Holly looked at Jens for confirmation, and he nodded.

'He'll be here after dinner to hand out presents for everyone. Like he does every Christmas.'

Tor smiled. 'I remember that. The adults would sit at the dinner table, eating, drinking and talking as if they would never finish, while all the children waited for Santa to deliver the presents. It was exhausting.'

'You were lucky. If Holly was home, she wouldn't get her gifts until tomorrow morning, isn't that right, Holly?' Jens beamed at her.

'Oh, yes. My little brother and I would wake up at five o'clock in the morning and sneak down to the lounge to rip up every gift there was. My dad put a stop to it by sleeping in the lounge and from then on we had to wait until eight o'clock. But we kept opening the door and peeping in. I don't think he got much sleep.'

Jens translated to Ole and the little boy gaped at her.

'Here.' Tor handed her another cookie, a diamond-shaped thin cake with a white almond in the middle.

'What is it?'

'I'm pretty sure it's made with golden syrup. They're called syrup snips.'

Some kind of gingerbread, Holly thought. *Good, but not as good as those little doughnuts.*

'I'm going to be full before dinner if I don't watch it,' she said to Tor.

He handed her a small sandwich cookie with pink filling. 'Try this.'

Holly popped it in her mouth. 'So good. What are they?'

Tor shook his head. 'No idea. My mum would buy our cookies at the supermarket, and all we wanted was marzipan anyway.'

They were interrupted by the doorbell ringing, startling Rosie who burst into tears. Frikk scrambled out from under the table and ran out of the lounge.

Ninni came out from the kitchen and picked up Rosie.

From the hallway came the sound of heavy objects hitting the floor and then someone muttering something Holly was pretty sure was swearing.

Ninni lit up in a huge smile. 'Come on, Rosie. Guess who has finally arrived.'

She went out into the hallway and Rosie's crying instantly turned into happy squeals.

A man came in, nodding at Jens who lit up when he saw him. He held Rosie with one hand and she had her arms around his neck, hugging him tightly.

'Lovely to see you, Petter. Say hello to Holly, Jack's sister, and to Tor, Holly's friend. He's been staying on the island for the last few weeks,' Jens said.

Tor stood to shake Petter's hand. 'Hello,' he said.

Holly did the same. 'Nice to meet you,' she said.

'And you. How are you doing out here?' Petter asked.

'I haven't been blown off the island yet,' Holly said.

Petter laughed. 'Good for you.'

He sat in one of the other chairs, and Rosie immediately

held onto his knee. Frikk claimed the other knee, staring adoringly at Petter.

Frøy hadn't moved from the fireplace.

Holly could hear laughter from the kitchen as Jens and Petter started talking rapidly in Norwegian.

Holly looked at Rosie leaning her head on Petters's arm. She looked so happy. It made her a bit sad that her own father was missing out.

'Holly, we need your help,' Ninni said with a huge smile, interrupting Holly's thoughts.

Chapter Twenty-Five

In the kitchen Britt and Sigrid sat by the table, chatting over an array of beer bottles. At the stove, Alma and Jack were having what looked like a heated discussion about something.

Britt pulled out a chair and Holly sat. 'Are they speaking only Norwegian in there?'

'Mostly,' Holly said. 'Is there anything I can do?'

'Yes, you can sit here and tell me what you think of my Christmas beer. I can tell you that some people don't appreciate good beer when they drink it. Here, taste this.'

She handed Holly a bottle.

Holly took a swig and let it roll for a second in her mouth.

'It's sweet and with a hint of orange and honey, I think,' Holly said. 'Like dark ale?'

'Pretty much. Jack claims it's too sweet.'

Holly took another swig. 'No, not really. It's lovely, actually.'

'I would use it in a stew,' Jack said.

'That's an insult. My good beer is not to be sloshed away on a sauce for meat,' Britt said.

'May I taste it?' Tor sat next to Ninni. 'I love Christmas beer.'

Britt handed him a bottle. 'Don't drink it all at once. It's perfect with dinner.'

Tor tasted it and smiled. 'It's really good. You made this?'

'Of course. If you weren't such a hermit, you could have tasted it weeks ago.'

Tor winked at Holly and turned to Britt. 'Did you know that they have been brewing beer here since the Vikings, and that it used to be illegal not to make beer for Christmas?'

'Yes, of course,' Britt said, rolling her eyes. 'Every larger farm had to brew their own beer or face fines. As if anyone needed to be punished into brewing.'

Alma interrupted her. 'Dinner is ready. Don't blame me for the mash, that's all Jack's fault. He insisted on mixing carrots and swedes, and added horseradish.'

'I did that because it's delicious, and I stand by it,' Jack said, smiling broadly at her.

'Well, that's true, it's delicious, but it's not traditional,' Alma said.

'I for one, am starving and if you don't feed me soon, I'll fight Frikk for his dinner,' Britt said.

'We have to wait for Olav and the girls before we sit,' Sigrid said. 'They'll be here any minute.'

As if on cue, the doorbell rang again and Frikk barked, followed by excited voices.

Anja came bouncing in to the kitchen. 'Pappa forgot to put the porridge in the barn, so we had to go back,' she said.

'Really? But everything was ready.' Sigrid gave her daughter a hug. 'Good thing you remembered.'

Alma pointed at Jack. 'Let's put food on the table.'

She started handing plates of food to those closest to her, and pointing at the door. 'Dining room, please. Jack will bring the meat.'

Holly took the beer bottles Britt gave her, and followed Tor out. He was carrying the bowl of mash. 'This smells amazing,' he said to her.

'What does it mean that they forgot the porridge? Anja didn't bring any into the kitchen,' Holly said.

'Oh, that. It's another old tradition. On farms, they put a plate of rice porridge in the barn. For the barn-*nisse*? If you don't he might get pissed,' Tor said.

'Right. I know this. Alma said that when she followed me into the house my first full day here.'

Jens had opened the doors at the end of the lounge to let them in.

'I love this,' Holly whispered when they entered the dining room.

Another fireplace warmed up the room and a long table stood in the middle, with chairs enough for everyone. Two huge candelabra lit up the table.

'You can sit where you want, Holly,' Alma said, coming in after her. 'It looks a lot more formal than it is.'

'It looks so lovely,' Holly said, smiling at her. 'Do you really do this every year?'

'Of course. Christmas is special.' Alma set down small bowls of some kind of jam.

'They're bringing the rest. Just sit,' Alma said.

Tor pulled her down next to him. 'I'm starving,' he whispered.

'Me too.' Holly smiled at him.

She took the napkin and looked at it. 'This is beautiful. Do you think she made this too?'

The napkin was embroidered with silver stars. Tor put his on his lap. 'At this point, it wouldn't surprise me if she built the house herself.'

Holly had Anja next to her and the little girl chatted with her in English, trying to explain Norwegian words for her.

She noticed that Tor was looking at her and leaned in. 'If they bring out the weird jellied fish or half a sheep's head, I'm leaving,' she whispered.

'I'll be right behind you,' he whispered.

Jack and Petter brought in plates filled with dark brown meat that reminded Holly of lamb chops. *I like those*, she thought and smiled at her brother.

'I'm making turkey on New Year's Eve, I promise,' he said.

'With all the trimmings?' Holly said.

'I promised, didn't I?'

Holly enjoyed the dinner. The meat was tender with a lovely smoky flavour.

'What do you think?' Tor sipped his glass, filled with Britt's beer.

'I like it. It's a bit fatty, but I hope nobody expects me to eat that.'

'Not at all. I don't. The food is rich, but that's what the beer is for. It helps with the digestion,' Tor said.

'And this will make it even better,' Britt said, hearing the last of his sentence.

'What is that?' Holly looked at the bottle she was carrying. It didn't have a label.

'This is the water of life, my friend. Aquavit. It will grow hairs on your chest. I mean, if that's something you want, of course,' Britt said with a naughty smile.

'I'll pass, thank you,' Holly said.

'No, you have to taste. I have made this myself, and you are all my guinea pigs. If this goes well, I'll up the production and perhaps have something to sell in a few years' time.'

She filled a small shot glass with the slightly golden fluid and handed it to Holly. 'Sip it, don't down it. You might have a heart attack.'

Holly looked at Jack who seemed to enjoy his glass.

'Okay, here it goes,' Holly said, taking a sip, Then she had a coughing fit that brought tears to her eyes.

'I'm having what she's having,' Tor said, holding a glass out to Britt.

'What is that? Moonshine?' Holly said, drying her tears.

'Yes, sort of, but it's also delicious, isn't it?' Britt said with obvious pride.

'I'm not sure.' Holly lifted the glass again, and to the delight of everyone else, took another, much more careful, sip. The liqueur was smoother now, but still strong enough to bring tears to her eyes. 'At least I'm not coughing,' she said, putting down the glass.

'It grows on you for sure,' Britt said, looking pleased.

Holly turned to Tor. He handled it a lot better than her, clearly enjoying the drink. 'Good for digestion, right?'

'It is, absolutely, just don't try to blow out any of the candles,' he said.

Holly giggled. She felt light-headed and happy, and so full she wasn't sure she could stand.

Tor enjoyed the aquavit. There were some interesting flavours in there. 'Did you put orange in this too?'

Britt nodded. 'Only a hint. I didn't want it to overpower the caraway seeds.'

'It doesn't,' he assured her.

'Mamma!' Ole sat next to his mother and had clearly run out of patience.

Holly nudged Tor. 'What's going on?'

'Oh, Ole wants to know when *Julenissen* comes –Santa Clause, I mean. Poor kid. It's going to be at least another hour. Sigrid is telling him it's not all about the presents. As if that ever helps,' Tor said.

Poor Ole looked so dejected.

'Dessert time, and then dish washing,' Alma said. 'Can't have *Julenissen* come in to a dirty house, now, can we? Ole, do you want to help me with something in the kitchen while the others clear the table?'

Ole nodded. 'Okay,' he said.

Tor stood at once, ready to help with clearing everything away.

'Please, sit. There's not room for everyone in the kitchen anyway,' Ninni said. 'Holly, can you take her while we do this?'

Holly lifted Rosie across the table, making funny faces to make her laugh.

Tor looked at the little girl and she grinned back at him.

'She's awfully friendly, isn't she?'

'Oh, not all the time. Like my father often says, she has a great pair of lungs on her,' Holly said.

Rosie's bow almost fell off, and Holly straightened it. 'So, are they really expecting us to have room for dessert?'

'Yes, they do. It's a...' He laughed when Holly stopped him.

'I know, I know. It's a tradition.' Holly leaned forward and kissed him lightly. 'Is there any moonshine in this dessert?'

'I'd be surprised if there was.' Tor didn't care about dessert. Not with her so close to him. He felt as impatient as Ole.

Holly smiled. 'What?'

'What what?' Tor said.

'Nothing. You had a peculiar look on your face for a second. Are you all right?'

He leaned over and whispered in her ear what he wanted instead of dessert, making Holly laugh. Rosie laughed too, delighted to be part of the joke.

The table clearing didn't take long, and the dirty dishes were quickly replaced by delicate porcelain bowls with a Christmas pattern

Holly showed hers to Rosie. 'Look. There's a *nisse*-brownie. See?'

Rosie put her face as close to the bowl as possible. 'Pus,' she said, pointing at a tiny cat next to the *nisse*-brownie.

'You're right. That is a kitty. Good girl,' Holly said.

Rosie clapped her hands.

The rest of them came back with serving bowls of what looked like cream and small mugs filled with red sauce.

'It's cherry sauce,' Jack said, reading her mind.

'That's a relief. I love cherries.'

Jack nodded. 'I know. But there is also raspberry coulis for those who prefer that.'

Rosie pointed at one of the serving bowls and started jumping in Holly's lap. Holly looked at Jack. 'You better give her something before she implodes.'

'Chill, Rosie.' Jack put a spoonful of the dessert in a bright red plastic bowl and handed it to her.

Rosie took it with both hands and put as much of the bowl as possible in her mouth.

Holly looked at the dessert. 'What is this?'

'Rice cream. It's made of the same type of porridge we had yesterday, but mixed with whipped cream and more vanilla,' Tor said.

'You can get a nut,' Anja said, using her spoon to chop at the cream in her bowl. 'I found it last year,' she said.

'There's a blanched almond in there somewhere, and if you find it, you get a prize,' Tor said.

Holly emptied the bowl, with no sign of an almond. Tor shook his head when she looked at him. 'Me neither.'

Ole suddenly jumped up from his chair, holding the little almond in his hand. 'Mamma!' he yelled.

Sigrid took his hand and talked quietly to him. Ole sat, holding the almond as if it was a precious gift, for a moment forgetting the presents under the tree.

Jens stood and came back with a little present for him.

'Here you go, Ole. I hope you share it with your sister. She shared it with you last year, you know.'

Tor translated for Holly while Ole opened the package and held up his prize: a big marzipan pig.

'What happens if you don't like marzipan?' Holly whispered to Tor.

'I don't think anyone has ever not liked marzipan,' he said. 'It's the most Christmassy sweet there is. Norwegians eat about forty million pieces of marzipan during the season, and there's only a little over five million of us. And then there's Easter.'

Holly laughed. 'Let me guess. More marzipan?'

'Yes, except it's yellow instead of green or red,' Tor said.

They were interrupted again by Frikk barking. This time he sped out of the dining room, annoying Frøy who jumped up in the nearest chair.

Tor leaned towards Holly. 'Look at the kids,' he said.

Ole and Anja stared at each other, wide eyed and excited.

Olav went to open the door. They could hear voices, and then he came back, smiled at the kids and said something in Norwegian. The two stood from their chairs and walked over to their father.

'What's going on?' Holly asked.

Jack winked at her, and stood with Rosie on his arm.

'Ho, ho, ho,' a happy voice said.

Holly had to stop herself from laughing when the new guest came into the lounge. His face was covered by the world's most fake white beard, topped with a red Santa hat askew on his head. He was wearing large boots and overalls that looked much like the one Tor wore in his boat. A long, red coat completed the outfit. He dumped a huge burlap sack on the floor, clearly filled with presents.

'Ho, ho, ho,' he said again, followed by something else.

Ole and Anja nodded and answered him.

Tor whispered in Holly's ear. 'He says, "are there any good children in the house?" And they tell him they have been so good all year.'

'This is Santa Claus?' Holly said, not sure what to make of it.

'This is *Julenissen*. He's one of Norway's old traditions; not Viking old, but old.'

'Okay. What's going on now?'

'He's asked the kids to be his helpers while he hands out the gifts. See, he has the big bag with him.'

Holly watched as *Julenissen*, otherwise known as Jens,

took out one of the presents, read the label on it, and then handed it over to one of the kids.

Anja came running over to her. 'For you, from Alma and Jens,' she said, before running back.

Holly was delighted when she opened the package to find a bright pink bobble hat. 'This is fun. Do you have an Easter *Nissen* too?' She pulled the hat over her ears, and was granted a huge smile from the *Julenissen*.

'Nope, that's all bunnies and chickens, I believe,' Tor said.

Holly could see Jens was enjoying himself as much as the kids. Rosie was curious about him, but cautious. She was standing at a safe distance, holding on to Petters's knee. When Jens read her name on a package, she looked at Jack who nodded. 'Go on, Rosie, get your gift.'

Rosie shook her head. 'No.'

Ole took the gift and gave it to her. 'For Rosie,' he said.

Jack had to help her. He took off the ribbons and showed her how to open it.

Holly had a lump in her throat. They were so adorable. She could see Ninni thinking the same. She had sat next to her father and was taking pictures of the two.

Good, I can send Dad some of her pictures too, Holly thought.

Rosie ripped off the paper and held up a fluffy sheep, her little face beaming at Jack.

'Is that your sheep?' Tor asked.

'Yes. I think she likes it.'

Holly didn't remember all the details. It took a good hour before there were no more presents left. The lounge was filled with wrapping paper and the kids were mental with happiness.

She had a few gifts herself after a while, and so did Tor, much to his surprise.

After the excitement, everyone had to wave off *Julenissen*, although they were told they couldn't go outside. The reindeer were wary of strangers and only *Julenissen* could handle them.

Afterwards there was coffee and more cake, and everyone had to have a taste of Jack's eggnog.

By the time Holly followed Tor into his house later that night, she was exhausted. They both were, and ended up falling asleep in Tor's bed with Frøy curled up on top of the duvet.

Chapter Twenty-Six

Holly was woken up by Frøy jumping up and tapping her lightly with his paw. She looked at him. 'What are you doing?'

The cat blinked at her. Holly smooched him and laughed when he wriggled away. 'That's what happens when you wake someone up too early. Remind me never to drink aquavit and eggnog ever again in my entire life, especially not with beer.'

Her head felt as if it was a size too small. The wine bottle she and Tor had shared when they returned to the house had not been a good idea. Not at all. She looked at the nightstand and smiled. The troll figurine Tor had given her had a manic toothy smile and she loved it. The troll book, too. Although right now, she felt more like a troll herself.

'Where's your butler?'

Frøy turned his head and looked at the door just as Tor came in, carrying a tray.

'I'm right here. I have the perfect hangover cure for us,'

Tor said and put the tray on the nightstand.

She couldn't see what was on it as he had covered it with a lid or something, but it was food. She hoped he didn't expect her to actually eat anything right now.

Holly tried to sit up, but her head pounded. 'Oh, my god, I'm going to die,' she muttered.

'Move over,' he said, and sat on the bed.

The smell of hot food wasn't that awful. 'What did you do?'

He handed her a bottle of water. 'Drink this first. It's carbonated mineral water. I've already had one bottle. You need fluids.'

Holly opened the bottle and took a sip first. It was ice cold and despite the slightly salty flavour, she drank half the bottle. 'That was lovely. Thank you.'

'Try to sit up again. You need to eat something.'

'Not sure I can keep anything down. I thought aquavit meant water of life, not death,' Holly said.

'Yeah, I'm not so sure about that one myself.'

Tor arranged the pillows behind them and she sat up, grumbling as she did so. 'This better be the best hangover cure of all time,' she said.

'Oh, it is. This is the food of my people,' he said, grinning at her.

'God, no more weird Viking food. I can't handle it,' Holly said, her stomach threatening a full revolt.

'No, this is a modern invention.' He took the lid of the tray and handed her a plate. 'I apologise for the toppings. You can pick off the pineapple. The rest is cheese and bacon.'

Holly stared at the slice of pizza he had put on the plate. It looked like the ones she bought at the supermarket. 'You have pineapple on pizza?'

'Yes, I know most people hate that, but it's my favourite. It doesn't really come like that. I always add it before cooking it, and I forgot this morning.'

Holly took a huge bite and closed her eyes. 'I love Hawaiian pizza. And you put bacon on it. God, this is so good.'

He laughed. 'There's more, but you might want to be careful. We can eat the rest later.'

'I also love cold pizza,' Holly said before kissing him and stealing his pizza slice.

'Hey, not fair. I'm hungry too.' Tor reached out to take it back.

Holly tried to cram it all into her mouth, but failed because she was laughing so hard. Tor took the slice back and finished it in seconds.

'That's so rude,' she said.

'That's my name,' he said, and pulled her under the covers. 'How's your head now?'

'Slightly better. How's yours?'

'I probably have a higher tolerance for aquavit and beer and wine, also I'm bigger than you.'

Holly snuggled into him. 'I need that nap so badly.'

Tor enfolded her in his arms. The room was cold and calm, and she closed her eyes.

When they woke up a few hours later, there was a text on Holly's mobile phone.

She read it while Tor was downstairs in the bathroom.

It was short, and she didn't know if she should be happy or sad.

Tor saw the indecision on her face when she came downstairs, dressed in his sweatshirt again.

'What's wrong?'

'They want me back at the hospital in two days,' she said, leaning against the door-frame.

Tor folded his arms across his chest. 'Oh. So soon?'

'Yes, I'll have to leave sometime day after tomorrow. If I can even manage to change my flight,' she said, trying to keep her voice steady.

'That's good, isn't it?' He didn't look like he thought it was good.

Holly nodded. 'It should be, but I was just getting used to the idea of staying here until New Year's Eve. With you.'

He came over to her and held her close. 'We knew from the start this would be short. The good news is that you haven't lost your job or your career. That's what you need to focus on.'

Holly nodded, pressing her nose against his chest. 'I know, but that doesn't make it any easier.'

She leaned in and they shared a long, very hot kiss, that made her weak at the knees and left her feeling light-headed.

Holly took a deep breath that made him laugh, and somewhere, in the back of her mind, came the realisation that in a very short time, she would probably never see him again.

'Holly?'

She felt embarrassed now. 'I'm sorry. I don't want to ruin our last days. I want to remember all the lovely things.'

He smiled, a bit sadly, she thought. 'So would I, but we knew that this would end all along, didn't we? From the beginning.'

'I know and I'm sorry. I'm ruining everything.'

'Only if you stay sad.' Tor looked into her eyes. 'We don't have much time, Holly. We shouldn't darken it by giving in to sadness. Let's take it one moment at a time. Let's just enjoy each other's company for as long as we can.'

'Can we go out in your boat again?'

'Yes. Today, and tomorrow,' he said.

'Good.' Holly sighed. 'As much as I would like to stay like this, we have to go for lunch at Jack and Ninni's,' she said.

Tor stroked her back. 'I think it's a bit late for lunch.'

'Then we'll go for tea later. Jack promised me a proper Christmas.'

'Do I have to drink tea?' Tor frowned.

'No, tea means dinner. If we're lucky, Jack has made turkey.'

Tor smiled. 'I like turkey, but I have to see to the nets first.'

'Then we better leave now,' Holly said, delighted at the idea of a boat trip.

Tor kept an eye on her as he turned the boat around, to return to the house. Holly was sitting in the aft, stretching her legs out in front of her, and Frøy was sprawled out across her lap. She had a peaceful look on her face, seemingly not so bothered by her news any longer.

A trip out in the boat, will do that to you, he thought. Or mostly it was the cool air and the quiet sea.

He knew she hid her disappointment that things were coming to an end. He was doing so himself. And it was stupid. It made him feel stupid, and he didn't like that.

Nobody knew how they felt about someone after barely a week. It was illogical and unrealistic, and all the other sensible words.

And still, there was nothing he dreaded more than saying goodbye to her.

'Do I have fish blood on my face?' Holly said, interrupting his thoughts.

'Sorry?' Tor frowned.

'You're looking at me as if there's something weird about my face.'

Tor laughed. 'No, not at all. Your face is perfect.'

Holly burst out laughing. 'Nobody has a perfect face, Tor.'

'I didn't mean perfect to everyone, but to me.'

'You are a funny one,' Holly said, carefully putting Frøy down, and coming over to him.

Tor smiled when she put her arms around his waist and pressed her cheek against his back. 'I'm going to miss this,' she said.

'Is it possible to drive this boat up the Thames?' he asked.

Tor could feel her giggling.

'I wouldn't know, but the estuary might be a problem. Or not. No idea how that works, I'm afraid.'

'I'm sure it would be a lovely trip,' he said.

'There are all sorts of boats on the river, and they have to come from somewhere, right?' Holly ducked under his arm and leaned against him. 'But it's not like here, you know.'

She waved at the open sea ahead of them. 'Not at all.'

Tor could hear longing in her voice. 'You will come back to visit, you know. You have family on the island.'

'Of course.' Holly smiled at him. 'But you won't be here, will you? Your life is in Oslo.'

'I might come back. If you're here,' he said.

Holly smiled at him. 'We could have one of those long love affairs where we meet once a year, here on the island, until we're too old to travel.'

'Sounds nice to me,' Tor said.

'Yes, it does, doesn't it?' Holly drew a sharp breath. 'But it won't happen, you know. We deserve better than a week every year, don't you think?'

Tor sighed. 'I suppose so.'

She was silent for a second. 'Let's not make this into more than it is, shall we? Let's just enjoy it while it lasts. Deal?'

He kissed the top of her head. 'Deal. Now, do you want to drive the boat?'

'I can?' Holly looked at the steering wheel. 'How hard

can it be? Is there a gas pedal, or more importantly, a brake?'

'No pedal, it's more like a motorcycle with everything on the dashboard. And it's not a speed boat, so be gentle, and don't hit anything.'

'As in don't hit any icebergs?' Holly was teasing him.

'Yes, although there are no icebergs here. There are, however, underwater reefs, and loads of other obstacles. Most are marked by buoys or on the sea charts.'

'Careful it is then.' Holly grabbed the wheel and held on so hard her knuckles paled.

'Relax. It's not going to bite you,' Tor said, putting his hand over hers. 'How do you drive a car?'

'As if brakes are optional, according to my dad.'

But she did relax her grip and the boat tugged gently forward. The water was choppy, with the wind blowing across the surface. Tor could see clouds building on the horizon.

'See that?' He pointed.

Holly looked at him. 'Are you telling me to head for the edge of the world?'

'Clever,' he said. 'No, the weather is changing. There might be a storm. We need to hurry. The boat will be safer docked at my pier.'

'Really?' Holly frowned. 'I can barely see any clouds.'

'Oh, they're coming. Better get Frøy inside too. I don't want him to get blown away.'

'Okay. You better take the wheel, then. I don't want to hit anything because I'm in a rush.'

He took over the wheel and increased the speed.

Chapter Twenty-Seven

By the time they had secured the boat, put an insulted Frøy in the house, and headed for Ninni and Jack's house, the wind was increasing. Tor held her arm and they ran most of the way, the wind pushing them sideways.

Inside the house it was warm and cosy, and so filled with Christmas lights it was dazzling.

'Are there any lights left in the entire country?' Holly said, peeling off her outerwear.

'Some,' Ninni said, greeting them in the hallway.

She put down Rosie who threw herself at Holly, who barely had time to catch her. 'What are you doing, you little maniac?'

Rosie pointed at Tor. 'Pus!'

'Of course he is,' Ninni said.

Rosie insisted. 'Fløy?'

Tor smiled. 'Frøy had to stay home today.'

Holly picked up Rosie and rubbed her nose on her chin. The little girl giggled. 'Holly silly,' she said.

'Yes, that's the privilege of aunties. We are supposed to be silly.'

'Thank you for inviting me, Ninni. It smells incredible in here,' Tor said.

Ninni smiled at Tor. 'It does, doesn't it? I've been banned from the kitchen for the last few hours. As if the turkey would explode if I looked at it.'

'Yeah, I know,' Holly said. 'It's the whole "artist at work" attitude.'

Jack put his head out from the kitchen door. 'Don't mock the artist. Dinner is ready, actually. You have impeccable timing, Tor,' he said.

'What about my timing? Isn't that impeccable?' Holly looked offended.

'Not so much. I have learned that Norwegians are freakishly punctual,' Jack said.

Holly followed him into the kitchen, and sat Rosie down in the highchair. 'I'm punctual. They'd fire me from the hospital for sure if I wasn't.'

'True.' Jack smiled. 'Okay, you're a freak too.'

'Oh, you think you're so funny, don't you?'

Jack narrowed his eyes. 'Did you hear from the hospital?'

Holly gaped at him. 'How do you always know stuff like that?'

'I'm you brother, and I know when something's bothering you. What did they say? Did you get bad news?' He sighed. 'Why would they give you bad news on Christmas Day? That's just rubbish.'

'No, I was asked to come back to the hospital by the 28th,'

actually. All is forgiven, and I get to keep my place in the program,' Holly said, not looking at him.

'But Holly, that's great news, isn't it?'

'Yes, of course it is. It's the best outcome I could hope for. Even if I suspect I only heard back now because they're under-staffed for the New Year's weekend.'

'Don't do that. You know they wouldn't take you back unless you were completely in the clear.'

'I know that,' Holly said, scowling at him.

Ninni sat next to Rosie and smiled at Tor. 'So, do you have any siblings?'

'No, I don't. Neither do you, I'm guessing.' He grinned at her in mutual understanding.

'I used to miss having a sibling, thought that it was bad to be the only one. Apparently it's not,' Ninni said.

Jack put a plate of mashed potatoes on the table and smiled at Ninni. 'The bantering will keep us from getting dementia in our later years. It's all good, I promise.'

'Did you cook Brussels sprouts?' Holly looked at Tor.

'Yes. I also made mash and the stuffing you like. And toast, just for you,' Jack said, bringing Brussels sprouts and cranberry sauce to the table.

'Good. I'm so ready for some proper Christmas food,' Holly said, pulling a face at Tor.

'Do you need any help?' Tor ignored her face pulling. 'Setting the table, bringing in more firewood? Taking out the trash?'

Ninni grinned. 'You're sweet. But no, we've done all that. All you have to do is eat, and warn me if Jack has put something weird in the turkey. Like Marmite.'

'Hey, Marmite is lovely, especially on toast,' Holly said, shaking with laughter.

'No, it's vile,' Ninni said, stopping Rosie from putting her hand in the mashed potatoes.

Tor shrugged. 'I like it,' he said.

Holly looked at Ninni. 'See, he likes it.'

Ninni turned to Tor. 'Marmite? Really?'

'I got a taste for it when I lived in Scotland for a year,' he said. 'Along with Scotch eggs and whisky.'

'You spent your time wisely then,' Jack said, returning to the table with a gigantic turkey. 'You have good taste.'

'You won't think that when you learn he likes pineapple on his pizza,' Holly said.

'Oh. I take it back then. Pineapple on pizza should be made illegal.'

'I'm a rebel,' Holly said.

'Pus!' Rosie said, pointing at the bird.

'No, that's turkey and you love it,' Ninni said.

Jack carved the bird and sat. 'Enjoy. Christmas supper is officially open.'

Ninni looked at Holly. 'How did you like Christmas Eve?'

'Oh, I enjoyed it. Not so much the aquavit though. I had a massive hangover that didn't really go away until we got in the boat,' Holly said, filling up her plate with turkey and all the trimmings.

'Fresh air cures everything, or so I've been told,' Jack said, handing Rosie a piece of turkey.

'I wish,' Holly said. 'But also I don't because it would make my job obsolete.'

It didn't take long before Rosie was happily smashing her spoon in the mash and Frikk had found a place on the floor next to her, safe in the knowledge that food would fall down sooner or later.

Holly tried the cranberry sauce and frowned. 'There's something different.'

'That's because that's lingonberry sauce. It's next to impossible to get cranberries here,' Jack said. 'It's almost the same.'

'It's not the same, but it's good,' Holly said, laughing when he stuck out his tongue.

Rosie did the same, making everyone laugh.

The wind was howling outside by the time dinner was over and the last of the dishes put away.

Ninni looked out of the kitchen window. 'I think you better take dessert to Tor's house, Holly. Unless you both would like to stay here tonight?'

Holly stood and walked over to the window. She could see the few trees in the garden bending almost to the ground.

'I think we should go back. Because of Frøy, you know.'

She looked at Tor who nodded.

'Sure. He doesn't really like being left alone for too long. And he gets really cranky if I'm not there to give him breakfast in the morning,' Tor said.

Holly managed to stay serious when she looked at him. There was no way she would spend one of the two nights she had left on the island in Jack and Ninni's spare room. 'Tor is Frøy's butler,' she said.

'Aha,' Jack said. 'Right. That explains it then. You'd better hurry.'

He exchanged looks with Ninni, revealing that they hadn't fooled anyone. Holly couldn't care less.

When they were dressed for the outdoors again and standing in the hallway, Jack handed each of them a bag. 'One with food, the other with your presents from Dad and Danny.'

'Thank you,' Holly said, knowing full well what he meant. 'I'll call them so they also know I'm coming home.'

'Good, and tomorrow you both come back here for dinner.' Jack shook his head. 'No arguments.'

'Fine. We'll be here.' Holly rolled her eyes, then gave him a hug. 'Can you make a turkey pie? You know, like you always do at Christmas? Please?'

'Yes, I'm quite capable of making a pie,' Jack said, grinning at her.

'You're hilarious,' Holly said.

Tor gave Ninni a quick hug, and said a few words in Norwegian, then shook Jack's hand. 'Thank you for dinner. I've never eaten turkey that wasn't dry.'

'Then I guess you were due a change,' Jack said.

Rosie held on to Frikk's collar. She pointed at the door. 'Out?'

'No, you two are staying right here. You'd be a tumbleweed in that wind,' Jack said, picking up Rosie and planting a kiss on her cheek.

'We're going. I'll let you know when we get to the house,' Tor said.

Jack handed Rosie to Ninni. 'I'll hold the door,' he said.

Ninni took Rosie and Frikk, and disappeared into the house, closing the middle door behind her.

Jack grinned. 'Ready?'

'Let's go for it,' Tor said, taking Holly's arm in a firm grip.

The wind hit them in the face the moment they stepped outside.

Holly laughed, then stumbled and then was really happy Tor was holding on to her.

Behind them, Jack closed the door in a hurry.

Tor looked at her. 'You okay? We can change our minds, you know.'

Holly leaned into him. 'No, we can't. This isn't too bad, is it?'

A gust of wind almost toppled them over, and gave Holly the giggles. Tor held her tight. 'We have the wind at our back. That's good. It makes it easier to walk.'

'I'll take your word for it.'

They managed to get up to the fork in the road and onto the pathway to Tor's house easily enough but the pathway was slippery and hard to manoeuvre. Holly almost fell twice, but Tor held on. *I'll probably have bruises in the morning*, she thought, but she was grateful he didn't let go.

Tor opened the door, and dropped the bags on the floor. Then he closed it again.

Holly looked at him. 'What are you doing?'

'I want to show you something. You okay with that?'

'As long as you're not taking me out in the boat or suggesting that we go for a swim.'

He held her hand. 'You don't want to miss this.'

Holly let him pull her up the small slope to the side of his house, and then on top of a big boulder.

'Are you sure this is safe?' The wind felt as if it was pushing her down.

'I wouldn't drag you up here if it wasn't. Just hold on to me,' Tor said.

He put his hand around her waist and pulled her up the last step, then enveloped her in his arms and kissed her.

'Nice. Did you bring me up here for this? I like it,' Holly said.

'Not just that. Look...' Tor turned them towards the sea.

Holly gasped. She could see waves crashing over each other, everything in shades of grey and white, and absolutely magnificent. 'Oh, my,' she said.

'Isn't it spectacular?' Tor smiled at her. 'It's one of the many reasons I like it here.'

Holly leaned against him, watching the weather rage. 'It's fantastic.'

They stood like that for a few minutes, swaying with the wind. Then the rain hit with a vengeance.

'Time to go,' Tor said.

He managed to get them back down and into the house quickly. Holly could hear the rain hammering on the roof and against the windows.

Her fingers were cold and stiff, and she struggled with the zipper on her coat.

Tor had an easier time with his, and he came closer to help.

'You're shaking,' he said.

'I'm cold.' Holly let him pull of the coat and help her with the overalls.

'I'm so sorry. I shouldn't have dragged you up there,' he said, rubbing her shoulders and arms.

'No, I'm happy you did. Aren't you cold?' Holly kissed him quickly.

'Not really. '

Holly laughed. 'Because you're hot?'

Tor took her hand and pulled her into the lounge. It was warm and cosy, the perfect place to warm up.

Chapter Twenty-Eight

By the time Tor turned the boat toward the beach below Jack's farm, it was dark again. Holly didn't want time to move. Not now, not like this. They only had one night left. She tried to tell herself, they only had to eat with Jack and Ninni, and then head back to the boat.

She was sitting at the aft, petting Frøy who somehow seemed to understand how she felt. He kept putting his nose to her face and even ignored the two buckets of crab standing next to Holly's feet.

'Holly? You need to see this,' Tor said over his shoulder.

She stood and came over to him. Frøy followed close by.

'Oh,' Holly said.

On the beach there were torches along the water's edge, and what looked like two huge fire pits about a hundred metres from the small boathouses. She could see people already there, kids running around with lights in their hands, and somewhere, someone was playing a flute.

'This must be why Jack wanted us to use the boat,' Tor said, laughing. 'He wanted you to see it from the sea.'

'It's beautiful. Do they always do this?' Holly looked at him.

'I have no idea,' he said, smiling at her. 'It's in your honour, isn't it?'

Holly couldn't help laughing at him. 'You are so funny,' she said.

'I'm really not. I couldn't tell a joke if my life depended on it,' he said.

'Believe me, you're funny. Even if it is by accident.'

Holly admired the lights. It gave the beach a magical atmosphere and she loved it.

'Look, there's Jack at the fire pits. I can't believe he's cooking outside.' Holly was delighted, but then she remembered something. 'What happens if it starts raining or snowing or another storm hits?'

Tor looked up. 'I think it will be nice tonight,' he said.

Holly wasn't convinced. 'It's bloody cold, and please don't tell me the not-rhyming poem about clothes again.'

'It's December, so of course it's cold, but the sky is clear, there's not even a hint of snow, and look, you can see the stars.' Tor sounded almost giddy.

'Are you okay?' Holly was concerned.

Tor frowned. 'Uhm, yes,' he said, sounding a bit unsure.

'I'm sorry, it's just that you sounded so different there for a moment. Almost happy,' she said.

Tor smiled. 'Since you ask, I am happy.'

'Even if I'm leaving tomorrow?'

'Yes, I have decided to live in the moment and not ruin this night. All your fault, by the way.'

Holly put her hands around his waist. 'Damn right it's my fault.'

He chuckled and bent down to kiss her, quickly, since they were almost by the boathouses now.

As soon as Tor had moored the boat, he jumped down on the little wooden pier and held his hand out for her.

Holly grabbed hold and let him pull her up, putting a foot on the gunwale and shrieking when she slipped. For one horrible moment she thought she would fall into the water.

Tor didn't let go of her hand and she soon found her footing. He pulled her up to stand next to him.

'Bloody hell,' Holly muttered.

'Almost everything in Norway is slippery in the winter,' he said. 'You want to watch your step.'

Holly looked down at her feet. 'Then how can I enjoy the stars?'

'Well, if you fall on your bum, you can look up, but then your back will be aching,' he said and made her laugh.

Holly waited while Tor picked up the buckets with crabs. 'I hope someone has brought bread and butter,' he said.

'Knowing my brother, I think they have everything and then some. Need any help with those?'

'No, they're not heavy,' Tor said. 'And even if they were,

347

I can't trust you to carry one. You might fall on your face, crushing the crabs.'

'Cheeky,' Holly said, secretly happy she didn't have to help. 'Jack is down by the fire pit. I'm sure he'll be thrilled to see those.'

'I'm keen to see what he will do with them, to be honest. He said he had an idea.'

'He loves everything he can eat,' Holly said, making Tor laugh.

A little figure came running up from the fire pit, clearly heading for them. Behind her Jack tried to make a grab for her, but Rosie was too quick.

'Fløy!' she shrieked when she discovered Frøy who had jumped from the pier down on the beach.

She lunged for him, and toppled both him and herself over. The cat jumped away and landed on all fours, but Rosie fell forward and began screaming.

Jack ran, but Ninni was quicker. She scooped Rosie up and hugged her.

The little girl stopped screaming when she realised her mother was holding her. She pointed. 'Pus!'

'Yes, sweetie, I know Frøy is a pussycat, but that's not the way to say hi to him,' Ninni said.

Frøy seemed unfazed. He sat and looked up at Rosie and Ninni.

Ninni sat as well, still holding Rosie. 'Be gentle, remember.'

Rosie stretched out a chubby hand and Frøy sniffed it gently. He also allowed the little girl to pet him on the head a few times. Then he walked away, following Tor and the crab buckets.

'Weird cat,' Ninni said.

Rosie looked at her mother. 'Fløy,' she said.

'Right. You want to go with Auntie Holly so I can help Alma with the food?'

'Kay.' Rosie held out her arms and Holly picked her up, putting her on her hip.

'Let's go see if there's anything yummy, shall we?' Holly said.

The other islanders stood around the fire talking and laughing, and greeted her with hugs and more laughs. Rosie had a great time, clearly thinking it was for her benefit.

Rosie seemed unfazed by the cold weather, but Holly made sure her bobble hat was safely on. 'Are you cold, lovely?'

'Oh, oh, oh,' Rosie said, waving her hand.

Holly turned around and discovered that someone had lit up a Christmas tree. 'Oh, that's so lovely. Look Rosie. There must be hundreds of lights on it.'

'See!' Rosie pointed at the tree, her eyes filled with awe.

'Yes, it's pretty, isn't it?' Holly took Rosie closer and discovered that Frøy found the tree equally fascinating.

'Frøy, don't climb the tree, please,' she said.

The cat ignored her and started cleaning his paw.

'He better not pull it down,' Britt said behind her.

Rosie started jumping when she saw her, waving her hand, and Holly had to hold her tighter.

'Hello, little weirdo.' Britt planted a kiss on the baby's cheek and made Rosie giggle.

'Frøy is far too well behaved to climb Christmas trees,' Tor said behind them. He smiled at Britt. 'Hi, nice to see you again.'

'Right back at you, Tor. I hear you're leaving tomorrow, Holly.' Britt turned to Holly. 'I'm so sorry. I hope you'll be back soon.'

'I'll certainly try,' Holly said. 'I never had a chance to see your brewery.'

Britt looked at Tor. 'Well, you were busy. We'll do that next time, then.'

'Food is ready,' Jack hollered.

'Yes, that's what I came to say.' Tor tickled Rosie under her chin.

Tobben appeared next to Britt and handed her a beer. 'It's what you wanted?'

Britt nodded. 'Thank you. Did you bring one for Holly too? And Tor?'

'Ehm, no. I'll go get it for you. Not for the little person, though. She's not old enough,' he said, bopping Rosie on her nose.

Holly looked at Britt. 'Did he just make a joke?'

'Apparently so. He can surprise you sometimes. Come on, I'm starving and I think Jack has made a feast.'

Tor put his arm around Holly's waist. 'I think your brother cooks like a mad scientist.'

Holly grinned. 'He gets that mad look in his face, doesn't he?'

Rosie talked and pointed, clearly enchanted with

everything. When they came down to the fire pits, Holly put her down, but held on to the hood of her winter suit.

Frikk showed up and licked Rosie in the face, making her push him away. '*Nei*, Flikk,' she said.

'Where's Frøy?' Holly looked for the cat.

Tor pointed to a folding chair close to the fire. 'There. He's watching the food. He looks like he thinks he's the king,' he said.

'Yeah, but he is, you know.'

She laughed and pulled Tor closer. The smell coming from the huge pan hanging over the fire made her hungry and Jack was busy filling plates and handing them out to people. His face lit up when he saw them.

'The guest of honour. I have something amazing here for you, Holly. Grab a plate.'

Someone handed her a plate and Holly took it. 'What is it?'

'Not sure you should know yet,' Jack said, taking the plate from her. 'This is just the appetizer.'

When he handed the plate back to her, there was one crab on it, turned on its back and lacking the claws. It was filled with... stuff, and had melted, grated cheese on top. Holly frowned. 'What's in it?'

'Crab meat. It's one of Tor's crabs. They are so delicious,' Jack said, handing Rosie a small plate with only crab meat.

She slunk down on the ground and gave one mouthful to Frikk, who patiently stood beside her, and then took one mouthful for herself.

'Why can't I get what Rosie gets?' Holly said, still not sure about the crab she was holding.

'Because you're not a baby?' Jack said, handing out crabs to other people.

'It smells unbelievable,' Tor said, waiting patiently while Jack handed him one of the crabs.

Holly used the fork he gave her to lift the cheese lid, and sniff. It smelled good, Tor was right about that.

'For God's sake, will you taste it?' Jack frowned.

'Don't rush me. Why won't you tell me what's in it?'

'Because you're picky. All right then. There's crab meat mixed with a splash of lemon, some wild garlic, double cream, and then parmesan on top.'

Holly scooped some of it into her mouth, pulling a face that made Jack laugh. 'You're a hopeless case. Tor, what do you think?'

'I can't believe you managed to improve on the crab,' Tor said, making sure the crab shell was cleaned out. 'Is this the kind of food you'll serve in the restaurant?'

'Yes and loads more. Scallops are good here, and there's all sorts of fish, and you should really taste the sea urchins,' he said.

Holly wrinkled her nose. 'No, thank you. Where's my pie? You promised me my Christmas turkey pie.'

Tor looked intrigued. 'Pie is good,' he said.

'Here.' Jack took a foil wrapped package and exchanged it for her plate. 'Share it with Tor, please.'

Holly looked at Tor. 'We'll see,' she said, holding the pie out of his reach.

She opened the package and almost burned her nose sniffing at it. 'Heavenly. I'll be over there, enjoying it.'

Someone had put down thick mats on the ground, and

Holly plonked down on one of them, close to Jens and Alma. She could see Britt was talking to Olav a bit closer to the water.

Tor found her quickly and sat beside her, stretching his long legs out in front of him. 'Mad,' he said, showing her his plate. 'Look at this. How does he manage to cook like this over an open fire like that?'

'No idea,' Holly said, inspecting her pie. It was filled with things she liked, with left-over mash and left-over turkey, creamy sauce and leeks, all covered with a buttery crust. 'You want to taste this, Tor? Jack always makes this for us every Christmas.'

She broke off piece and handed it to him. Tor took a large bite. 'It's good, right?'

'Delicious. I've never had anything like it.' Tor looked at the plate he had. 'I'm not sure what this is, but it smells delicious.'

He tasted it and a slow grin appeared on his face. 'There's chanterelles in this and meat, I actually think he's used left-over *pinnekjøtt* from Christmas Eve.'

Holly looked at the stew and shook her head when he offered the plate to her. 'I want to enjoy my pie.' She looked around. 'It's so beautiful here. Cold, but very beautiful.'

Jens must have heard her, because he handed her a thick, woollen blanket. 'We have more if you need it,' he said.

Holly pulled it over her lap, and made sure Tor was covered too. 'This is better,' she said.

On the beach, the music played up again, this time with

a flute and violin. It was light and slow. 'What are they playing?'

Tor listened, then smiled. 'Christmas songs. You probably won't know the words but it's nice though, isn't it?'

She nodded. 'Yes, very much. A bit sad, maybe.'

'I think that's the violin's fault,' he said, smiling at her. 'Are you still cold?'

'No, I'm fine.' Holly lowered her voice. 'I was just wondering how long it's going to last.'

'Until everyone gets too cold, I'm guessing,' he said.

Holly leaned her head against his shoulder. It felt so good sitting like this, not worrying about anything.

The music changed its tune, and she could see Ninni dancing with Rosie on her arm. Jack came over to them and kissed her, getting a pat from Rosie on his face.

'He's settled in here so well,' she said. 'As if he's been here all the time.'

Tor put down his plate and took her hand. 'He's happy,' he said. 'They both are.'

'They're lucky,' Holly said, feeling a bit sad.

'I know,' Tor said.

The music changed again, and Tor stood, pulling her up with him. 'Come.'

Holly followed, still holding his hand. She soon discovered who the musicians were. Sigrid and Olav played together, their children dancing in front of them, Ole with a hotdog in his hand.

Tor looked her. 'Would you care to dance?' he said, trying to sound posh.

Holly laughed and curtsied for him. 'Thank you, my lord.'

He pulled her gently towards him and they swayed to the music. When the tune changed, the dancing changed. Tor twirled her around, grabbing her just before she almost slipped on one of the rocks on the beach.

She caught a glimpse of Britt and Tobben, dancing tightly together. They looked like they were having fun.

Holly held on to Tor. 'Don't let me fall,' she said.

'I won't,' he said in her ear.

At some point, Ninni came over to say goodnight.

'It's Rosie's bedtime, I'm afraid. Jack's staying a bit longer though, to make sure the fire is out.'

Holly gave Rosie a kiss, but she was half asleep on Ninni's shoulder.

'Did you have fun?' Ninni asked. 'I hope you'll come back soon. Next time I promise we'll be here the whole time.'

'I'll hold you to that. I've had a wonderful time. It's such a special place,' Holly said.

Ninni smiled at Tor. 'I hope we see more of you, too.'

Tor nodded. 'I'll be here for a while longer,' he said.

The house was rented until well into January, but he didn't say that. It would be strange without Holly now. He probably couldn't go back to being a hermit again.

When Ninni left, it seemed to be the end of the party. The other families went home right after, all of them making sure they said goodbye and wished her a safe journey home.

Jens and Alma hugged Holly, then him, before leaving.

'I think it's cold now,' Holly said.

'We better see if Jack need any help with the firepits,' Tor said.

Jack, it turned out, had everything under control.

'You going back?' he asked.

Tor nodded. 'Yes. We have to get up early tomorrow, as you know.'

Jack smiled. 'It's a surprisingly long trip to London from here. Come for dinner before you leave, too, Tor. The door is always open, you know.'

'Thank you. I appreciate that.'

He stepped back and let Holly say goodbye. She would be up early the next morning to catch her flight to Oslo, so this was the last time she would see her brother before she left.

'Do you want me to let Danny and Dad know you're coming?' Jack said.

'No, I'll call them from the airport in Oslo. I'm flying into London so late anyway, I'm just going straight home from the airport. I'll see them over New Year's,' Holly said.

Jack hugged her and made her laugh when he swung her around.

'I'm sorry we didn't get much time together while you were here,' she said.

'You were busy,' he said, grinning at Tor.

'And you weren't here when I arrived.' Holly kissed him on the cheek.

Tor looked at the fire pit. He could still see embers in the ashes. 'Do you have to stay here long?'

'Nah, I'm just about to pour seawater over it and pack my stuff,' Jack said. 'Most of it I'll leave here, like the pan and the table, and come back for it tomorrow.'

Holly took Tor's hand. 'He'll be fine, I swear.'

'She's right. I'll be fine. I love this,' Jack said, smiling at them.

Tor helped Holly on board the boat and discovered Frøy was taking a nap on the cushions in the aft. 'Clever you,' he said.

Jack was almost a shadow on the beach as the torches were out now as well.

Holly shook her head. 'Look at him. We'll never get him back to London again.'

'Did you think you could?' Tor started the boat, turned on the lanterns, and they headed for the pier by his house.

'I haven't really thought about it. I guess I just assumed he would at some point.'

Holly turned to Tor. 'But he's here to stay now. I wish I could stay longer, too. With you.'

Tor pulled her closer to him. 'I wish the same.'

The hours went too fast, Holly thought when they walked through the glass doors at the little airport. Neither had slept much, and it was still dark outside when they headed out from Tor's house.

Tor pulled her suitcase for her, all the way from the

marina where he'd docked his boat not too far from the airport. The boat had brought them there faster than the ferry and the airport bus would have.

Inside there were a few travellers waiting for security to open so they could go into the coffee shop.

Holly looked at the board. It was close now.

Tor handed her the suitcase and smiled. 'You'd better check in.'

Holly took a deep breath. 'I really don't want to go,' she said.

'I don't want you to go either, but this was always going to happen. There's not much to be done about it. I'm happy everything was sorted out for you.'

Holly put her hand on his cheek. 'Will you grow a beard again?'

'I might. To keep myself occupied, you know.'

'I'll miss you,' Holly said, trying to regain control of her voice.

Tor put his hand over hers. 'I'll miss you.'

'Kiss Frøy for me, will you?'

Tor kissed her first. 'I will,' he whispered against her mouth.

'And... and let's not stay in touch. It will be too painful, and after a while it will only turn awkward. I would hate that.'

Tor nodded. 'I agree.'

The metallic voice over the speaker rattled them.

Holly took a deep breath. 'This is a holiday I won't be able to forget,' she said, forcing a smile.

'I don't want to forget it,' Tor said.

His eyes were so serious, and Holly had to force herself to let him go. All the way through security, she could see him whenever she turned her head. He didn't wave. He just stood there.

Holly almost turned back, but forced herself to go on.

On the other side of security, she turned to catch one last glimpse.

He smiled and lifted his hand.

Holly waved back, and then he was gone.

An hour later, Holly was in her seat on the plane. The plane was half-full, so she had been able to move to the window seat.

There was no snow or rain; the skies were clear. When the plane lifted off, she could see a boat bopping in the water just beneath the wing.

It was just a glimpse, but she imagined she could see Tor looking up to see her off.

Holly pressed her eyes together. It wouldn't do to bawl her eyes out here. She had to keep it together.

Chapter Twenty-Nine

L ondon felt strange. Holly went through security at Gatwick and wound her way through the masses of passengers on their way to the trains. She wasn't sure what to feel. It had all happened so fast.

One minute she had been with Tor, and now she wasn't.

She pulled her suitcase behind her, and walked over to the other side of Victoria station. Her train would come in at any minute.

All the familiar signs of Christmas were still there. The coffee shop still sold Christmas biscuits and spiced lattes, WHSmith had tinsel over their counters and somewhere, someone was singing 'Jingle Bells' out of tune.

She took a deep breath and got on her train. It was only a ten minute ride, but it felt endless. All she wanted was to crawl under her own duvet in her own bed, and forget about everything.

Tomorrow I'm back at the hospital, and this whole holiday thing will soon be nothing more than a nice memory.

Finally the train pulled into Beckenham Station and she could get out. She dragged the suitcase across the parking area, and along the little park.

It was raining, but it wasn't cold, not like on the island.

From outside, she looked up and noticed that the lights were on in the apartment.

She hoped Jocelyn was alone. Their friends were nice and great company, but Jocelyn was the only one who had known her for so long that they were practically sisters.

The elevator wasn't working again, and so she had to drag the suitcase up three sets of stairs. In the hallway, almost every door had some kind of Christmas decoration, and the one on their apartment made her smile.

Darth Vader in a Santa hat.

'Perfect, Jocelyn,' she said, and unlocked the door.

The first thing she saw inside was Jocelyn sitting on the settee with a cup of tea in her hand. When she discovered Holly, she hastily put down the cup and jumped up.

'You're here!'

She threw her arms around her, and Holly burst into tears.

The dark skies gathering at the horizon promised rain and probably another storm. Tor sat on the deck of his boat, drinking coffee, and wondered if he would have time enough to return to the house before it hit him. Still, he didn't move.

Frøy jumped down from the bow and trotted over to him.

Tor rubbed his head. 'What do you think? We could always try to reach Shetland. They probably won't let us into the country, you being a cat and me without my passport, but we're halfway there.'

The cat looked unimpressed. He sniffed Tor's cup, then turned around and looked at the empty buckets.

'Sorry, mate. No fish in the net today. No crabs either and I think the bait is off. For you, anyway. If you were a lobster it would be okay, but you're not.'

Frøy jumped up on the bench next to him and leaned against him. Tor looked at him, a bit surprised. 'You're being weird. Why are you so cuddly all of a sudden?'

The cat put a paw on his arm and Tor stroked the silky fur on his head. 'You're a strange cat, Frøy. Really strange.'

He looked at the stormy clouds again; they were getting closer by the minute.

'Time to make a decision, Frøy. Here it comes,' he said. 'We will ride out the storm, and then go home to Oslo before New Year's. I don't want to sit here, moping with my cat and have the islanders be nice to me because they feel sorry for me,' he said.

He thought about Holly. How was she doing? They had agreed not to be in contact and though it had seemed sensible yesterday, he ached for her now, and that made him feel like an idiot.

There was no such thing as love at first sight, was there? He looked at Frøy who was busy cleaning his head. 'What do you know, you're a cat, and if you weren't spayed, you'd be making baby fluffs all over the island.'

He stood and walked over to the helm, pressed the engine button and steered towards land. Oslo would be good. Oslo would be a return to normality. His island holiday was over.

Chapter Thirty

O utside the windows in the hospital they could see fireworks already starting to colour the sky. *It isn't midnight yet, for God's sake,* she thought. People were such idiots.

Holly looked on as another rocket exploded and coloured the sky green. The hospital canteen was filled with people, some having their first break in hours and eating as if they had starved for weeks.

'I hate those,' she said when Jocelyn brought a tray over with hot food that smelled acceptable. 'We all know the damage that fireworks do, and I wish they would stop selling them.'

'Yeah, we all do. They've brought in two idiots already. One had his fingers scorched and another barely missed his eye. It's barely nine in the evening, for God's sake.'

Holly nodded, taking the plate of korma from her. 'Thank you. There's going to be more of them before our shift is over.'

'God, I wish I had stayed home,' Jocelyn said.

She broke a poppadom in half and handed it to Holly. 'They didn't have any more left.'

'You volunteered, remember? I'm here as part of my punishment,' Holly said, smiling at her.

The food was bland, but hot, and sometimes that was enough. Holly knew it could be hours until they had a chance to eat again.

'I'm here to keep an eye on you,' Jocelyn said, shovelling rice into her mouth. 'I don't want you moping around as we enter the new year.'

'There's no time for moping, you know that.' Holly lifted her spoon. 'This is about the only break we'll get until tomorrow morning.'

'I bought plenty of chocolate and a few bags of crisp too,' Jocelyn said, patting her bag. 'We'll be fine.'

'Thank you, Joc. I've been a mess since I came back, and you've been a rock. I'm sorry for ruining your New Year's Eve.'

Jocelyn chuckled. 'Yes, I'll remind you of that next year when I need a day off.'

'Any time.' Holly finished the last of the korma and snapped up the brownie before Jocelyn could.

'That's mean,' Jocelyn said. 'Also, that was the last one they had.'

Holly broke it in two and handed half to her, then changed her mind. 'Here, take both. You deserve it.'

'Yes, I do.' Jocelyn ate the brownie, laughing as Holly tried to grab it back.

The loudspeaker interrupted the fun.

Doctor Greene, please come to the reception.

Jocelyn looked at her. 'Now what did you do?'

'Nothing. I just got here, remember?'

The loudspeaker croaked again and Holly stood. Jocelyn did the same.

'You don't have to come with me, you know.'

Jocelyn grinned. 'I'm your designated protector. I have to see what's going on.'

They raced each other through the corridors, almost running, but not quite, since running was strictly forbidden.

When they went through the doors to the reception, they were out of breath and laughing at the same time.

Holly walked over to the desk to ask for the message, but stopped midway there. A man turned around and suddenly she couldn't move her feet.

'Oh, my god, is that your Viking?' Jocelyn said, still half out of breath.

'He's not mine,' Holly said, staring at Tor.

But he's here. She walked over to him. 'Tor, what are you doing here? And how did you find me?'

'Jack told me. I had to convince him to do so, but he did. He didn't tell you?'

'No, he didn't.' Holly looked at him. She couldn't believe he was for real. 'You didn't drive your boat here, did you?'

'No, that would be crazier even than this. I took a plane from Oslo.' Tor took a step closer. 'If you want me to, I can leave. I know we agreed on no contact, but I missed you.'

Holly blinked. 'I've missed you, too,' she blurted.

Tor smiled, relieved. 'Thank goodness. I'd feel incredibly stupid and intrusive if you hadn't.'

'How long are you here for?' Holly didn't dare touch him just yet.

He shrugged. 'I have to earn enough money to pay for the plane ticket back and that might take a while. Do you have any idea how insanely expensive it is to fly from Oslo to London on New Year's Eve? I might have to sell my boat. Or Frøy.'

She knew he was joking. 'Don't, please. It wouldn't be the same without either of them.'

Tor put his hands around her face and looked her in the eyes. 'The day after you left, I was sitting in my boat, with Frøy, and I realised I'm in love with you. I think we should see where this leads. No strings, no pressure, and if it doesn't work out between us, it doesn't. I have a place to stay, so there's no hassle about that. What do you think?'

'Shut up and kiss me, you idiot,' she said.

Holly didn't hear Jocelyn whooping behind them, or see the receptionist making googly eyes at them or even more fireworks filling the dark sky.

He was here, kissing her, holding her, and that was enough for now.

Acknowledgments

Thank you to my brilliant and lovely editor, Charlotte Ledger, and the whole One More Chapter team, who have had to deal with my crazy deadlines with a lot more patience than I probably deserve.

Thanks again to Sue Davison, who proofreads and encourages in equal measures. I wouldn't manage without her.

Thank you also to the amazing Romance Novelist Association, who managed to go digital when we all had to go into lockdown. You are an inspiration.

And even more thanks to my Cariad Chapter friends who help and encourage and make me laugh. You are the best.

Finally, thank you to my lovely Aunt Berit, who still reads everything I write – and likes it.

Author's Note

Dear reader,

Christmas Island is set in winter, when Norway is dark and cold most of the time. But winter isn't Noir as in dark and depressing, it's also filled with light and fun, warmth and love. Nordic Romance is still romantic even in the middle of winter, and I hope my book has shown that to you.

Happy Holidays

God jul

Recipe: Aunt Berit's Christmas Cake

This is a family recipe my aunt got from her cousins in America – hence the cups. Aunt Berit makes this every Christmas, and if I happen to come home for a visit in December, I always leave with two of these in my luggage. It wouldn't be Christmas without it.

What to put in the cake:
('ts' means teaspoon here)

> 1/2 cup of melted butter – let it cool before adding it
> to the eggs
> 1 cup of sugar
> 1 egg – separate egg yolk and whites
> The egg whites need to be whisked stiff and added in
> at the end
> 1 cup of kefir milk – or buttermilk/thin yoghurt or
> something else fermented (not cabbage)
> 2 cups of all-purpose flour

1 cup of raisins
1 ts of baking soda
1 ts of grounded cinnamon
1/2 ts of grounded clove
1/2 ts of grounded nutmeg

How to do it:

1. Mix the dry ingredients together – sieve into a mixing bowl, and add raisins. Then mix the egg yolk, the milk and melted butter in another bowl.
2. Pour half of the wet ingredients into the mixing bowl with the flour. Stir gently, then pour in the rest.
3. Finally, whisk the egg-white until it's stiff, and then fold it gently into the mixture. It's a sticky dough, so don't put in more flour.
4. Grease two bread tins (1–1.5 ltr) well, or line them with baking paper, pour the mixture in and put it into a cold oven at 200' Celsius for about 30 minutes. It might take longer, or not. It's done when you poke it with a fork or a knitting needle and it comes out dry.
5. Let it cool on a rack.

Recipe: Delfia Cake

This is a staple cake for Christmas with us. The name is derived from the brand of coconut oil everyone uses. The recipe is also printed on the package.

When I tried to find out about substitutes for coconut oil for those who don't live in Norway, the translation gave me *hydrogenerated coconut oil*, which sounds a fright. It means the coconut should not be liquid.

It's also possible to use butter, but I have no idea how that would turn out. Pretty good, I guess.

I discovered that in Australia *Copha* is used for *White Christmas Cake* – which sounds delicious by the way.

Crisco is also named as a substitute, but that's not made from coconut oil, so I have no idea how it would taste.

What to put in the cake:

12,3 oz. / 375 g cooking chocolate
12,3 oz. / 375 g coconut fat (not oil)
6 tablespoons strong coffee
4 eggs – should be room temperature
4 tablespoons sugar
12 sweet wheat biscuits
About 5,3 oz. / 150 g coloured marzipan, thinly sliced
7 oz. / 200 g jelly tops
For a more adult version, add 1/2 dl of whiskey or
cognac, or Old Baileys – or something else

The filling is all about what kind of sweets you like with chocolate, so there are no rules. Kids love this cake too, but maybe without the booze.

What I like in my cake:

- Thin slices of marzipan or chopped up marzipan figures.
- Chocolate buttons (like Smarties or M&Ms) in different colours – if I'm in a really festive mood, I only use the red and green.
- Some kind of jelly sweets. Norwegians have *stick men*, which are jellied sweets covered in sugar.
- Some kind of marshmallow sweets. We have marshmallow Santas.
- I love dark chocolate and sweet soft liquorice, but that might just be me.

How to do it:

1. Dress a bread tin (about 1.5 ltr) with baking paper/greaseproof paper – so that the cake doesn't stick in the tin.
2. Melt the coconut oil in a small pot, take it away from the heat, break the chocolate into pieces and stir into the oil until it melts. Or you can use a waterbath, or the microwave.
3. Add the coffee or booze when the chocolate has melted.
4. Set it aside to cool while you prepare the eggs and sugar.
5. Whisk the eggs and sugar together until it's fluffy.
6. Add the chocolate mixture to the egg mixture and mix well until smooth.
7. Add layers of chocolate, sweets – or biscuits. Then decorate the top of the cake as you please. I use whatever sweets are left.
8. Serve the Delfia cake in thin slices. Wipe the knife between each cutting for a prettier result.
9. Delfia cake keeps well in the refrigerator and can also be frozen. Which is what I do, otherwise it won't last.

Recipe: Norwegian Wort Cake

Freshly baked Wort Cake is fragrant, sweet and just scrumptious. It's in my house every Christmas – makes the flat smell like Christmas. I love a slice with butter and brown cheese, but they go well with other cheeses too. And fig jam is delicious on this.

What to put in it:

500 g/1,1 lb rye flour, sieved
500 g/1,1 lb flour
1 ts of ground pepper
0.5 ts of ground clove
1 ts of ground coriander
1 ts ground aniseed
3 dl/0,6 pt milk
1 dl/0,2 pt golden syrup, Lyle's or similar
50 g/1,75 oz yeast
2 dl of raisins

1 bottle of wort beer (0,33 l/0,7 pt)

How to do it:

1. Mix the rye flour with half of the flour. Add the ground spices. Dissolve the yeast in lukewarm milk mixed with golden syrup. Add wort beer and stir the lukewarm liquid into the flour mixture.
2. Knead the dough well and add more flour until the dough releases the side of the bowl. Cover with plastic and let the dough raise in a warm place to double in size. This takes about 1 hour.
3. Divide the dough into two large or three smaller dough pieces. Knead and shape into round loaves. Place the loaves on the baking sheet with baking paper and let rise for about 30 minutes. Bake the bread at the bottom of the oven at 200 C/390 F for about 40 minutes. If you want shiny cakes you can brush them with water or eggwash.

The recipes for *Norwegian Wort Cake* and *Delfia Cake* are taken (mostly) from the blog:

recipereminiscing.wordpress.com

If anyone tries the recipes, please share a picture on Instagram or Facebook. I would love to hear and see how it worked out.

Instagram: instagram.com/natalienormann

Facebook: facebook.com/NatalieNormannAuthor

YOUR NUMBER ONE STOP

ONE MORE CHAPTER

FOR PAGETURNING BOOKS

One More Chapter is an
award-winning global
division of HarperCollins.

Sign up to our newsletter to get our
latest eBook deals and stay up to date
with our weekly Book Club!
<u>Subscribe here.</u>

Meet the team at
<u>www.onemorechapter.com</u>

Follow us!

 <u>@OneMoreChapter_</u>
 <u>@OneMoreChapter</u>
 <u>@onemorechapterhc</u>

Do you write unputdownable fiction?
We love to hear from new voices.
Find out how to submit your novel at
<u>www.onemorechapter.com/submissions</u>